T0323891

STITCHING A LIFE

STITCHING
A LIFE

An Immigration Story

MARY HELEN FEIN

SHE WRITES PRESS

Published 2020
Printed in the United States of America
ISBN: 978-1-63152-677-0 pbk
ISBN: 978-1-63152-678-7 ebk
Library of Congress Control Number: 2019919409

For information, address:
She Writes Press
1569 Solano Ave #546
Berkeley, CA 94707

She Writes Press is a division of SparkPoint Studio, LLC.

Book design by Stacey Aaronson

I dedicate this book to my husband, Stuart Allen Clancy.
His support is unwavering. He is my true soul mate.

PREFACE

The Lower East Side of Manhattan was Plymouth Rock to the two-and-a-half-million Jews who came to the New World between 1880 and 1920. Three quarters of them were Russians. So wrote Lawrence J. Epstein in his inspiring book *At the Edge of a Dream.*

My grandmother, Helen Breakstone Fein, was one of the millions who made the epic journey. In 1900, she came from Russia, from what is now Lithuania. Her family was poor, and as Jews in Lithuania, had no prospects for improvement or higher education. Jewish boys were drafted into the Russian army at the age of twelve. For decades prior, conscription had been for a term of twenty-five years. By 1900, boys were still taken at the age of twelve, although the term of service had been shortened. They might be taken for six years, or for an arbitrarily longer time. For these young Jewish boys, their years in the Russian army were harsh, filled with abuse and beatings. At the end of their ordeal, the boys returned home as pathetic figures, stripped of their memories of all things Jewish—stripped of their humanity.

Families felt great urgency to protect their sons from this fate. My grandmother Helen had four younger brothers. Her parents, Devorah and Chaim Breakstone, envisioned safety for their sons. They envisioned a better life for their family in America.

This is an historical novel, and also a true story, as true as I could make it. I drew on family history, as well as online resources such as ships' manifests and genealogy sources. As I stepped into the world of historical records, I didn't know if I would find the names I sought, but, amazingly, on line eleven of her ship's manifest, there it was in handwriting: "Hinde Breakstone," to be met by "father." I felt I was reaching back in time. I imagined her standing before the ship's official as he wrote those words on line eleven, the writing before me the same writing that was before her more than one hundred years ago.

I wove in family stories passed down from previous generations. I imagined scenes and conversations between characters from what I knew of their situations, personalities, and values. I visited Panemunė, Lithuania, where the Breakstone family dairy compound once was, and I saw the stork nests and the beautiful, lazy Nemunas River that my grandmother must have walked along.

The story is based on events pertaining to my family's immigration. It relies on a mix of sources: family lore, documents, and photographs, as well as historical research. To the best of my knowledge the stories of my family history are true. I've taken some liberties with historical chronology in order to make the story more readable and to better communicate the difficulties faced in both the old country and the new. My aim is to tell the essence of my own family's immigration story, but this is not just the story of my family. It is also the story of so many immigrant families who came to America for safety, opportunity, and better lives.

My parents divorced when I was four. Stability always eluded my mother. I attended different schools every year, sometimes for only a few months. The one constant in my life was spending the summers at my grandmother's house, on a leafy, residential street in the North Bronx. My time with Nana was filled with her generosity and sense of fun, so unlike my winters with my mother—tempestuous, dramatic, and unstable. Nana offered me consistency and kindness. Her humor and her humanity made my days with her a joy. I had a sense of belonging to a group of courageous and wise people. Above all, with my grandmother, I knew I was loved and valued.

This story revealed itself to me as I researched the time when Helen was a young girl in Lithuania. I read about the impoverished existence of the Jews. I delved into the nearly universal hatred faced by Jews in Russia. I visited her village of Panemunė and took in the sights she would have seen along the Nemunas River across from the city of Kaunas. Gradually, a picture emerged of what drove my grandmother and her family to escape to the New World, of what drove over two-and-a-half-million Jews to flee Eastern Europe at that time. They fled poverty and anti-Semitism. They sought safety and prosperity. They came to start lives anew in the *Golden Medina*, the promised land.

I

PANEMUNĖ, LITHUANIA

APRIL, 1900

It was springtime, and small green plants pushed up from the earth alongside the dirt road. The small town of Panemunė stretched along one side of the road. The other side of the road was grassy and lightly wooded for about thirty feet, then dropped sharply down to the beautiful, slow-moving Nemunas River. The name of the town, Panemunė, meant "along the Nemunas." You could see the big town of Kaunas across the water.

This same road led to the Breakstone family dairy farm just outside Panemunė, in Lithuania. Twenty or more Breakstone families worked together in the dairies and lived in the compound, each family close to all their aunts and uncles and grandmothers and cousins. Their ancestors, one generation after another, had lived and worked here for more than one hundred years. The families lived close together in small wooden houses.

It was late in the day, and most of the houses were empty, awaiting the return of the families for the evening.

All the adults were still hard at work in the dairies. Classes at the compound school were over for the day, and most of the children were still playing in the schoolyard.

Fifteen-year-old Hinde Breakstone was preparing dinner in her family's modest home. Her younger brother Max was with her, sitting at the rough wooden table, frowning over his mathematics homework. Hinde noticed his long legs sticking out from under the table, and she thought how fast he was growing. Max was no longer a little boy. At twelve years old, he looked tired from the eight long hours he had spent in classes.

The two siblings resembled one another physically. They both had deep, brown eyes and shining, dark hair. Max was lean and tall, whereas Hinde was strong and sturdy. Though not tall, she looked capable, especially her hands. She was enjoying making dinner for the family. Her hands moved skillfully as she chopped the carrots and onions and celery that she knew would give the pot of soup a wonderful flavor. The two siblings were also alike in the intensity with which they concentrated on their work. With her full attention, Hinde stirred together the vegetables that would simmer on the stove. Max once again crossed out the wrong answer to the mathematics problem he was trying to solve. In frustration, he bore down so hard on the pencil that the point broke off, and not for the first time this afternoon. A small knife had been pressed into pencil-sharpening service. He reached for it and began to make a new point for his next try.

Mama and Papa were still at work at the Breakstone dairy, but they were expected home for dinner within an hour or two. Mama worked feeding and caring for the dairy cows, and Papa handled records in the accounting office. Papa was an important person in the compound, and he knew a lot about the dairy business.

Hinde stirred chicken pieces and matzo balls into the soup. She closed her eyes as she inhaled the warm and comforting aroma that began to rise from the pot. She stirred everything with a long wooden spoon that Papa had carved years ago. The familiar spoon fit perfectly into her hand, and as Hinde held it, she thought of the many things her father did so well.

Chicken was normally too expensive for their family dinner, but Mama had been able to afford it this time because a special order had come in from a family in Kaunas, the big city across the river. This wealthy family was having a wedding, and they wanted fancy cheeses and creams for the event. All the Breakstones had been paid to work overtime, to make and to pack up the dairy products needed to fulfill the order. Although Jews in Lithuania were never prosperous, the Breakstone families were more fortunate than many. They had enough to eat and warm places to live. It was true that sometimes all they had to eat was spoiled milk or old cheese, but for Hinde's family, tonight was special. Tonight, they would have chicken.

Hinde and Max kept a companionable silence in the one-room home. Hinde stood at the stove, and Max sat at the table. From time to time, he would ask a question. She was the oldest, and her siblings regarded her as the smartest one in the family. In fact, Max said she was the smartest one in the entire Breakstone compound school.

As she stirred the soup, Hinde daydreamed a bit about a boy she liked named Leonard. He was handsome and had been paying attention to her for some time now. She enjoyed their conversations, and it was easy to imagine that a romance might spring up between them. Maybe they would kiss soon. It would be the first time for her.

Max was studying geometry, and Hinde was good with numbers. He interrupted her reverie. "I don't understand this Pythagorean Theorem," Max said. "There's a quiz tomorrow."

"It's about how triangles with a right angle are special," Hinde explained. "There are always certain relationships between the three angles and the three sides."

"Ok, but I don't understand the relationships. For example, what's this A squared plus B squared equals C squared?" Max asked. Hinde patiently explained the geometry.

Suddenly, Hinde stopped talking as she felt something through her feet, like the earth was trembling. The vibration turned into a sound, a sound of galloping horses racing straight toward their tiny home. Her heart began to race in time with the thudding hooves.

Max jumped up and ran to the window, Hinde right behind him. The sound got louder and louder. Though she couldn't yet see the horses, a cloud of dust rose above the nearby trees. Her shoulders tightened, and her breath quickened.

Hinde knew who was coming and why. For months, the entire family had lived in dread of this moment, and now it was happening. This was the Russians, and they were coming for Max, to take him away. Forever—or as good as forever. A cold rush of fear gripped Hinde's chest. They were only a few minutes away, but she was ready. They had practiced, and everyone knew what to do. Max's future depended on acting quickly.

Hinde whispered sharply, "Quick Max, run to the hideaway hole!"

Max had already run across the room and was dragging a huge wooden chest to one side. He struggled with the weight of it, but finally it moved. Next, he crouched down in the corner where the chest had been and began to work at the floorboards. Hinde grabbed Max's school books and papers from the table. She ran over as he slipped his fingers into the crevices and lifted a piece of the floor, revealing a hole in the exposed dirt.

Max could slide, feet first, down into this hole. It was exactly big enough for him. He stepped into the dark opening and wriggled himself down, wedging himself against the dirt, from his toes to his shoulders. Only his head was free to move. The rest of his body was trapped.

Hinde knelt down, dropping his books and papers on the dirt next to him. The hole came right up to the top of his head, which he could tilt back enough to look up at his sister. He was pale, his eyes wide with fear. Hinde patted his cheek and said, "Be very still and don't worry. I'll get rid of them. It will be all right." She wasn't sure she believed this, but she wanted to reassure him and help him to stay calm.

Once the boards were back in place, Max was hidden. Then, as she had practiced many times, Hinde stood up and tried to drag the heavy trunk back on top of the floorboards, tugging and pulling. It refused to budge. She ran around to the other side and pushed. The trunk was almost too heavy, but Max was depending on her and she wasn't going to let him down. She shoved it with all her strength. Finally, it shifted a little, then slid back into its proper place. The thundering hooves were now directly outside the door.

Hinde rubbed her apron over the floorboards so that

there were no marks or fingerprints in the dust that might give them away. Then in one moment, the sound of the galloping horses stopped, leaving an ominous silence.

Someone banged on the door. She gave one last look around to make sure there was no evidence of Max. Shaking inside, she forced herself to walk calmly across the room with her head held high. She opened the door.

Five soldiers stood in front of the house. They wore the uniforms of the Russian Army, black fur hats and dark blue jackets with red and gold trim. Crisscrossing gold bands made diagonal X's across their chests. Each soldier had a long, curved sword at his left side. Hinde watched the afternoon light glinting off the dangerous blades. The horses stamped and blew their steamy breath into the air.

Three of the soldiers still sat astride their horses, but two had dismounted and stood near the door. One took a step toward Hinde, stopping a few inches in front of her. She hunched her shoulders and contracted her chest as she took an involuntary step back. The soldier looked toward his leader for direction. The leader was a big blond officer still on his horse out in the lane. He unrolled an important looking scroll of paper, holding it up as he read in a commanding voice.

"We have come for one Max Breakstone, having now reached the age of twelve, and hereby officially drafted into the Russian Army for a term of twenty-five years. Anyone who tries to prevent this Jew from entering the Army is guilty of a crime punishable by imprisonment and will be taken into custody immediately." The paper slid back into a roll with a loud snap.

The leader lowered his arms, then reached out and aimed an accusing finger at Hinde.

"Girl, bring the Jew Boy Max Breakstone to me now."

For a moment Hinde thought she would collapse to the ground. She reached out her hand to touch the wooden wall of the house, steadying herself and allowing the loud proclamation to fade away into the air.

"Max is not here," she croaked in as calm and dignified a voice as she could. "He has gone away on a trip and will not return for ten days." Her voice quavered. "But he is not yet twelve years old. He is only eleven. I can prove this to you. I have his birth certificate, issued by your own Kaunas Government, and I can get it for you right now." Mama and Papa had documents ready for this moment, as had almost every Jewish family in Russia with a boy who was twelve years old. The leader shouted at Hinde, "We do not believe your papers are real, and we do not believe your brother is away. Officers, search this hovel."

Hinde stepped aside as the two soldiers pushed roughly past her into the one-room home. There was nothing obvious for them to see, the bare wooden table, palettes on the floor where the family slept, and the kitchen area with the wood stove on which the chicken soup still simmered. Hinde realized she could not even smell the soup anymore. The menacing presence of the soldiers consumed all her senses. Her every cell was on alert.

The men walked around the room and peered everywhere. They knew Max was here, and they weren't leaving without him. They stomped their loud boots on the floor listening for a hollow sound. Violently, they flung open the lid of the heavy trunk, seeing that it was large enough to hide a small boy, but inside were only a few papers and the clothing the family saved for special days.

These soldiers knew all the tricks. The burlier one of

the two gave the trunk a shove, but it did not move. Hinde felt a wave of relief, as it seemed he had decided it was too heavy for her to have moved it by herself.

A mental picture of Max crammed into the dirt came to her. He would be listening to the sound of the soldiers' boots on the wooden floor over his head, not knowing if these were his last few minutes of freedom. Her knees felt wobbly, but she could not allow herself to surrender to the panic that grew inside. There was too much at stake. The only chance of saving Max was to appear calm, sincere, believable. She would not give him away by shaking and cowering.

One of the soldiers went back outside, but the other one went over to the stove where the chicken soup bubbled away. With a sneer he looked at Hinde, then drew his heavy sword from its scabbard and raked the flashing metal across the stove top. The blade caught the pot with a loud clank, then threw hot liquid and chicken and matzo balls in every direction. The pot and lid crashed loudly onto the floor. The fire in the stove sizzled as liquid poured down. The precious chicken pieces, broken matzo balls, and carefully cut vegetables lay steaming everywhere.

Hinde froze, wanted to cry, wanted to scream. She stood completely still, knowing instinctively that this was a time to be as invisible as possible. She had heard stories of women and children being subjected to terrible cruelty by these soldiers. The man looked at her with a leer that told her he could do whatever he wanted to the soup, to the house, to her. She bit the inside of her lip as she realized her powerlessness in the face of this thuggish invader. Finally, he turned and went out the front door.

As she took several large, involuntary gulps of air, she realized she had been holding her breath. She followed the soldier outside. He raised his empty palms and shook his head to indicate to the officer that they had had no success in finding Max.

"Girl, go and get the fake birth certificate," ordered the officer from high on his horse. He waved his hand through the air, shooing Hinde back into the house. She went to the trunk in the corner. The soldiers had left the heavy lid open with the pile of papers right on top. It took her only a moment to find Max's birth certificate.

The officer knew it was a fake, and so did Hinde. Max was twelve years old, despite this document that showed that he was only eleven. She went back outside with the papers and handed them to the soldier near the door.

He lowered his head to read the document, then looked up and said to his officer, "It says that Max Breakstone is only eleven. Born in 1889, just eleven years ago. It looks valid, with the usual stamps." The family had paid dearly for those stamps.

The officer brought his horse a few steps closer to Hinde. He leaned toward her. He bared his teeth at her, scowling. She felt his white-hot hatred as if she were standing too close to a raging fire. "We shall leave for now, but we will be back, filthy little Jew girl, you can be sure of it." With that, he jerked his horse's head so that its eyes went wide, and it turned back the way they had come.

The soldier who held the birth certificate gave one more sneer, then threw the valuable paper down on the dirt and ground his boot into it, all the while keeping his leering eyes on Hinde. He turned and leapt into his saddle.

"Ah yes, be sure of it." The soldier raised a finger and

pointed at her to make his point. "We'll be back for little Jew brother Max."

Dust rose up again as she stood outside the door and watched them gallop away. It was a long time, watching and waiting, until she felt sure they were truly gone. Suddenly, she started to shake all over as if everything she had held in while the soldiers were here was now coming out at once. She didn't want to show her fear to Max; she wanted to be strong for him, but the shaking wouldn't stop.

She bent down and picked up the paper that had been ground into the dirt. Despite the soldier's boot marks, everything was still legible, and the valuable stamps of authenticity were not damaged. Hinde dusted off the birth certificate and smoothed out the wrinkled paper as best she could. She went back into the house and closed and barred the door.

"It's okay, Max," she called out loudly to her brother. "They're gone."

Crossing the room, Hinde placed the fake papers back into the trunk and closed the lid. She leaned her whole body against the trunk and pushed with all her strength, but it resisted. She pushed harder, but it moved only an inch. She had to get him free, and now. She leaned again, and gathering all her strength, pushed so hard she let out an involuntary cry. Finally, the trunk gave way and slid over to the side.

On her hands and knees, she pried at the floorboards. "I'm moving the boards now, Max. You'll be free right away."

In a moment, Hinde could see Max's dark hair. He didn't move or even look at her. His face seemed frozen into an angry mask.

"It's okay, Max. Look at me. You're safe."

Hinde lifted the books and homework as Max wriggled himself up until his arms were free. He lifted himself up and out of the hole. "It's a coffin," he said. He got to his feet, and she pulled him to her, and her tears began. He was covered with loose dirt, but she hugged him anyway, then dusted him off with her apron, her tears falling. Max was still and didn't move at all, as if he had been frozen. Gradually he moved his head and looked around the room. When he saw the soup on the floor, his trance broke.

"The soup," Max cried out.

"Soup? What is soup when my brother is safe?" Hinde said, smiling through tears. "You are all right, my brother. You are safe." She didn't tell him the officer's words about coming back.

Together, the brother and sister reset the floorboards and dragged the great trunk back into place. They picked the pot up off the floor, then washed it out. They rinsed off and salvaged whatever they could from the mess of the soup vegetables and chicken pieces. Soon a pot of soup simmered on the stove once again. It was nowhere near the soup it had been, but at least the family would still have something for dinner.

Max said forlornly, "It was such a wonderful soup."

Turning to face him, Hinde looked him in the eye. "Have faith, Max. There will be many more pots of soup in our future. You and I will have soup in America before this year is out."

2

THE PLAN

Within half an hour, Mama and Papa rushed into the house. Neighbors and cousins had seen the soldiers. Word had flown through the compound, and soon everyone knew that the soldiers had left without Max, that he was still safe at home. Both parents burst in the door, needing to see him with their own eyes to know that he was safe. The four younger children also heard about the threat and came running home. Soon the whole family of eight was gathered around the big table.

Papa sat at the head, and Mama sat at the other end, near the stove. Mama was sturdy and even shorter than Hinde. She had long brown hair piled on her head and held in place with hairpins. She wore a long skirt and boots and an old woolen shawl that was heavy and warm. Mama was practical and down to earth. People who knew Mama were never fooled by her small stature. Everyone knew she had strong opinions and was not afraid to speak her mind. She was also regarded as something of a wise woman, old enough to have gained life experience so that she was a good judge of character. She sometimes seemed to know what was coming when no one else expected it. Mama had warm and friendly eyes and was deliberate in everything she did.

Hinde was so happy to see her parents come in the door. She was still shaken by the soldiers, and she could see that Max was as well. He was not his usual relaxed self; instead he seemed to be frozen in a state of shock. The two siblings sat on the wooden bench that ran along one side of the table. Ten-year-old Selma came over and sat between them. She stretched out her arms to pat the backs of Hinde and Max in unison, then leaned against Hinde. Hinde reached out her arm to comfort her sister. Selma was small and had light hair, unlike anyone else in the family. She was pretty and delicate, unlike her adored older sister.

The three younger boys lined up on the other side, Bernard, age nine, Milton, eight, and Julius, only six years old. After a few minutes, Julius slipped down from his seat and crossed over to Hinde. He climbed onto her lap and put his thumb in his mouth, something he hadn't done for years. He curled up against the safety of his big sister, and she patted him reassuringly. It was dinner time. Hinde wasn't hungry and doubted that anyone else was either. The remains of the chicken soup sat covered on the stove and would stay warm until later.

"Chaim." Mama looked pointedly at her husband as she began the discussion with Papa's real name. Everyone called Papa Hymie, so it was clear Mama was serious. Her voice was unusually tense, her face wrinkled in concern. Papa returned his wife's look. He was tall and broad shouldered with dark hair that was usually a little too long and would fall into his steady brown eyes. Papa had a way of inspiring confidence in everyone. He dressed more formally than most of the men in the compound, a reflection of his important position. His family looked up to him in all things.

"Devorah," her husband replied. "Today was a terrible day. Max, my dearest oldest son, we are so relieved that you are safe and did not get taken away to the army. From now on, you must never be alone in this house. Someone else must always be here to help you to hide. Be careful from this day on." Max nodded his understanding.

"Now, everything must change. We must act to keep all you boys safe from being drafted. You could be taken away from us for many, many years. Your mother and I have had long talks, and we have come up with a plan. It won't be easy, but it is the only way to keep our family together and out of danger for the long run."

When Papa spoke of danger, he was referring to changes in how Russians were treating the Jews. For many years, Russia had been ruled by a good man, Tsar Alexander II, known as Alexander the Reformer. He had freed the serfs, a class of Russians who had been slave laborers to the landed gentry, and he had never acted against the Jews.

Sadly, Alexander II had been assassinated about 20 years earlier. The tsars who came after him were hostile to the Jews. The current tsar, Nicholas II, hated the Jews. He told the recently freed serfs that their problem wasn't that they had been slaves for centuries. Their problem was the Jews, these hateful foreigners with strange customs, outsiders who prospered with what rightfully should have belonged to the serfs. Tsar Nicholas did everything he could to spread bad feeling toward the Jews.

For more than fifty years, the Russians had drafted Jewish children into the army. Once a Jewish boy reached the age of twelve, he was vulnerable to conscription. If drafted, he would serve many years in the army, up to thirty-five years at some points in time. Once in the army, treatment was miserable. The boys were taunted for being Jews, forced to eat pork and other foods against their religion, ridiculed, abused, endlessly punished for no reason, and condemned to a life of misery. Everyone in the Breakstone compound had heard terrible stories not long ago; a Jewish boy had escaped the army, and the Breakstones had helped him, giving him a hiding place for a few days.

Sometimes the army would come to the house, as they had for Max, today. Other times it would be local kidnappers working for profit. The Tsar employed these *khappers*, locals who knew where Jewish boys lived and just how old they were. Khappers had to deliver a required quota of boys to the army, or they would face heavy fines. They kept track of every boy in the village and knew the exact date when each would reach the age of twelve.

The khappers would forcefully enter the house, find the boy who was on their list, tie him up, and carry him away. The family might never see their son again. Khappers weren't careful about the minimum age of twelve, happy to kidnap boys as young as eight years old and turn them over to the Russian army to fulfill their contract. Only Papa's importance in the community had kept them away from Max, so far.

When released from the army, so many years later, a boy would be ruined. He would return to his family a pitiful figure, beaten down, without any sense of or pride in his Jewish heritage, without any humanity remaining in his character. Family connections were weakened beyond repair, ill health would set in, and there were no prospects for a reasonable life. He would be forever altered, always to carry the traumatic memories of violence and the emotional scars of a cruel life.

There were few ways to escape the draft. Some boys would cut off their index fingers. The army wouldn't draft anyone who was missing their "trigger finger." Max had asked Papa what he thought of this, and Papa forcefully replied that he would not have his sons mutilate themselves. One Jewish family in the area was so frightened of having their boy taken away that they had raised him from birth as a girl. No one knew this tall girl was a boy, but people did wonder how she got to be so strong.

Many of the Breakstone cousins had gone to a forger in Kaunas who was sympathetic to the Jews. He had made Max's false birth certificate. Hinde knew that both Mama and Papa were uncomfortable doing anything illegal. They prided themselves on being contributing, law-abiding citizens, but in this case, they told the children an exception had to be made. They had to save Max. They had been lucky that the army came for the boy, rather than the khappers. False papers were useless against Khappers, but often worked with the army.

The anti-Semitic Tsar Nicholas instituted a vicious campaign to discriminate against Jews in as many ways as possible. Newspaper articles, rallies, posters, and speeches incited discrimination and violence. These were not only tolerated but encouraged.

Higher education was restricted so that almost no Jew qualified. Jews were no longer allowed to live in the heart of any town but were forced to move to the outskirts. Fortunately for the Breakstones, their compound was already outside the town.

Hinde remembered how frightened she had been when Papa had told her about the pogroms. Jews were killed just for being Jews. Rough people would go on a rampage into Jewish neighborhoods where they would break windows, smash furniture, and burn homes. Jews were beaten, sometimes killed, and the police did nothing. She knew Papa would not mention this tonight, as it was too scary for the small children.

Papa continued, "My children, your Mama and I have a plan. A wonderful plan, and we are all going to be safe soon." Then Papa began the hard part of his talk. "I have to leave Panemunė. We all have to leave. We must get Max out of the country quickly. Mama and I have saved enough for my ticket to America." His voice cracked as he continued, "I will leave you all in just one week."

Selma reached across and put her hand on Papa's arm. She cried out loudly, "Don't go, Papa. We need you."

Papa's soft eyes met with hers. He covered her small hand with his own. "We will all be together again soon, my sweet girl. As soon as I arrive in New York, Cousin Rose will help me find a job. After five years in New York, she's a big success." Papa patted Selma's hand as he spoke. "I will be able to work for the Breakstone cousins. They have started a New York Breakstone Dairy business and will hire me right away. Rose says there's also lots of work in New York's garment business. She writes that I can save enough money for Hinde to come over within three months.

"Now you may be thinking, 'Why not bring Max first?' He is the one in the most danger, but Max is only twelve years old and he won't be able to earn much money. Hinde, on the other hand, is old enough to make a good salary. All the boys will get to New York faster if Hinde comes first and helps me to earn Max's fare. Together we can make twice as much money and get Max over to New York fast, and then all the rest of you."

"Hinde will have to take the boat by herself," Papa smiled at Hinde with a wink, "but my oldest daughter is smart and resourceful. She can do it."

Hinde glowed with the compliment. She loved that Papa felt he could rely on her. She need wait only three months. The prospect of leaving for the New World thrilled and frightened her so much that a shiver ran through her body. Mama and Papa had shared this plan with her a few days earlier, so she was not surprised. Both parents looked at her with confidence and admiration. She felt a warm feeling that went a long way toward dispelling her fears. Mama reached over and patted Hinde on the back. Their eyes met, and Mama's gentle tears and soft smile said everything.

Papa added, "The two of us will be able to earn enough to send Max a ticket before his next birthday. Soon there will be three of us in New York, all working. We will be links in a strong chain, each one working to bring the next. Together we three will save the money to bring all five of you over, Mama, Selma, Bernard, Milton, and you too, little Julius." Papa chucked his youngest under the chin, and Julius giggled and nestled himself deeper into his sister's lap. "We will send for all of you. That's our plan."

There was a moment of silence as everyone took in what would be their lives for the next few years.

"It's a good plan," Mama nodded her agreement. "But one more thing. Each of you must keep this a secret and not mention it to anyone outside of our own little family. If everyone finds out, someone might alert the authorities that we are trying to save a boy from the draft, and we might get in trouble. So, remember not to talk about this to anyone.

"You may even have to tell someone a white lie. Tell people that Papa is travelling in Lithuania selling dairy products. Don't mention the New World or that we must save our twelve-year-old Max from the soldiers. All your lives Papa and I have taught you never to lie, but this is a special case. Our safety and our future depend on all of us keeping this secret together."

Mama paused and looked at each of her six children. "It will be hard to pretend, but remember that our lives, and especially Max's life, may depend upon it.

"When we get to the New World, everything will be better. Most of the people there are immigrants like we will be. There are already millions of Jews in New York. We will escape the tsar and his wicked army, and we will all start a new life together."

The children voiced their understanding of the plan, each at his or her own level. Every one of them trusted Papa and believed that this plan would work. Each of them promised to keep the secret.

3

BLACK BREAD

Hinde walked down the only street in the village
of Panemunė, past the wooden houses with their small
front yards and gardens. The air was fresh and cool today,
and the sky was perfectly blue. There were yellow flowers
at the sides of the road and, once in a while, a few beautiful purple rye flowers. Sometimes the smell of honeysuck-
le wafted through the air.

She was on an errand to buy a loaf of black bread for
dinner. As she walked down the town's only street, she
could feel that things had changed. There was a new hostility in the air. Trees all over the town displayed posters
with angry accusations against the Jews, how they
couldn't be trusted and would steal if given a chance.

Visiting Russian officials had recently come to Panemunė from the capital in St. Petersburg. They checked
every house to make sure that no Jews were living illegally
in the town itself. They spoke to every shop owner,
spreading frightening lies about the Jews. They told how
Jews hoarded money and were dishonest business people,

how they made outrageous profits lending money to desperate people. They even warned that Jews would kidnap Christian children and kill them to use their blood in the recipe for matzo, Jewish unleavened bread. These were terrible untruths, but people believed them. Everything had changed for Jews in Panemunė.

Would this be the last time she ever walked through the town? Hinde would miss the houses and the gardens, but she would not miss how mean people had become because she was Jewish. She would be happy to leave, happy to work to bring the whole family to a new country where Jews were not hated.

Each day she looked for Papa's letter to arrive. Would today be the day? She imagined him writing a letter to tell her that the time had come. Her heart beat faster at the thought of crossing the Atlantic Ocean and starting a new life. It had been more than three months since Papa left, an eternity. Every day she waited to hear from Papa. Every day no word.

Hinde wanted the letter to arrive, but she was also afraid. She had never even been far from home, only to Kaunas a few times, the big city across the river. She had never been on a boat, only the little ferry to Kaunas. America would be different from this small place. People there spoke English, ate different food, wore different clothing. Nothing would be familiar. Would people there like her? Would she find a way to fit in and make friends? She walked faster as she thought of all that was ahead of her.

Hinde continued down the familiar street. She remembered walking down this street with Mama when she was a little girl, when she still had to reach up to grasp Mama's hand. Would this be her last walk through the only town she had ever known? Deep ruts carved the dirt road, cut by the wooden wheels of horse-drawn carts. There were tall oak and maple trees across the street along the river. As she took in the familiar weeds and flowers by the side of the road, she wondered if they would have these same plants in America? Would the houses look like these houses?

This end of Panemunė's only street was sandy. The other end was smooth with dirt and grass and tall green trees all along. Everyone called their own end of the street "this street," and the other end "the other street." There was only one street, but people didn't think of it that way.

She walked past the family homes, small wooden houses on either side, painted gray or brown, with steep roofs so the snow could slide off in winter. Most of them had kitchen gardens enclosed by rough-hewn wooden fences. Vegetables ripened in the warm days of summer. Onions and potatoes grew out of the rich soil. Stakes held strong vines that climbed toward the sun. A brown and white cow tethered in a yard looked at Hinde with big wet eyes.

Hinde knew the families who lived in each house. Although she lived outside of town in the Breakstone compound with the Jews, and although they had different ways of doing things, the Breakstones had always been good neighbors, enjoying friendly relationships with the townspeople. But no more. Now Jews were unwelcome. Everything had changed, and this new hatred had driven Papa away.

Hinde missed Papa desperately. She remembered the day last fall when he left. How tightly he had hugged her, his strong fatherly arms surrounding her, his words comforting her. "Hinde, my dear daughter," he said just to her, quietly so no one else could hear. "You'll be the next to come to America. My heart will be waiting until I see you. Together we'll earn enough to bring Max and then the whole family. Our plan will work, you'll see."

She remembered how he smelled like clean laundry, how safe she had felt with him, how much she loved him. He held her out in front of himself with both his arms so that he could look at her, almost like he was creating a picture in his mind that he could look at later. Again, he said, "Hinde, my dear, dear daughter." Hinde saw the tears in his dark eyes, tears that matched her own.

Why hadn't the letter come? Had something bad happened to him? Maybe they hated Jews in America, too, and some bad Jew-hating men had attacked him and he couldn't work or even write a letter. Hinde felt tightness in her chest as she thought of every terrible thing that could have happened. After a bit, she realized she was allowing her imagination to run wild, and she admonished herself for having silly thoughts. Papa was fine. The New World was safe for Jews; everyone knew that. The letter would come soon.

She brought herself back to the business at hand. She was in town to buy a loaf of black bread from the bakery where the family had bought bread for years. Lithuanian black bread was even better than Russian black bread. It had a special sweetness to it. Hinde knew Mama was planning to bring home some special butter the Breakstone Dairy always made, so the bread would be even better. Mama had given her the kopecks, and they jangled in her pocket. It would be a special treat for the family.

As she came to the shop, she bent down to smell the

beautiful purple roses that had always grown here. Then she went into the shop. A gold colored bell was hung with a red ribbon on the door knob, and it jingled to announce her arrival. The baker's wife was behind the counter, and she looked up with a smile, but as soon as she recognized Hinde, her smile vanished.

The woman had known Hinde all her life, had even given her cookies when she was a little girl and came in with Mama. They had always been friendly, but now it was different. Hinde wondered if shopkeepers could get in trouble just for being friendly. The woman averted her eyes.

Hinde politely asked for one of the big black breads on the shelf. The woman took it down and wrapped it in paper. She tied it with string but did not immediately hand it over. "That will be five kopecks," the woman said. "I'm sorry, but we have to charge you people more, now. For regular people it is only three kopecks." Reaching into her pocket and taking out the money, Hinde counted out the coins onto the counter and took the bread in return.

Hinde felt terrible as she left the bakery. She let her head hang forward and her posture became slumped and round. She kicked a small rock down the road. How could anyone treat her like that? How could the woman blindly believe all these lies after knowing Hinde for her whole life? It was hard to stay proud when everyone said you were no good. She hung her head as she walked. The idea that maybe Jews truly were bad people crept into a little corner of her mind.

Hinde walked only a few feet before she realized how crazy that thought was. The Jews were a great people, and she had always been proud of her heritage. She lifted her head up and reminded herself that she was a good person, that she came from a family of kind and honest people, from generations of kind and honest people. She swore to herself she would always stay proud of who she was, no matter what anyone said. She took a deep breath and straightened her back. Lifting her chin, she continued down the street, forgetting to kick the little rock of un-happiness.

Hunger knocked at Hinde's belly, as usual. She was always hungry, and there was rarely enough food to fill up. She tried to resist, but hunger won out. She reached into the bag and took a little pinch of the rich black bread from the bottom of the loaf where no one would notice. She put the delicious morsel into her mouth, enjoying the rough texture and strong flavor. However wrong their attitudes, the bakers still made good bread. She wondered if they would have bread like this in the New World.

Tonight was a special night. The family usually ate in the compound's communal dining hall with all the other Breakstones. The fare was simple and inexpensive. Some-times, all they had to eat was potatoes and milk from the dairy. Sometimes it was sour milk that was too old to sell. Often there were pickles and plain bread, and sometimes even *tzimmies,* a stew made with potatoes and prunes. They rarely had anything as good as this Lithuanian black bread.

Tonight, Mama had planned a treat for the family. They would eat together at home, only Mama and the six children. Hinde quickened her step.

She was very curious to check up on the new bird's nest that had appeared in the family's yard. It was the first thing she saw as she walked around the last curve in the road. The nest was several feet across. There was the enormous mother bird on top of the tallest tree in their yard. The bird was a white stork.

Stork nests were frequently seen in the spring and early summer. In Lithuania, the stork was held in very high regard. People celebrated Lapwing Day, the day the storks returned from their winter migration. They still told the old story that the stork brought new babies, but no one would dare to harm a stork. It was regarded as very good luck if a stork chose your yard to build its nest.

The mother stork stood up as Hinde approached. She flapped her wide, black-tipped wings to announce herself. Hinde could see several little storks at the mother's feet. The bird had arrived and started her nest the very day after Papa's departure. To Hinde and to the entire family, it was a sign that the family's plan was going to succeed. Storks were always a good sign.

Hinde could see that Mama was back from work now. She was hanging laundry out to dry in the warm air, whilst keeping an eye on her four boys roughhousing in the yard. Hinde waved and went inside the cabin. Immediately, she saw a letter on the wooden table. It was written on blue air-mail paper, the thinnest of paper, so that it would not contribute much to the weight of the mails from America. This had to be the letter from Papa. He had used blue-black ink, the same ink Hinde used in school. She recognized his handwriting, fluid and strong. Papa had a good education; you could tell from looking at how he made his letters.

She put down the precious loaf of black bread, then took the remaining kopecks out of her pocket and put them on the table too, all the while not taking her eyes off the letter. She hung her coat on a hook and then walked back to the letter and sat down beside it. She sat on her hands so that they would not reach down and open the letter without permission.

4

THE LETTER

Mama came in from work and immediately saw the letter on the table. Knowing that both she and Hinde would think of nothing but the letter until they opened it, she came right over and sat down at the table close to her daughter. She picked up the letter.

"I waited for you before opening it." Hinde held her breath as Mama loosened the edge of the envelope and then unfolded it into the letter itself, a kind of puzzle that used the back side of the letter for the envelope, saving the extra weight of an envelope.

Hinde could hardly contain herself wanting to know what Papa had written. Mama began reading.

My Dear Family,

I miss you all terribly, but I am happy to be here in New York. This is a busy and fast paced city. There is always too much to do and not enough time. My job cutting fabric for clothing is good, honest work. When I'm not working, I spend time with Cousin

*Rose and her children, and our other cousins who
are here.*

*Here Jews have every opportunity, and anti-
Semitism is rare. There is no military draft, so young
boys can study and plan their lives without fear.
Recent arrivals like me are filled with hope. It was
hard at first. I didn't know my way around and I
kept getting lost, but people helped me. However
long a person has been here, it is not so long that
they don't remember what it was like when they
themselves first arrived and didn't know how things
worked.*

*The hardest thing here is that I worry about the
soldiers or the khappers coming for Max. We must
get him to safety. Money is much easier to make here
than in Panemunė. My original plan was to get a job
here in the Breakstone Dairy. I met with our cousins
Joseph and Isaac, who started the New York dairy
almost ten years ago. They offered me a job, but they
understood when I discovered how much more the
schmatta trade pays. I know you will laugh when
you read that, because a schmatta is an old piece of
cloth to tie around your head, but this is how
everyone in New York refers to the booming garment
industry. In Yiddish of all things. Even people who
aren't Jews call it that.*

*I can get Hinde an excellent job. Aunt Rose has
already found her a place nearby where she can
work a sewing machine. I have now made enough for
Hinde's ticket. My dear daughter, you can come to*

*New York now. You must be very careful on your
journey as there are real dangers. Once you are here,
between the two of us, we can have Max safely in
New York within a month or two.*

*Love to all of you. I think of you constantly,
especially you, Devorah, my loving wife. We will be
together soon.*

Papa

Papa's letter also included Hinde's ticket. It had cost
thirty dollars.

At that point, Mama got a worried look on her face,
but Hinde put her arm around Mama. "Don't worry about
this. I will be careful and do everything to arrive safely in
New York. You know I'm practical about people, and I can
tell who is reliable and who is not."

Mama hugged Hinde back and said, "I don't want you
to go away."

Hinde replied, "But you will come soon. We will all
start our new lives soon." Hinde felt a little afraid, but she
wanted to appear confident. Her remark made Mama feel
better, and the two of them managed to grin at one another.
Hinde felt a shiver of excitement from her head to her
toes. Soon her adventure would start.

5

ALL THAT MUST BE
LEFT BEHIND

A wind had sprung up, and Hinde's hair blew in a swirl. She retied the *schmatta*, the scarf that had slipped off her head. It was the day after the letter. She was on her way home from a walk in the woods, wanting some time to herself to think about her upcoming journey and how life was about to change.

Most of her days were spent in school, and school was Hinde's great love. She knew she would miss it terribly. Her parents encouraged all their children to excel in their studies. The school had been set up inside the compound, and all the dairy workers' children attended.

She especially loved learning about the Jewish people, learning the history of her ancestors. More than two thousand years ago the Jews lived in their own country, called Israel. Now they lived all over the world because of the great diaspora. The Rabbi had taught them that the diaspora was the scattering of Jews, in wave after wave, over a period of more than two thousand years.

Hinde also loved mathematics and was the best in her

geometry class. Homework was never a chore for her. She could usually do every problem, and if she didn't know how to do it, Papa would explain and help her to solve it. What would it be like not to be in school? She knew she would always be learning new things, but no more history and mathematics.

There would be no more school in New York. It was time to become an adult, work hard, and make money. Everything depended on it. As much as she loved school, she loved her brothers more. She was torn between anticipation of her new life and sadness over what she would leave behind.

The Breakstone compound had its own rabbi, Rabbi David, and where there was a rabbi, there could be a school. Hinde admired Rabbi David. She loved how smart he was, and how learned. He taught them history, literature, Greek mythology, and geography. He hung precious color copies of beautiful paintings on the walls and explained to the students why the paintings were important.

He also taught them the Bible stories, and this was the one thing that bothered Hinde about Rabbi David. He insisted that every word in the Bible was literally true. Papa had said not to worry about this, that even though he was smart, even though he was a rabbi, he might not be right about everything. Papa said that these stories were symbolic and not meant to be taken literally. She listened respectfully as Rabbi David insisted that the Red Sea had parted for Moses, and she didn't argue when he talked about how God had impersonated a burning bush. She wondered if rabbis were required to think such things, no matter how smart they might otherwise be.

As a teacher, the rabbi was a good communicator. Best

of all, he spoke fluent English. He had been giving interested children special English lessons for some years. Hinde and Max and Selma attended every class and were getting better and better at speaking and understanding English. Together they would practice, and after Papa revealed the plan, they practiced more than ever.

Everyone in the Breakstone compound spoke Yiddish, and few people could speak any other language. Some Russian words were needed to get by in a Russian village, but at home it was always Yiddish. Hinde and Selma would speak English whenever they were together, at the table or on the way to school.

Hinde felt a special place in her heart for little sister Selma. They were close despite their age difference, but Hinde was getting too old to play with the handmade cloth dolls that Selma still endlessly enjoyed. The dolls had pink fabric faces with small dark buttons for eyes and a mouth that was only a line of red stitching. Hinde had also outgrown playing dress-up, but would still play with Selma sometimes, just because it made Selma so happy. They would drape themselves in old musty curtains, and when she wasn't looking, parade around in Mama's high heeled shoes. They were glamorous brides and princesses.

Papa had brought back the two dolls one time when he went to Kaunas to the Jewish bank to do business for the dairy farm. You could see Kaunas across the river, it wasn't far. She had learned in school that Kaunas was Lithuania's largest city. Lithuania had been part of the Russian Empire now for over one hundred years. Being part of Russia was not a good thing for the Jews, now that Nicholas was the tsar.

Would she ever see Panemunė again? Would she ever see

her sister Selma again once she left this town? She began to feel heartbroken, empty, like her whole life was being taken away from her and her new life had not yet arrived.

As she neared the compound, she saw a familiar figure coming her way. She wiped away her tears and felt her sadness fading as she saw who it was. It was Leonard, the boy she liked, and Hinde felt a little thrill to meet him accidentally this way. Leonard had paid special attention to her for almost a year now. He worked in the dairy and would often catch her eye and smile at her. The two of them talked about everything, from common gossip to the recent political changes. She had grown very fond of him and knew she was going to miss him. She wished she could confide in him that she was leaving, but she knew she could not. She was happy for this chance to see him for what might be the last time.

Leonard was blond, unusual for a Jewish boy, and handsome, tall with broad shoulders. Hinde enjoyed looking at him. When she went to America, she would never see him again. She wanted to go so much, but it meant leaving everyone behind. Brothers and sisters, cousins, aunts, uncles, grandparents, the rabbi, her friends in school, the whole town, her whole world, all of it, all left behind. Even Mama left behind.

Most girls in Panemunė got married at Hinde's age, but there were few Jewish boys now, with the Russian army drafting them all. The few who were left were the only sons in families with no father. These boys had to support the entire family and were therefore excused. This was true of Leonard.

As he came closer and recognized her, he smiled and said, "You're looking pretty today." Hinde looked down and blushed a bit at the compliment. She wasn't sure "pretty" was the right word for her, but she knew her features were clear and regular and that her skin was bright. She wasn't delicate or petite like some girls, but she was shapely. She liked being shapely and sturdy, like her mother. She also liked hearing Leonard say she was pretty. His hair was golden in the sunlight, and he looked even more handsome than usual today.

She liked Leonard not only because he was handsome and always complimented her, but also because he was responsible and smart. He had a sparkle in his eye that drew other people to him. Hinde thought maybe they were similar that way. People liked her too. Most of the other students at school liked her, and, like Leonard, she was often chosen as a leader. Hinde had no trouble organizing a team for a game or deciding what game they would play next.

Leonard stepped a little closer to her. "I'm so happy to see you here. Will you walk with me a ways?" He reached over and tenderly tucked in a few strands of her shiny dark hair where it had escaped from under her scarf. Wisps blew around in the light summer wind. Hinde smiled and shyly looked at the ground as he touched her hair.

Together they walked toward the river. After a few minutes, Leonard reached down and took her hand. Hinde felt happy, and she did not pull away. She gave his hand a little squeeze and blinked back a tear before he noticed it. She felt happy that he liked her and wanted to hold her hand, and she felt sad that she was leaving and could not even tell him.

"I am always so glad to see you," he said, smiling down at her, and reaching an arm around her waist as they walked. "There is a dance next month for all the Break-stone teenagers. Will you go with me?"

"There are very few things I would love more than to go with you to the dance," Hinde replied, squeezing his hand, and choosing her words carefully so as not to tell a lie, but also to keep the secret. When the dance came, and he discovered that she was gone, she hoped he would re-member her exact words and the warm smile she gave him. She hoped he would understand why she had had to keep the secret. Perhaps he would even know how she had truly meant what she said, how much she would have loved dancing with him.

They came to the fork where they had to part. He turned to face her and said, "See you soon, my dear Hinde."

"I am very happy you asked me to the dance," she replied. She leaned forward and rested her head against his chest for just a moment. Then she looked up at him, and they gazed into one another's eyes for one moment more. Then he turned and was gone. She watched him as he walked away, until he disappeared into the forest. She thought that she would never see this friend again. She wondered if any boy would ever again like her as much as Leonard did.

As she neared the river bank, she could see the ferry-man rowing people on his barge over to Kaunas. Hinde had been to the big city a few times with Papa. She loved all the excitement of the crowds, the horses and shops and things for sale. Right here on the river bank was exactly where she had stood when Papa left for America. She had waved and waved as Papa in his heavy coat had gotten smaller and smaller. She kept on waving as the ferry boat itself shrank into a small smudge on the sparkling water.

Hinde kept walking toward Petamushelis, the location of the Breakstone compound. Straight white birch trees lined the road on the riverside and continued as she turned away from the river. She could hear the summer wind as it moved through the leaves making the branches bend and the leaves quiver. As she neared home, Breakstone cousins waved to her. Here were the shoemaker and the tailor and the blacksmith, men she had known her entire life as shoes wore out or Papa needed a new suit for work. She passed the dining hall where most meals were served communally. The fields were full of cows that gave milk each day for the Breakstone dairy business. She passed the ice house. Here dairy workers brought blocks of ice cut from the river in winter. This kept dairy products fresh until they could be sold. There was no ice to cut in summer, but if winter ice was carefully wrapped in sawdust, it would keep through the summer.

Hinde's mind wandered back to her friend Leonard. He was a special person, and it was easy to dream about him. In an imaginary world where Jews were treated well, they might have grown closer and built new lives together. That was not to be.

6

OVERLAND JOURNEY

It was a few weeks since the night of the letter and the Lithuanian black bread, the night that was the start of everything. Despite her growing nervousness, Hinde was thrilled that her adventure had begun. Today she would leave behind everything she had ever known: the Breakstone compound with the dairies, her little brothers and sister, the one-room wooden cabin that had always been home, and most of all Mama, the one person she relied upon most in this world.

Mama would travel with her to the ship, but then Hinde would be on her own. She would travel to America by herself, like a real grown-up. She had the papers she needed. Papa had paid a man at the bank in Kaunas to help each member of the family get their emigration papers when the time came for them to leave. Mama had visited the banker last week, and he had been as good as his word. Everything was in order.

As she came out of the house, her brothers and sister all gathered around her to say goodbye. Hinde watched as

Max reached into his pocket for something, then shyly extended his hand toward her. As he opened his palm, she saw a small green stone. The green color was vivid and streaked with brown lines. She remembered that he had found it months ago, and that it was one of his treasures.

"This is for you to keep," Max said as Hinde took the gift from him. "Forever," he added, looking up at her to be sure she understood. Hinde solemnly nodded to her brother.

She took the stone and held it up to the light. The beautiful markings looked like a landscape. She reached over and pulled Max close. She hugged him to say thank you, to say goodbye. Then she slipped the stone deep into her pocket. She had sewn hidden pockets into her skirts for the trip. The treasure would be safe there, along with her ticket and her emigration papers. "When I touch this stone, I will think of you," she said to Max.

Selma cried as she took her big sister's hand. She, too, had a present, a dried hepatica flower that she had pressed between the pages of a book. The delicate flower was carefully wrapped in heavy paper, so it could travel without getting damaged. Hinde loved this present, too. She opened her canvas bag to tuck it into a safe corner. She hugged Selma, and her heart ached.

Hinde knew that the three little boys regarded her like a second mother. Whenever they needed direction or reassurance, they turned to her as they turned to Mama. Each hugged her close. She realized they didn't fully understand what was happening today, but they knew she was leaving, and that had to be difficult for them.

One by one, each little boy reached into his pocket and extended a small gift to Hinde. There was an eagle feather from Bernard, light brown with stripes going across it. Milton gave her a tooth he had found in the woods, barely white but recognizable as the tooth of some wild animal. Julius looked up at her accusingly and started to cry as he handed her a gift that Mama had helped him make, a tiny crocheted bag to keep all her treasures in. Hinde tucked everything into the crocheted bag which then fit into a corner of her larger bag. As she reached out to hug Julius, tears ran down her own cheeks. One by one, she embraced each of her little brothers.

Hinde felt sad that none of her Breakstone cousins were present, but the family had kept its secret well, and no one knew she was leaving. She would miss her extended family. Max would be in charge at home for the few days it would take Mama to accompany Hinde to the ship and then return. He would watch out for the younger children. They all looked up to him and would listen to him. Selma knew how to cook a few things that would be enough. The family would be fine for a few days.

For luggage, Hinde had a large bag she had made from an old piece of canvas she had found in the dairy. She had carefully cut out two large matching rectangles for the front and the back, and then stitched them together on three sides, leaving the top open. Though the fabric was old, it was still strong, and the bag would hold up. She had used smaller rectangles of canvas to make pockets inside the bag to hold special things. The bag had a long strap so that she could wear it across her shoulders and leave her hands free.

This bag carried everything she would take to the New World. She had the clothes that she wore, plus a clean blouse and a second skirt. She had extra underwear and socks, two handkerchiefs and two scarves for her head. Her only shoes were the ones that she wore, hand-me-downs from another cousin. The shoes were already a bit tight, when only a year ago they'd fit perfectly. They would have to do. There was bread and cheese in one of the pockets for Mama and Hinde to *nosh* as they travelled overland to the boat. In Yiddish, to *nosh* meant to snack.

Hinde was barely herself that day. She felt like she was leaving behind this person named Hinde. For a moment, she had the crazy idea that she should have a new name, that she was becoming someone else entirely. It was only a fleeting thought, and she let it go.

Soon she heard horses trotting down the road toward them all. She was excited to see the troika pull up in front of their yard. This was a special carriage pulled by three horses. Most people never had a chance to ride in a troika, least of all a young girl like Hinde. The special carriage was used for important business only. Many times, since she was a child, she had stood by the side of the road and watched the great troika pass.

This troika was always driven by a Breakstone cousin who sheltered and fed soldiers for the Russian army. In return he was allowed the use of this special wagon. It was an expensive and impressive vehicle, and the cousin was proud that the army allowed him to use it. It was drawn by three perfectly matched white horses, harnessed side by side. All the harnesses and other livery were bright red with little bells sewn on, so the troika always passed by with silvery sounds floating in the air, over the deep thuds of hooves hitting the ground. Usually only the rich and the upper class could ride in such an elegant vehicle. Russians were proud of the troika, a symbol of their country. Of course, that meant that Jews and other poor people like Hinde rarely got a chance to ride in such a fancy carriage. Hinde was thrilled to ride in the troika, but at the same time her heart ached as she left her home.

Once each week the cousin drove the carriage to Kaunas to bring the Breakstone Dairy products to the synagogue and to the Greek Orthodox Church where they could be sold. Today Mama had paid the driver a little extra to drop them off at the train station. The driver got down to help Hinde and Mama climb up. Hinde sank for a moment into the luxury of the carriage's soft black leather seats, but then quickly sat up to look at her home and her family one last time.

All the children stood lined up in the yard. They waved goodbye to Hinde and Mama as the three horses trotted down the road to the ferry. Hinde turned around in her seat to keep waving a little longer. Finally, they came to the bend in the road, and the family disappeared from sight. Hinde could not bear that they were gone, and she closed her eyes, holding onto the picture of them waving goodbye.

Soon the cousin drove the horses onto the ferry, and they crossed the Nemunas River. Once they arrived in Kaunas, he took about an hour to make his deliveries.

"Mama, I'm nervous driving around town in this elegant carriage. What if someone sees us and realizes we don't belong in such finery?"

The cousin was inside a building, making his last delivery. Mama said, "You are right to be nervous. Look at these soldiers standing on the corner across the street. They have noticed us." Hinde saw that some of the soldiers were indeed looking at them, one of them pointing right at them with a long arm. Just when it looked like they would come over and ask what a Jew was doing in a troika, the cousin returned.

"*Oy vey iz mer*," Mama said to the cousin, Yiddish for "Oh woe is me."

"Thank heaven you are back," Mama said to him, gesturing toward the soldiers. The driver grasped the situation immediately and leapt up into the carriage. Reaching for the reins, he snapped the horses into a fast trot down the street.

Once they were far from the soldiers, Hinde realized she and Mama were clutching one another's hands. She saw Mama realize this at the same moment, and they exchanged a relieved smile with one another as they both let go. Hinde let out the breath she had been holding and allowed her tensed shoulders to drop down an inch or two.

She felt even more relieved when the cousin let them off at the train station. The troika had been exciting when they first got on, but it had almost ended their journey before it started. She was glad now to leave it behind.

They walked quickly through the large and busy train station. Hinde remembered stories she had heard of Jews being accosted in train stations and prevented from travelling, even though they had all the proper tickets and papers. Hinde and Mama's eyes met without words, their anxious glances expressing their vulnerability. They found the correct platform for their train and stood back against the wall, doing their best to be invisible. Soon the train arrived in clouds of smoke. It made screeching noises louder than anything Hinde had ever heard.

Whistles blew, conductors ushered them aboard, and finally they found a place they could sit together. Hinde took the window side and tucked her canvas bag under the seat, keeping one foot atop it at all times.

She had never been on a train before. The view out the window was so mesmerizing that she forgot to be afraid as she watched the city fly by. Almost immediately, the train crossed the Nemunas River on a high bridge. As they continued, the area was very hilly, and soon the windows went black as the train entered a long, straight tunnel. When they emerged, the landscape was flatter. Hinde and Mama gradually relaxed and settled into their seats.

After an hour or so, they came to Vilnius. The city streets they passed looked much like the streets of Kaunas, with a few grander buildings and boulevards. They walked across the platform, changing trains to the one that would take them across Europe to the boat. Soon they were back in the countryside, heading west to Warsaw in Poland.

For the first few hours Hinde gazed out the window, pointing excitedly at a flock of ducks or a field of horses. The train rushed along across the Lithuanian landscape. Hinde was entranced looking out the window at fields and houses. They passed through villages and made stops in the larger ones. People got on the train and people got off. Finally, Hinde fell asleep, safe in the knowledge that Mama would keep an eye on her and her things.

After a long time, the train came to Warsaw. A Polish conductor walked through all the cars announcing that they were coming into the city. Mama and Hinde stayed in their seats, bound for the next big stop, Berlin. Hinde's ship would leave from Bremen, and this train continued on to Bremen. They would travel all night until early morning.

They ate some of the bread and cheese from Hinde's

bag. They took turns sleeping and keeping watch. As Mama slept, Hinde looked at her face, resting now, but still worn with worry. She memorized every line, wanting to be able to summon up Mama's beautiful face once they were parted. Hinde tucked a shawl around Mama.

In the early morning, Mama tapped Hinde's shoulder to awaken her. Hinde looked around the train car and saw that all the nearby passengers were asleep. She realized that Mama wanted a private moment, and now Mama was handing her a small folded paper package. Mama whispered, "Keep this in the special pouch I made for you and never leave it unguarded." Mama had sewn a special deep pocket into each of Hinde's two blouses. This pocket was in the front center of the blouse where Hinde could reach into it from the neck. Her blouses fit loosely, so no one would suspect she had a pocket in such an unusual place. It was a safe place to keep valuables, right where she could see them.

"There are thirty rubles in that package," Mama whispered into Hinde's ear. "One day you may need this to get yourself out of a dangerous situation. Never forget that your safety is more important than any amount of money." Mama's words sent a shiver down her spine, but she realized she needed to pay attention.

Hinde tucked the money down into the special pocket in her blouse. She felt grateful to Mama. Thirty rubles was a lot of money, more than both her parents together would earn in a month. It felt like a fortune. She had never had that much money at one time.

"Thank you, Mama," Hinde said, leaning her head onto her mother's shoulder, feeling the comforting warmth of Mama's body. She had never known a time when Mama was not there for her. She tried to imagine life without Mama by her side. In that moment, she realized she would soon not have to imagine it. That life was about to begin.

It was morning and the train had arrived in Bremen. Papa's letter sat safely in her bag. He had included his address in New York City, in case something unforeseen prevented them from meeting as planned. He had also written some good advice for getting through United States Immigration at Ellis Island. Hinde planned to study this later. The immigration process brought worries. If you were not approved, you could be sent right back to Europe on the same boat that had brought you to America. If that happened, then all Papa's work would be for nothing, and Max would lose years of his life to the Russian army.

In Bremen, Mama and Hinde made their way across the station. The waiting room was an assault of noises and the smell of unwashed bodies. Hinde had never seen such a great hall. It was painted white, with high, arched windows all around and dozens of wooden benches filled with all kinds of travelers. A man with softness in his eyes approached them.

"Are you Jewish?" he asked in Yiddish. Hinde backed away from the man, but Mama looked carefully at him. Hinde could see Mama was deciding if he was trustworthy. Yes, he spoke Yiddish, but still, he was a stranger. Mama nodded to him slightly. The man showed Mama and Hinde a card that said he was an advisor from the German Jewish Agency. "Don't be afraid, I'm here to help you. It's my job."

Hinde felt that the man was sincere. Apparently, Mama did, too, as with some hesitation, she began to walk tentatively alongside him. Hinde walked along with them. "Follow me, I will help you find your train. It's only an hour's ride to Bremerhaven. 'Bremerhaven' means 'Harbor for the city of Bremen,'" he explained. "It's one of Germany's biggest ports on the North Sea. Most ships to New York leave from Bremerhaven." The three of them walked along, up stairs, down other stairs and finally onto a platform by a waiting train.

"This is your train," the man said, stopping before the open doors of a coach car. The man turned toward Mama and leaned forward with a stern face. "It's good you were careful before you spoke to me. Be careful with all strangers who approach you. I recommend you talk to no one, no matter how friendly they may appear. These stations and trains are filled with confidence men. They will try to swindle you because they know that passengers boarding these ships are likely to be carrying valuables. You don't need their help, and someone trying to help you when you don't need help is worthy of your suspicion. People are robbed every day, so beware." They thanked the man for his good advice. "*Shalom,*" he said, tipping his hat and then disappearing into the crowd.

They boarded the train and found seats for the short ride to Bremerhaven. Within an hour, the train pulled to a stop, and the doors opened onto an outdoor platform. Mama and Hinde got off and walked into the town. After the long journey, Hinde enjoyed being outside and walking. The sun was shining, and the air was fresh with sea breezes.

"Look at these huge houses, Hinde," Mama said, pointing out elegant three-story houses with tall windows and big doors, much bigger than any house Hinde had ever seen. She felt that Mama was trying to distract her from their impending separation. She didn't mind being distracted. She felt a terrible emptiness in her belly. Parting was going to be hard.

They walked along the docks, looking up at ship after ship, trying to find Hinde's. A man approached them and spoke to them in Yiddish. He politely offered to be a paid guide to help them make their way. Mama said strongly, "We are fine, and we know where we are going, thank you very much. We have no need for a guide." The man stayed with them for a few moments longer, but then he gave up and left them alone.

Finally, they came to Hinde's ship, the SS *Barbarossa*. Together, Mama and Hinde gazed up at the enormous ship. They had to lean backward and shade their eyes with their hands to take in the ship's soaring black sides and pointed bow. Sisal ropes a few inches in diameter tied the boat to large iron moorings on the dock. Two great smokestacks towered atop the boat, spewing clouds of blue-gray steam and smoke. Papa had written that this was a new ship with the latest design and the fastest speed. The smokestacks were raked back sharply, almost diagonal to the hull, emphasizing the speed and the long lines of the ship.

Crowds of people swirled around them speaking languages Hinde had never heard. The ship was scheduled to leave in a few hours, but Hinde needed to board the ship now. Both Mama and Hinde had tears in their eyes, and it was not from the smoke.

"Mama, I love you so much. I will do everything I can to help you and the other children come to New York soon, and our whole family will be together again. It won't take long, I promise. Papa and I will work hard and make lots of money. But I will miss you so much while we are apart."

"My dear daughter," Mama's voice cracked as she spoke, and her eyes were shiny with tears. "I will keep you in my heart until we meet again. It will take more than an ocean to separate us. We can be together in our hearts, even if we are far apart. Safe journey, my daughter, and know that my love goes with you."

After one final hug, Hinde turned and made her way up the wooden gangplank. At the top, she turned and waved to Mama one last time. Mama stood surrounded by a large crowd of people, many of them looking like they might also be someone's mother. Mama was still smiling and crying and waving. All the women surrounding her were smiling through their tears and waving. Hinde waved one last time and blinked away her own tears as she took the last few steps onto the ship.

SS BARBAROSSA

AUGUST 3, 1900

The officer at the top of the gangplank appeared to be a few years older than Hinde, perhaps nineteen or twenty. He had dark hair and blue eyes, and he wore a smart navy-blue uniform with brass buttons and a matching cap. He looked at Hinde with a business-like expression and put out his hand for her papers.

Hinde had felt more and more tense as she walked up the gangplank. She clutched her emigration documents, as well as the *shifskart*, the prepaid ticket that Papa had purchased. She could not stop thinking about a cousin who left for America, only to return the next day to Panemunė; he had been rejected because of some problem in his papers.

Hinde held everything out to the officer, and he reached over and took her documents, immediately becoming absorbed in his review. Every few moments he looked up at her as if he might discover something that was not right about her. She waited quietly as he inspected her papers, making sure she was who she claimed to be.

She felt more and more afraid that something might not be in order and that she would never even board the ship. Finally, the officer looked up at her.

"You are Hinde Breakstone?" he asked in German.

"Yes, I am," she replied, her voice squeaking a little. She attempted to put more courage into her voice. "From Panemunė."

"You are travelling to America alone?"

"Yes, but my Papa will meet me when the ship docks. He lives in New York." Hinde felt her fingernails digging into the palms of her hands.

The officer looked at her closely. Finally, he folded the papers and handed them back, nodding curtly at her. It was only a small, efficient movement of the head, but she was flooded with relief to see it. She had passed. She was to be allowed onto the ship. She hadn't realized she was holding her breath until this moment, and she felt herself relax as she breathed normally again.

"You will be travelling in steerage class," he said. He was not unfriendly, but he was not friendly either. Hinde understood a little German and got most of what he said. She assumed he knew she was Jewish, but he was not exactly rude to her. Only very efficient, like she was not quite a person.

Papa's letter had described the ship in detail. He had written that the SS *Barbarossa* was indeed one of the world's most modern ships. Travel between Europe and America was growing, Papa had explained, and new ships had been designed to accommodate more people more comfortably, and to make the trip much more quickly.

Papa wrote that "barbarossa" meant "red beard" in Italian, and that there was a pope named Barbarossa and also a few pirates. She thought she would prefer her ship be a nice prayerful pope rather than a boisterous pirate.

The SS *Barbarossa* was the first passenger ship ever built with multiple decks. These decks allowed the ship to have three classes, a few hundred in first class cabins on the highest deck, and a few hundred more in second class on the next deck. There was never any mixing between first and second class, as passengers on each deck were prohibited from the other decks.

Hinde knew that her ticket was the cheapest possible. That meant third class, also known as "steerage." The ship would carry sixteen hundred passengers in steerage. There was plenty of money to be made by the shipping companies, ferrying Jews and other persecuted peoples to the New World.

Steerage was located directly beneath the main deck of the ship. Hinde knew what a "steer" was in English, so she had imagined that steerage was a reference to cattle. It made sense, because steerage consisted of hundreds and hundreds of people being herded aboard the ship, then stowed in row upon row of beds, but Papa had explained that the ship's steering devices used to be in this very space, so Hinde realized that was the more likely reason for the word.

The ticket to America had cost about thirty dollars. With sixteen hundred steerage passengers, the shipping company made around $50,000 for a one-way trip, and this must be enough to buy all the jewels in the Russian Imperial Crown that Hinde had read about in school. She had spent hours and hours considering every aspect of the ship and her journey. And now she was finally here.

Passengers would be fed during the journey, but people

said that the shipping company spent only pennies a day per person. The food was expected to be terrible. For the return voyage, to net even more profits, the company would fill the steerage area with exports from America to be sold in Europe. Hinde had inherited her Papa's eye for business, and she could see that this ship was a profitable enterprise.

The officer motioned to a young sailor standing nearby, then gestured to Hinde that she should follow him. This sailor was a little younger and not quite as handsome as the officer. He led her along the ship's deck until they came to a large open space where a crowd of twenty or so passengers stood holding their luggage and waiting.

The sailor said, "Please join this group, which I will now escort to the steerage area." Hinde nodded her understanding. The sailor said loudly, "Everyone please follow me." Hinde assumed the sailor waited for a large enough group so that he did not have to make too many trips to the sleeping area.

He led the group across more of the ship's large open-air deck until they came to a big metal door flat in the decking. The door lay open. They climbed about six feet down a steep wooden staircase into the steerage area. It was much darker, and her eyes blinked as she tried to see this place that would be her home for the next week. The air seemed thick, and she had difficulty catching her breath.

As her eyes adjusted, she was amazed to see row upon row of rough wooden bunk beds lined up like unfriendly soldiers, with narrow aisles between them. Enough beds to sleep over a thousand passengers. Some beds were big enough to sleep five people. Hinde felt that all the passengers were being treated like just another kind of freight. Stowed away below decks, transported, and delivered.

The sailor led the group to an older woman in a white dress, and then took his leave. The woman stood amidst the bunk beds with a sheaf of papers. "I am one of the matrons here in steerage," she announced. Then she asked the first passenger for his name and gave him his bunk number. She pointed in the general direction he should go. Apparently, the ship employed these matrons to take charge of the steerage passengers. She was middle-aged, thick waisted, with strong freckled arms and a detached expression. She wore white stockings and shoes, and she had white hair pulled tightly back in a bun. Her eyes were a watery blue. When Hinde's turn came, the woman did not look directly at her as she recited the number "815," and pointed to the right. Hinde walked in that direction, looking at the numbers on each bed.

Finally, she found her bed, a top bunk with a ladder to climb up. Just then the matron appeared, saying "These lower bunks are reserved for older passengers not able to climb a ladder. You are young and won't have any trouble getting up top."

"Thank you," Hinde said.

The matron made no reply to Hinde's thanks, but instead continued sharply, "You stay away from the boys on this boat." The woman was now looking directly at her and shaking her finger in Hinde's face. "I don't want any trouble. I get all kinds of people in this low class of travel, but everyone behaves, or I move them to the beds over near the toilets where the smell is very bad. No one wants that." The woman finally retracted her finger. Hinde was intimidated and nodded to show she understood. The woman's job was not just to assist the steerage passengers but to make sure they behaved, especially young women travelling alone.

Hinde climbed up to explore the bed, glad to leave the scolding woman behind. It was a single bunk, and she was happy she wouldn't have to sleep next to a stranger. A small plaque with her number was attached to the bed post. She worried she might forget the number and not be able to find her way back later. Making an association with something else was always a good way to remember. She thought of the eight people in her family, that she was the first-born child, and that she had five siblings. That was it, 815. She tucked her heavy canvas bag into the foot of the bed under the thin mattress, relieved to finally put it down after carrying it for so long. She felt as though she had been carrying a bag of bricks everywhere she went.

She realized at that moment that the bag was going to be a problem for the entire trip. She was going to have to take it with her everywhere, for as long as it took to cross the ocean. It was the only way to protect her possessions. With so many people in steerage, there were bound to be a few who would steal her bag if she left it unattended. When she got to New York, she would write to Max that he should bring as little as possible, because he was going to have to carry it with him all the time.

Hinde looked out over all the other passengers. Near to her were other young women and girls who travelled alone. Everyone sat on their bunks and looked around at everyone else. She couldn't sit up straight because the bed was so close to the ceiling. She had to slump down to not knock herself on the head. She knew that she would forget about the ceiling one night and sit up suddenly and bang her head.

The mattress was straw and smelled fishy. Hinde laughed to herself as she imagined it might be stuffed with seaweed. She tucked some things into corners and tried to organize her bunk into a tiny home that would work for the next six days.

Farther away she could see families, mothers and fathers with children. There were hundreds of people sitting in the top and bottom bunks. At the greatest distance from the young women, all the way across the huge room, were the young men travelling alone. Whoever had planned the sleeping arrangements had done their best to keep shipboard romances to a minimum. Hinde was quite sure she would not be tempted by any boys. She was on a mission. Although she did pine a bit for Leonard.

She held tightly to her bag. She patted her chest to be sure the hidden pocket in her blouse was in place, holding the banknotes that Mama had given her. All was well.

The ship was gleaming and new, but nothing was clean enough to prevent the smells already drifting over from bathrooms. Toilets must have already overflowed, and people had even been sick on the floor between the bunks.

As Hinde became accustomed to the dim light, the huge space and the enormous number of people, she felt a return of excitement. She pushed away the longing for her mother and the sadness of leaving the only home she had ever known. She tried not to concentrate on the odors that increasingly filled the air. Her great adventure had begun. She had never experienced anything like this. She knew she could do it. It would only be six days, and then she would be reunited with Papa. She could endure worse than this, she thought proudly. The din of hundreds of bedfellows speaking dozens of languages blended into a background of sound as she lay back and closed her eyes. She promised herself she would do fine as she crossed the ocean.

After a short rest, she sat up and looked around again. There to her left, about twenty feet away, was another young girl about her own age. She also sat in a top bunk surveying the situation. The girl had long dark hair like Hinde and was dressed similarly. She, too, clutched a canvas bag. The girl waved to Hinde and motioned that they should get down and meet. They both jumped down and made their way toward one another.

"Hi, my name is Rebecca," the girl said in Yiddish.

"Hi. I'm Hinde."

"Where are you from?" asked the new friend.

"Panemunė, near Kaunas," Hinde told her.

"Oh! I'm from near Vilnius," replied Rebecca. "We are both from Lithuania, practically neighbors," she said, giving Hinde a big smile. Hinde smiled back.

"How old are you?" Rebecca asked.

"I'm sixteen."

"Me, too."

A friend for the journey, Hinde felt sure. What could be more fortunate?

"Let's go up on the deck and look around," suggested Rebecca.

"OK, but I have to get my bag first. I'm not looking forward to carrying it around everywhere with me, but there seems to be no other option."

"You're right, I was just realizing the same thing. We have no choice but to carry everything with us all the time," replied Rebecca.

The two girls got their bags, then made their way back up the staircase to the deck. Hinde took a deep breath of air. The weather was perfect, and the sky a clear blue. The deck was crowded, but the girls managed to find a spot at the railing where they could hold on and also watch the ship's progress. Above all, the air was fresh and breathable. She strained her eyes toward the crowded dock, hoping to catch one last glimpse of Mama, but she saw only a sea of uptilted faces and hands waving goodbye.

Suddenly her ears were pierced by the ship's loud horn announcing their departure. Both girls jumped at the loud sound. The noise of the engines changed, and Hinde held on tight to the railing as she felt the boat lurch into movement. Her new friend also grabbed onto the railing. The girls looked at one another, smiled broadly, and then they both started laughing. Now was the moment they had waited for.

Slowly, slowly the ship began to move out into the water. The horns blasted again. As the ship moved forward, it made all kinds of unexpected movements. Sometimes Hinde felt pushed to the right, sometimes to the left. The boat seemed to fall away from under her feet for an inch or so, then lift up again. All of these little movements left Hinde feeling lightheaded. She was grateful for the railing to hold onto.

Soon they were making their way down a channel with buildings on both sides. The ship's deck was high enough for them to see the town spread out along the shore and pierced by the occasional church spire. Dozens of boats lined the waterway, sailing ships, big steam boats, little fishing boats, but nothing as big or as modern as their own SS *Barbarossa*.

The channel got wider and wider, and after a time they passed a few small islands on either side, but then there was only water in every direction. Hinde realized they had entered the North Sea. She had never seen open water before and was amazed at the undulating waves stretching all the way to the horizon. She had looked at maps in school, and she had traced how they would sail along the north coast of Europe and then into the English Channel and out into the North Atlantic. Hinde was glad that the trip would take only six days. She imagined what it must have been like for Papa, spending weeks on board with the terrible odors. She was lucky to be on such a fast ship.

After an hour or so of watching how the boat made its way, the girls found a bit of deck out of the way of everyone else and sat down on their bags. The bags at least provided a soft place to sit. They traded their stories about how they came to be making this journey. Rebecca was the youngest child. Her Mama and Papa and her four siblings were already settled in Texas. When Rebecca arrived, the entire family would be together once again. Hinde was pretty sure Texas was not near New York, which Rebecca confirmed.

"Texas is out west, I've heard," Rebecca said. "It's got lots of lakes and trees in the eastern part where we live. There are plenty of jobs and everybody is working. My family wrote that they like it there and have even found a synagogue."

Hinde did not know if there was a synagogue near where she would be living. Her mind travelled back to her final meeting with Rabbi David. He had once again insisted that every word of the Bible was literally true. Hinde was astounded that her intelligent teacher could have such a simple-minded point of view. She had read the Bible as part of her schooling, and she could not for a minute believe that it was all literal truth. In her strong but respectful way, she had expressed her opinion to Rabbi David.

"*Rebbe*, I will always be a Jewish girl. I love our traditions and our strong values, and our food and our whole way of life. I love the Bible and all the stories. To me these stories are beautiful metaphors, where one thing stands for another. They aren't meant to be taken literally. I will never believe in the Bible the way you do, the way you want me to, and in this, I must follow my heart and my mind." Hinde did not mean to shock the Rabbi, but thought that she had, especially when he made disapproving noises.

Hinde's family had told everyone that Papa had gone to Vilnius for a long trip hoping to expand the dairy business. Everyone had accepted this, and now they were telling everyone that Hinde would soon leave to join him and help with the new business he was establishing. Since Max was still at home, no one suspected that these absences were related to his age and the draft.

Hinde thanked the Rabbi for his years of teaching, and for the worlds of learning he had opened up for her in history, mathematics, and the English language. He seemed mollified by her gratitude, and she politely said goodbye and left.

Mama and Papa were not happy that Hinde spoke her mind so freely with the Rabbi. They had told her for years to be quiet and listen to the learned man. Privately Hinde thought her parents agreed with her, and sometimes they let down their guard and said what they really thought, which was the same as what Hinde thought. They were the older generation and were respectful of the Rabbi above all others and would never disagree with him to his face. Both parents had admonished Hinde and suggested she keep her opinions to herself, but she felt so strongly that she had not been able. She had little conflict with her parents, but this was an area where they did not all agree.

Hinde knew her life would not change if the New York synagogue turned out to be far away from where she would live. She wasn't planning to go every week anyway. As she thought about it, she realized the many Jewish immigrants in New York would probably mean there were lots of synagogues. Still, it was not a factor for her as it was for Rebecca. Hinde kept her thoughts to herself, not knowing Rebecca for even a whole hour yet, although she seemed so familiar and already such a close friend.

The two girls sat together and talked about their journeys to Bremerhaven and what their lives had been like in Lithuania. Rebecca had stayed with cousins until the family sent her ticket. She was the last one of her family to set out for the New World. Hinde was leaving most of her family behind. She felt a heavy heart as the ship's progress put more and more distance between her and Mama and her siblings. The two girls understood one another, the particular mix of excitement and grief that comes with leaving a cherished home and setting out for a new one.

They traded stories of anti-Semitic incidents they had experienced as Lithuania became more and more intolerant. Hinde told Rebecca about the bakery lady, whom she had known her whole life, and who suddenly treated her badly. Rebecca said her family had lived in the city of Vilnius, but when the new laws came, they had been forced to move out to the countryside. Her brother had been studying at the university, but he had been thrown out as the new laws prohibited Jews from receiving higher education. They were both happy to leave these memories behind.

The evening came on, and both girls were tired from all the excitement of their travels. They gathered up their bags and returned to their bunks. Hinde climbed up into number 815. She settled down and pushed and pulled her bag until it resembled a pillow. She put her head down, feeling tired after the long journey and this long day. She had just started to drift off, but suddenly felt a small panic as she realized that she was all alone in this bed. At home, the whole family had slept near one another, on palettes on the floor, made soft with blankets. Nighttime had always meant that she could reach out and touch Selma's arm or her hair, or that she could hear her brothers breathing. Tonight, for the first time in her life, Hinde was going to sleep all alone. She stretched out in the bed. It was a treat to have such a big space all to herself, and she was happy to be finally on her way. But at that moment, those happy feelings were overwhelmed by the ache she felt for everyone she had left behind.

The days went by. The communal bathrooms had sinks and running water. The bathrooms were new, but inadequate for so many people. Although the ship's crew tried to keep them clean, they could not keep up with the more than one thousand people in steerage. The toilets continually overflowed, and the smells were intense, often filling the entire steerage area. Every time Hinde entered the bathroom, she made sure not to accidentally set her bag down in some foul puddle. Dragging the bag around was a burden, but necessary.

There was no way to be alone on the ship. Hinde had always valued quiet time alone, taking walks in the woods outside Panemunė. Here it was never quiet. Even in the night, so many people made a lot of noise just sleeping. The only privacy was in the women's toilet stalls in the bathroom, but the odor there was unbearable. Hinde could huddle down in her bunk to change her clothes so that no one could see her. That was as private as it got.

Everyone in steerage was poor, and many people did not look trustworthy. Each day at some point, Hinde and Rebecca took turns guarding the bags for one another. This allowed one of them to enjoy half an hour of freedom walking around on the deck outside without any heavy baggage. Hinde discovered that if she made her way to the very back of the ship, she was often the only one there. She could stare out over the bubbling wake that the fast-moving ship carved into the green ocean water. After a time, she would once again feel that precious sense of being alone.

Hinde knew she should be grateful to be on a new boat. Only a short time ago, many boats had taken as much as a month to cross the Atlantic. Conditions were so bad that one in ten steerage passengers would take sick and die during the voyage. The very young and the very old were always the most vulnerable. She knew she was lucky to be young and strong and travelling on the new SS *Barbarossa*.

Meals were served in the dining salons, located off the huge sleeping hall. You didn't have to go outside to get there. There were long wooden tables where everyone sat, and Rebecca and Hinde usually ate together. Both girls enjoyed the chance to strike up conversations with other passengers and hear their stories. Everyone had a story, many of them exciting tales of escape from prejudice and danger. No one undertook this journey without strong forces motivating them.

The food was cheap, but it was better and more plentiful than at home. Hinde was always hungry even though there was plenty of food. She drank the cold milk that was served. It was cold and fresh, not like the frequently spoiled milk at the Breakstone dairies, served to family because it was too old to sell. There was also a dark German bread, a treat to Hinde. It was perfect for dunking into the German stews that were served every day. These stews had only scraps of meat, but they were tasty with spices and potatoes or noodles. To Hinde the stews were a luxury.

For the first few days, the weather was bright and warm with sunshine every day. The steerage passengers all crowded onto the deck during the day, taking in the ocean air. It was hard to return to the evil odors of steerage at the end of the day. The girls held their noses against the smells. Neither of them experienced seasickness, but others did and would throw up in their bunk or on the floor. Sailors came to clean up the floor only once a day, so walking to the toilets meant being careful where you stepped. With each day, the odors got worse and worse.

One night as they returned to their bunks, Rebecca turned to Hinde. "Just walking to our bunks is a nightmare. I feel sick from the smells of everyone else getting sick."

"I know," Hinde replied. "I sometimes wish my sense

of smell would stop working. I don't need it for anything, especially at night. I would like to keep it in the daytime, however, to smell the salt and sea air."

Rebecca gave Hinde a smile and a hug goodnight. "At least we don't smell things while we sleep, a small blessing."

Day after day, the two girls became inseparable, spending time together, talking about what it would be like in America. They always sat in a little corner of the deck in a place they regarded as just for them. They sat on their bags and talked for hours. They watched the sea and the sky and the clouds.

Hinde took Rebecca to her favorite place at the rear of the ship. The girls worked out a way to stand on the straps of their bags to keep them from falling overboard. Then they leaned out over the railings and watched the ship's wake streaming away from them, boiling with white foam. Each moment brought them closer to America. They told each other more about the lives they were leaving behind, and their hopes and fears for what lay ahead.

Eventually Hinde confessed her reservations about Judaism and in particular that she didn't accept the literal truth of every word of the Bible. Rebecca was not shocked. She simply said that she didn't worry about all that. She was happy to light the candles and observe *Shabbat* with her family. Hinde was relieved that religion was not an issue between them.

The two girls watched the handsome young sailors as they went about their jobs. Hinde didn't mind when these boys seemed to enjoy watching them as well. She did mind some of the older passengers. These men stared at them covertly and lewdly, not pleasant at all. Hinde was glad to have a friend in Rebecca with whom she could flee when one of these predatory men looked like he might come over and try to strike up a conversation.

One the third day, Hinde brought out her letter from Papa, and the girls talked about the looming trials they would face at Ellis Island. Rebecca also had gotten letters from her family sharing tips on what to expect. She told Hinde they would have to climb a steep staircase with inspectors watching them to make sure they were healthy. Everyone called these the "Stairs of Separation." If you didn't climb the stairs briskly, you could be separated out. Hinde imagined this happening to her. What if she got sick that day? What if she got the flu like she had a year ago and could barely get out of bed? Rebecca told her that the inspector would chalk mark an 'X' on your clothing if you did not look well. America did not want the ill or disabled. This was especially frightening for families travelling together. If one family member failed a test, they would be separated from the others and might be sent back to Europe all alone.

After the staircase came the examinations. Everyone was examined by a doctor to be sure they were healthy. This was the so-called the "Six Second Examination." It was a cursory once-over, nothing in-depth. There was also a mental examination. The doctors would ask twenty-nine questions to be sure you were mentally healthy. Hinde knew that she and Rebecca were both young and strong and mentally healthy. Papa's letter told Hinde not to be afraid, that she would do fine. Still, whenever they talked about Ellis Island, Hinde noticed a little note of panic in her own voice and in Rebecca's, too. She reassured Rebecca, in part just to reassure herself. She was grateful to have a friend in these moments, someone else who would be tested in the very same way, who had the very same fears. It was such good fortune that they had found one another.

$\mathcal{Life}$ in steerage was bearable until the fourth day when the ship encountered a storm. A team of sailors came down and closed the big doors up to the deck. All the steerage passengers were locked in. Any small hatches or air passages were shut tight as well. By midday the air had become fetid. Without any breezes from outside, the air quickly went from stale to putrid, dominated by the smells of urine, feces, and vomit.

The boat rocked more and more violently. Hinde held onto the edges of her bunk to avoid being thrown to the floor. Locked in the dark with all the others, she heard the wails of children and adults alike, moaning with terror. Suddenly, the ship lurched and seemed to fall through space. A chorus of screams arose from the bunks all up and down the huge hall. Hinde was surprised to hear her own voice cry out with everyone else's.

The next day, the storm continued to rage. The doors remained locked. Everyone was trapped in the dank foulness of the steerage hall. Although there was food in the dining room just a few steps away, few people ate anything. Hinde worried that if she ate, she would become sick. She couldn't afford to be sick with Ellis Island only two days away.

Someone was always seasick, and the smell of vomit was everywhere. That second night of the storm, she tossed and turned and had trouble falling asleep. This wasn't surprising since all she had done that day was sit in her bunk and hold on for dear life.

In the middle of the night, there was a huge roll of the ship, and half asleep, Hinde found herself lifted out of her high bunk and thrown to the floor. Everything seemed to happen in slow motion, and she felt herself sailing through the air for what seemed like a long time. Then she landed on her right side with a great jolting force, and abruptly, time switched back to normal as she rolled several feet across the floor. She heard other people who had also been thrown from their bunks crying out from the floor.

Hinde lay still, terrified that the ship was about to sink. She waited for the huge waves of water that would come rushing across the room and drown them all. But nothing happened. After about five minutes, she decided she was going to survive. She pulled herself up tentatively, not sure how hurt she was. As soon as she moved, her right arm began to throb. She felt panic, immediately thinking about the examination at Ellis Island. What if she were rejected because of an injured arm? Slowly she sat up, reorienting to where she was and what had happened. Nothing else hurt, but she wasn't sure about her arm. She could barely move it. She wiggled each finger to be sure they all worked. She gently rocked the arm, checking to see how bad it was. She decided it wasn't broken. The pain seemed bearable, so she carefully got to her feet and climbed back into her bunk. As the ship continued to toss, sleep was fitful. She was grateful she hadn't been hurt badly, but her arm throbbed through the night. She swore she would be better before they got to New York.

That night, Hinde became seasick for the first time. Like so many others had, she vomited on the floor next to her bunk, as there was no place else. People walked through vomit all over the steerage hall. Hinde ran to the bathroom where the odors were so intense that she retched from the smell, even though she had already vomited. She threw up over and over until she was empty and exhausted. Making her way back to her bunk, she felt weak and wretched. She held onto the other bunks to keep her balance. There was simply no way to keep herself and her clothing and her shoes clean. Rebecca was not doing well either and was no help, staying in her own bunk to be sick in peace. The only thing to do was to lie as still as possible in the bunk and pray for the storm to be over.

Finally, the sun came out and the seas calmed. The sailors returned and soon the great doors to steerage were opened. Light and warmth streamed in, and the stifling odors dissipated. Hinde fell asleep at last. She awakened after a few hours, still feeling weak. She made her way over to Rebecca's bunk to look in on her friend. Rebecca looked a bit green but otherwise ok.

"Are you alright?" Hinde asked. "Do you want to go outside? It looks like they have opened the doors. I would love to breathe some fresh air."

Rebecca climbed down, looking just like Hinde felt. The two girls dragged their clumsy bags up the steps and out into the open. The freshness outside was invigorating. They stood next to one another and held onto the railing while inhaling huge gulps of the precious air. Hinde had never before appreciated how valuable it was to breathe fresh air. Her arm wasn't hurting too much. She closed her eyes and inhaled deeply. Gratitude filled her along with the air.

The waves were still very high from the storm, reaching almost to the level of the deck. They were lucky to find a spot where they could hold onto the ship's railing, as so many people poured onto the deck just to breathe good air. It was awkward holding onto their bags and the railing, too. Older people did not venture outside, as even the young and agile could stumble and fall as the ship pitched up and down. Gradually over the hours, the seas subsided, and there seemed to be more room on deck as people moved about freely. There was no damage to be seen. The SS *Barbarossa* had held up well, even if her passengers had not.

The last day of the journey finally arrived. Rebecca grew more and more excited. She couldn't stop talking about seeing her family. "Once we land in New York, I have a train ticket to Texas. My whole family will meet me at the station when I get there. I can't wait. It's been almost a year."

Hinde said, "I will take the ferry from Ellis Island over to Manhattan. Papa said there is a park where I can wait for him safely. I haven't seen him in three months." They exchanged addresses and promised to stay in touch after they were settled.

As America neared, the girls grew more and more anxious about the looming trials at Ellis Island. They rehearsed the questions they expected from immigration officials. They reviewed all the well-known reasons why some people were rejected and deported back to Europe. Groups of passengers spontaneously gathered for English lessons, and the girls joined in. They made sure they knew every answer that would guarantee their entry into the New World.

Early the next morning, August 8, 1900, Hinde and Rebecca crowded on deck with all the other passengers. Everyone waited for landfall. Warm sunlight streamed down on them, and little white clouds skittered against a fresh blue sky. That morning, crew members had given each person a name tag on a string to wear around their neck. The tag had a number written on it that corresponded to their entry on the ship's manifest. Hinde was number eleven. Eleven. Hers had been one of the first tickets sold. Today she would walk off the ship into New York.

The sky looked different now. Hinde kept her eyes on a thin line of white clouds that stretched all the way across the horizon ahead. Slowly, a dark band of land appeared beneath the clouds. As they got closer, she could make out the horizontal stripes of sandy beaches, and soon she could see the dark shapes of trees. The ship slowed and finally entered the Narrows into New York Harbor. Even though they were not in the harbor yet, Hinde could now see the statue that she had heard so much about. It was visible, but still small in the distance. Gradually it grew as they made their way across the water. Hinde could feel her heart pounding with excitement. They might still be on the ship, but they had arrived.

Everyone was transfixed with watching the great lady who faced them from hundreds of feet above the water. She had only been in the harbor for ten years. While the statue was expected to age to the beautiful blue-green color of weathered copper, that process could take thirty years or more. Today, her original copper still gleamed. Hinde had read all about this lady and knew her history. Her full name was Liberty Enlightening the World. But nothing had prepared Hinde for the actual sight, the flowing grace of her robes, the nobility of her proud head, the one arm raised high.

The statue was a recent gift from the people of France. People all over France had donated to help create the gift. It was given to welcome everyone who came to the New World. A similar fundraising project in America had raised the money to build the pedestal, with most donations being from working people, the amounts less than one dollar.

The lady faced out to sea so that she greeted everyone who arrived. With her arm reaching toward the sky, she raised the torch of freedom, of democracy. Lady Liberty conveyed her welcome to everyone who came into the harbor, Hinde included. Her welcome was as warm to those in steerage as to those in first class. Hinde felt tears in her eyes. She clutched Rebecca's hand, and as they exchanged glances, she saw that her friend was crying, too.

Soon everyone around them was either laughing or crying. More and more the sounds of joy predominated. Whole families joined in song. Everyone was hugging and kissing. It was as if a spontaneous celebration had broken out. No more tsars or kings in America. From now on the people would know best what the people wanted and needed.

Hinde bent backward to better look up at the statue. She was moved by the gently draping folds of the golden robe, the seven star-like rays of her crown, and most of all the strong stance with her arm raising the torch and defying anyone to try to rule over her and the people of this New World. Liberty was big, and she was powerful. Hinde knew she had come to the right place.

For some reason, she thought of Helen of Troy, another lady of another harbor long ago. Helen, whose beauty had launched a thousand ships. In that moment a new thought came to her. Her new name would be Helen. No more Hinde from Lithuania. She would now be Helen of New York. She would be strong and free and powerful. This was where she was meant to be.

ELLIS ISLAND

August 8, 1900

Every passenger crowded onto the ship's deck. Everyone craned their neck to see the harbor. Adults, children, entire families all held onto their belongings, ready to move on to the next steps of their journey. The bright morning sun promised a warm summer day. A light breeze blew small white clouds over the buildings of New York. The fresh air was exhilarating after the days of stench.

With one hand Helen clutched the cloth bag that she had guarded so closely since the moment she left home. It held everything she owned in this world, the treasured gifts from her brothers and sisters, her clothing, Papa's letter, everything. With the other hand, she held onto her new friend, Rebecca. The girls' time together was running out, and they held onto one another as if they could prolong the hours.

The great ocean liner blasted the air with the sound of its horn. The ship slowed and pulled in close to shore. They were just inside the Narrows, the entryway channel from the ocean into New York Harbor. The ship's engines wound down to a hum. At some point in the last six days, Helen had stopped hearing their thundering din. She felt her breath release and her shoulders drop as the tension from the noise subsided.

A small boat of visiting medical inspectors pulled up alongside them. Helen watched as nimble young sailors clambered down ropes and tied the smaller boat to the great ship. A gangplank was set up, and the team of inspectors came aboard. A few went into the first and second-class areas, making sure no one was obviously sick, but those passengers were automatically admitted with only cursory inspection. U.S. citizens were not inspected at all.

Everything changed when the inspectors came down to the steerage area. Helen and the others were herded from the deck back into the sleeping area. Rebecca reminded Helen to pinch her cheeks to look healthier for the inspection. Each passenger had to stand next to their bunk. The inspectors began to move methodically around the great hall.

If you had a rash, you were marked for further checking. Americans did not want measles, or worse yet smallpox, entering their country. Anyone who looked pale or too red or a little ashen was under suspicion. Helen was shocked when she saw a woman bite through her cuticle and use her own blood to rouge her cheeks so that she would look healthier and more youthful. People were desperate to get through these examinations.

An inspector walked by Helen and looked directly into her eyes. She was frightened that she would be singled out, so she tried to radiate good health and even managed a lopsided smile. Thinking a show of good English might reassure him, she spoke, "Good day, sir. I hope you are doing well." The man nodded to her without expression. A wash of relief swept over her as he moved on. She watched as the same inspector approached Rebecca and felt a second wave of relief to see him pass by her friend.

Eventually the inspectors climbed the stairs out of steerage, returned to their boat, and departed. Everyone came back out into the air on deck, except for those the inspectors had marked as suspect. Helen felt badly for these poor unfortunates, but knew she was powerless to help. Those who had been marked were kept below. Sailors guarded the great doors in the main deck, so they could not rejoin the crowd. The engines of the ship started up again. Finally, they sailed all the way into the harbor itself, and the boat docked at the lower tip of Manhattan.

Once again, the agile young sailors swung themselves down to the pier and tied up the ship with the thickest ropes Helen had ever seen. Gangplanks were brought out, and everyone crowded toward them. It was six days since she had left Europe. It seemed a world away, and the promise of America was right before her.

U.S. citizens, along with first and second-class passengers, now debarked directly onto Manhattan Island. These were the affluent. They would not end up in hospitals or be a burden to the country. They would pass through customs here at the pier, and then their journey was done. They were free to travel wherever they wished within the United States.

But the sixteen hundred steerage passengers now faced their most feared obstacle, Ellis Island, the Island of Tears. Gradually they shuffled forward. Eventually, it was Helen's turn. She held her head high as she walked down the gangplank, toward what she hoped would become her new home. When she reached the bottom, she paused and looked down at her foot, feeling a thrill as she took her first step onto American soil. She did not look back at the great ship; what mattered most was what was in front of her.

As she stepped off the gangplank, she planted both feet on the new continent and stood still for a fraction of a moment. She had arrived. Even though the ground seemed to sway under her, she flashed on the future, on what her life would become. Mama and all the other children would come soon, and they would all be reunited. Helen would be an important wage earner for the family. Then what? What would her future be once her family was together again? She rarely thought about it, her focus always on the family. Of course, she had dreams. A husband, a home, her own children, her own family? With her feet firmly in this New World, anything seemed possible.

She snapped herself out of her reverie as everyone was herded onto barges for Ellis Island. She heard smatterings of different languages. Rebecca was right behind her. The two girls stood at the railing of the barge and watched as Ellis Island came into view. For each of them, for all these immigrants, this small island in New York harbor was the object of all their fears and all their hopes.

As they came closer, Helen was surprised to see an elegant brick building. It was new, and looked like a palace, the biggest building she had ever seen. It had four gleaming copper cupolas, large windows, imposing doors, and green manicured lawns. She had not expected this. She had imagined more of a dark stone prison. This was the gateway where the thousands of immigrants who came to the New World each year would be processed and sorted. Some would be accepted, and some would not. The thought of being turned away was daunting, but Helen felt an urge to stand up tall, to ready herself to join those who would make it through. She lifted her head and straightened her spine. Just changing her posture bolstered her spirit. And it might communicate confidence to those who would soon be watching and judging.

On a tall pole before the main entrance, the flag of the United States waved with its forty-five stars. Huge crowds of people now formed a winding river into the front door of the building. Helen had heard Ellis Island itself called "the front door to freedom."

The barge docked near the entrance. Helen and Rebecca let go of one another's hands to walk single file down the small gangplank. Two uniformed guards came up immediately and reached for their bags. Helen panicked and jerked her bag away from the guard. He was in uniform, and his sudden appearance reminded Helen of the soldiers who had come to the house that day for Max. Helen fought down her panic as she realized she was overreacting. The soldier smiled down at her and said kindly, in English, "It's alright. Don't worry. Everyone gets their bags returned to them. We have to take all luggage at this point." Helen handed over her bag reluctantly, as there was no choice.

The guard tore off half of a piece of paper and handed it to her. He then tied the other end of the paper onto her bag. She wondered if she would ever see her few possessions again, especially the precious gifts each of her little siblings had given her. She felt grateful to Mama for sewing the secret pocket inside her blouse. She tapped her chest lightly, and she could still feel that the precious thirty rubles were safe.

The two girls lined up with more people than Helen had ever seen before. Gradually they moved toward the large main doors of the building. After an hour on the slow-moving line, they finally entered the building.

They found themselves in an enormous red-tiled room with tall ceilings and great staircases up to a second level. Piles of baggage were stacked everywhere, each with a string and a number. Cloth bags and suitcases were all thrown together, waiting to be claimed by their owners. The red ceramic tiles that covered the walls created echoes and reverberations. For another hour, everyone moved slowly in long lines through this baggage room.

Soon they came to a group of interpreters, calling out in different languages. They moved toward a young man speaking perfect Yiddish, explaining that he would be their interpreter. This was a relief as the girls didn't want to make any mistakes by not understanding the instructions. The interpreter led about thirty of them toward a steep stairway. He explained that they would need to go up the stairs to the registry room. Once there, they should find seating until they were called by the inspectors. They started up the crowded stairs, but it was slow moving. A few minutes later they heard their interpreter guiding another group over, this time speaking a completely different language that Helen could not even identify.

Gradually they ascended. As they climbed up, Helen realized she was climbing the dreaded "Stairs of Separation." The stairs and the walls were covered with the same dark red tiles so that everyone's footsteps and conversation echoed in the air. Helen was feeling exhausted from standing in line for so long. She was hungry and the air felt stale with so many people. Despite how she felt, she forced herself to step lively. She wanted to display lots of energy because she knew they were all being watched.

At that very moment, she noticed a short, heavy man in a dark suit with his hat pulled down over his eyes. He stood to one side and watched everyone with a critical eye as they went up the stairs. A few feet in front of the girls was an older woman with a cane, breathing heavily and wheezing a bit. The man waited until she passed by, then approached her from behind and quickly and inconspicuously marked the back of her jacket with white chalk, drawing a large X near the shoulder. The woman did not even know she had been marked. Rebecca reached out and squeezed Helen's hand. Helen knew they had both witnessed this unknowing woman's future fall into jeopardy. Her heart ached for this poor woman and for the others who would be turned away. She knew what they had risked getting here, and the horror they would return to.

Getting the X meant you would be separated out from everyone else, even from your own family. You would then be scrutinized to see if you were healthy enough to enter the United States of America. No one wanted to get that X.

The girls finally arrived at the second floor where there were long wooden benches. They found two seats together. Rebecca asked the lady next to her how long she had been waiting, and the lady replied it had been three or four hours.

"At least we can sit," Rebecca said, trying to be cheerful. "We can watch all the people."

"Yes, everyone looks as nervous as we do," Helen laughed.

"We don't have to worry," Rebecca said bravely. "We're young and smart and strong."

"Yes, we are lucky," Helen agreed. "I wonder where we

will be tomorrow? Will you be on the train to Texas? Will I be in my new home in New York City? I only hope that the people I'm going to live with are nice. They are relatives, but I don't remember them."

Rebecca replied, "I can hardly wait to see my family. I know I will miss some things about the old country." Helen noticed that it was already the "old country" before they had even fully arrived in the new.

"I miss my little town and all those relatives too, but I am so excited that I will see my Papa soon," Helen said. "It's been months since I last saw him."

The girls sat for a long time, and Rebecca even fell asleep for an hour or so. Finally, Helen's name was called by an inspector at the far end of the room. She squeezed Rebecca's hand and got up and moved quickly toward the inspector.

"Do you speak English?" he asked.

"Yes, but maybe not quite so well as you." Helen smiled as she replied in what she hoped was a friendly and easy manner.

"Your name, miss?" he asked in English.

"Hinde Breakstone," she replied, leaving off her new name so as not to confuse things.

"Are you in good health, miss?" he asked.

"Excellent," she replied, grateful now for the endless hours of tutoring in English at the school and the extra English practice on the ship.

He filled out a form and ushered Helen to a small space behind his desk where a second doctor finished up with the previous person. This was the so-called "six-second examination." The doctor held a large stick of chalk in his hand. More chances for the dreaded X. The doctor reviewed the form, looked Helen over, and asked her to sit on a small white painted stool.

"Open wide," he commanded, taking a metal tongue depressor out of a glass jar, and inserting it into her mouth. Helen opened wide as he looked into her mouth. He looked at her face and her neck, and into her hair. He asked her to extend her hands and turn them over, so he could examine both sides. And that was that. He was done. Face, hair, neck and hands.

She watched as he stamped the form. All she knew was that she did not see the word, "Denied." This was the word you did not want to see on your form. "Denied" was the same as the chalk mark X.

Next, she was ushered further behind the inspector's desk to another doctor. This doctor was interested only in her eyes. Helen knew he was called the "eye-man." Eye disease was the number one cause for deportation, and Helen had heard that even the slightest pink color to the eye could send someone back to Europe. The doctor used a light to examine Helen's eyes, motioning with his finger for her to look this way and that. Apparently, she passed, as he gestured for her to continue down the line.

Finally, she came to the third and last doctor. He sat on a high stool and had before him the ship's manifest. This was the document that had been filled out in Bremerhaven during boarding. Helen had been asked her name, her age, who would be meeting her in New York, and other questions. All the answers had been written down on line eleven of the form.

Helen realized she was about to hear the famous "twenty-nine questions," designed to make sure you were mentally healthy.

"What is your name, miss?"

"Hinde Breakstone," Helen again answered this question.

"Where did you come from?"

"Lithuania," Helen replied. "Near Koanas, the village of Panemunė."

"How much is two plus two?"

"Four," Helen replied with a small smile. She was proud she had worked so hard on her English. She had no trouble understanding the questions or formulating her replies.

"Who's meeting you?"

"My father, Chaim Breakstone. He came a few months ago. Everyone calls him Hymie."

"Where are you now?"

"In America at Ellis Island," she replied.

The inspector continued to verify her answers, mixing in questions to which any sane person would know the answers, so long as they spoke English. Once he had asked all twenty-nine questions, he seemed convinced that Helen was of sound mind. He put away his chalk stick, stamped her form once again with something Helen could not read but was pretty sure did not say "Denied," and gave her a curt nod of dismissal.

Helen turned around and walked back toward the seating area. She felt relief, for she knew if she had been found to be physically ill or mentally incompetent, she could either have been put into the Ellis Island Hospital for days of observation and more extensive testing, or she could have been sent back home on the SS *Barbarossa's* return voyage. Looking up, she saw Rebecca heading toward her with a big smile. Both girls had passed.

A guide came by and herded all those emerging from their examinations back down to the baggage room. Here they handed over their baggage stubs. It seemed a miracle to Helen when she was reunited with her bag. She opened it and reached inside, feeling around for the special trinkets from her siblings, the small piece of paper with her father's address, her clothing. Everything seemed to be there, untouched. Finally, she closed the bag again, satisfied that nothing had been taken. Rebecca was also looking relieved.

In the baggage room there was a window with an iron grating. A large sign hung over the window that said, "Money Exchange." Papa had told her she would need to change any money she brought from home, so Helen took the rubles out of her secret pocket and went up to the window. The teller took her rubles and handed her back United States money. Helen looked at it with curiosity, as it was the first she had ever seen. She now had about fifteen U.S. dollars. This quickly went back into the secret pocket in her blouse.

Rebecca changed money as well, which she quietly tucked into a deep pocket in her skirt. The two girls had never mentioned their secret pocket money, and they both smiled and understood one another's previous discretion.

They moved with the crowd out the front of the building toward the railroad ticket office. Here Rebecca would wait until it was close to the time of her departure for Texas. Then she would be taken by barge to the train station in New Jersey.

As they walked along, they passed several outdoor food stands advertising boxed lunches. They seemed expensive to Helen, two dollars each, but then she had no idea what things cost in America. The girls had not eaten since early that morning, but they agreed that two dollars seemed like much too much money to spend. They would take their chances on finding less costly food later.

They sat down on the grass beside the crowded walk-ways to enjoy a final moment together. They noticed a man nearby with one of the lunches they had passed up. They could see him eating a large section of bologna sausage that looked good. When he finished that, he brought out a small fruit pie and smelled it to see if it was fresh. He made a bad face and put the pie back into the box uneaten. Finally, he brought out a tin of sardines, but he didn't seem to have a way to open it. Both girls were happy they had resisted buying the lunch. They were hungry, but they would get through the rest of the day.

Helen and Rebecca said their goodbyes. Rebecca had her train ticket to Texas. The two girls held hands with one another. Helen felt like she had known Rebecca her entire life. Even though it had been only six days since they met, they had shared a life-changing experience. They had crossed an ocean together, been through a terrible storm, and had supported one another through the frightening trials at Ellis Island. They had shared their dreams and worries. No one else in the world understood their journey. Helen felt that Rebecca was her best friend.

"We'll write, and one day we'll visit one another," Helen said.

"We'll be best friends forever," said Rebecca. "No one else will ever understand what you and I have shared."

"I will write and tell you everything that happens," Helen promised.

"Me, too."

Helen gave Rebecca Papa's address so she could send a letter. The two girls parted ways, and Helen stood and watched until Rebecca's form was lost in the crowd.

⇌

Papa had said in his letter that he would know her arrival date and time because ship arrivals were printed in the newspaper every day. Helen boarded the ferry to Manhattan, such a small boat after her days on the *Barbarossa*. The ferry smelled like burning coal. She could hear nothing over the deafening noise of the engine. She didn't mind the noise. She didn't mind anything now. The worst was behind her, and she was on her way to meet Papa.

Manhattan came closer and closer. After a short twenty-minute ride, the ferry docked at Battery Park. Helen walked down her last gangplank, still holding tightly to her cloth bag. Finally, she was free in the New World.

The park was crowded with people from all over the world getting off the ferries, as well as with New Yorkers arriving from the neighboring streets to enjoy the park. Everyone scanned the crowd for relatives and loved ones. Young boys stood on top of fences or climbed gaslight poles for a better view. Helen found a bench with an un-obstructed view of the entire park and sat down, tucking her bag under the seat.

For half an hour, she watched as other families reunited, couples, children, parents. They would shriek and run to embrace one another, crying, tears and smiles all at once, like summer rain. It was easy to tell the new arrivals from the New Yorkers. The new people were roughly dressed, their clothes neither clean nor neat, all of them carrying heavy bags or suitcases. Their faces looked tired but eager. In contrast, the New Yorkers looked confident and at ease in their surroundings. Many of the women wore pretty dresses and matching hats with exotic curling feathers, and the wealthier men sported suits and natty black homburg hats.

Some of the locals were just out for a walk with their dogs, including a little white dust mop with raisin eyes and another that looked like a German sausage with legs. Helen had never seen such clean and pampered looking dogs, only the mutts that wandered the streets of her village.

For the reuniting families, this was a happy ending to an important chapter of their lives. So would it be for her, the end of a long journey to the New World, the beginning of a new life. She was ready for anything. Her eyes scanned the crowd for Papa's tall form. She knew he would come. You could rely on Papa.

9

THE LOWER EAST SIDE

Helen sat on her bench and continued to watch for Papa. The little park presented more new impressions in one place than she had ever experienced. So much was happening at one time: conversations in many languages, the clip-clop of horses on the surrounding streets, people finding relatives, shouting, laughing, hugging, embracing. She hoped Papa would find her, as her chances of finding him in the crowd were not good. Helen stayed put on her park bench and took in her first impressions of New York. Her body was tired from the stress of a long day and her endless worry over the inspections at Ellis Island. She wanted to close her eyes and rest, but of course that was out of the question. The moment was too important, and the day was not yet done, and too much was going on. She watched the people in their strange clothes, speaking their strange languages.

After an hour or so without Papa's appearing, she began to feel a bit alone and vulnerable. Men loitered around the park, and it seemed some of them were watching her. She realized how easy it would be for someone to overpower her. After all, she was only sixteen years old and not yet familiar with the ways of this country. She had been warned not to trust anyone, so she was careful not to make eye contact with any of these men.

The park was at the southern-most tip of Manhattan, surrounded by water on three sides and a busy New York street on the fourth. Most of the park was a large grassy area with benches where one could sit and enjoy the shade and the breezes off the water on this hot August day. The grassy area was as big as the entire Breakstone compound she had so recently left behind in Lithuania. A profusion of white roses bloomed around the edges of the park.

An older lady came up and sat near Helen. She had white hair and a kind face. Helen thought she was someone who had lived in New York for a while, a local person enjoying the park. The woman smiled and said, "Faith and Begorrah, I'm completely knackered after walking all afternoon in this heat. It's a pleasure to sit down for a minute, if ye don't mind?"

Helen nodded back sympathetically at the lady, although she had no idea what "begorrah" meant. "Do you live in New York?" she asked.

"Oh yes, I live on the Lower East Side. It's hot in our apartment today, so I thought it might be cooler down here by the river. Did you just arrive from Europe?" Helen figured the woman could tell she had just arrived, that she looked more like someone from another country.

"Yes, I'm waiting for my father. He will be here any minute. He also lives on the Lower East Side. I'm going to live there as well, with my cousin."

The lady smiled back and said, "You must be so excited.

I know you will love it here. Now you be careful," she went on. "There are terrible men around here lying in wait to get their hands on the baggage of someone like you. Don't let any of those men get close to you."

"Thank you for that warning," Helen said, feeling an increase in anxiety. "I will have nothing to do with them." She jutted out her chin and sat up a little straighter to better look like a brave young woman who could not be taken advantage of.

She sat back for a moment, trying to calm down and enjoy the fresh air and the tall green trees, their leaves shimmering in the gentle New York breeze. For the last week, she had breathed nothing but noxious air below decks in a ship with sixteen hundred other people, and she had seen nothing but water.

"So, they stamped your papers, and officially admitted you to the United States?" the chatty lady asked with a smile.

"Yes," Helen answered, smiling back. "They told me I could wait at Ellis Island with the other women travelling alone, but my father wrote to me that I should meet him here in Battery Park. I just came over on the ferry."

Helen looked out at the dense crowds of people who, like her, had come on the ferries from Ellis Island. From her time on the boat, Helen was used to the sounds of unknown languages filling the air. She could make out Yiddish being spoken from several directions. What English she heard was decorated with an unfamiliar accent that she realized must not be any accent at all, but the right way to speak English here in New York.

"Where did you come from?" Helen asked the lady.

"I came from Ireland," she replied. "I've been here ten years now, and I love it."

Just then Helen's attention was attracted by a few fashionable New York couples who came strolling along the pathways of the park.

The chatty lady smiled and said, "Those are the rich ones. New York's most wealthy out for a walk."

Elegant ladies with parasols walked slowly by, their arms held firmly by gentlemen in expensive suits and homburgs. Often nannies followed behind with baby carriages. The ladies were beautifully attired in long dresses and artful hats. Helen had never seen such impressive-looking people. She admired their self-assurance and tried to imagine their lavish lives. Maybe one day it might be her in a beautiful dress strolling through the park with a parasol and a calm smile on her face. Wouldn't that be something? She smiled to herself and thought how anything could happen in America.

"It's a beautiful park, isn't it?" asked the lady.

"Yes, more beautiful than I imagined, with the name Battery Park. A battery is a row of guns, isn't it?"

"I think you're right," replied the lady. "See those cannons over there? I believe this park used to be a fortress to guard New York."

Helen lifted her hand to shade her eyes from a shaft of sunlight coming through the trees. She gazed out toward the end of the point. Cannons stood at the ready, aimed out into the harbor to protect the city.

"And that is the Public Aquarium," added the lady. "You can see fish there." Helen could see a building with "Castle Garden" carved over its arched entrance. Clearly it was neither a castle nor a garden. The sturdy building was built with rough dark stones and brick. It was a fort, with a cleared area around surrounded by trees. It was open to the water on the far side where, in the past, it could have protected the city from naval attack. The fort was three stories high, each story smaller than the one beneath, like a three-layer cake. The United States flag flapped away at the top. *That's the flag of my new country*, she thought, noticing the stars and stripes more carefully, now that she had realized it was *her* flag.

A sign outside Castle Garden read, "New York Aquarium." People lined up outside waiting to enter to see exhibits of live fish. Children played with one another as they waited in line with their parents, and their voices floated in the air. She heard a little boy ask in English, "Mama, can we feed the fish?"

"How nice that a fort could change into a place to have fun and see fish," Helen said to her bench mate. "A place where people can enjoy themselves."

The lady nodded kindly at Helen. "You take care of yourself," she said as she stood up. "I hope your papa comes soon. Remember not to talk to anyone or let any of those rough men over there get anywhere near you."

Helen stood up and thanked the lady, then said goodbye and sat back down.

Another half an hour passed, with Helen looking carefully at the faces of every tall dark-haired man who passed by. A young man Helen had not seen previously approached her.

"I can take you to a friendly place where you can get a room for the night, with a nice lady, real pretty place," he said with an accent like the lady who had departed. He reached out to take Helen's bag. Helen jumped up and snatched her bag away from the man's hand.

"No!" Helen said loudly. "Stay away from me. I am not

interested in your room for the night. My father will be here in only a moment. You back up and get away from me, or I am going to scream."

Helen was panicked, but the man seemed frightened by her vehemence and did back up. "I don't mean nothing bad," he said. "Just trying to help."

"I don't want your help, so please leave," Helen said. The young man turned and moved quickly away through the crowd. Helen panted, clutching her bag tightly. Gradually she calmed down from the encounter. After a few minutes, she returned to scanning the crowd for tall darkhaired men.

Questions began to arise. *What if Papa never comes? What if he forgot the date and is not coming until tomorrow? What if something bad happened to him, and he can't get here?* Helen commanded the "What if's" to cease. She knew that she didn't need to make up scary things to get upset about. Papa would come. She was confident in him.

Then, just as she thought of her confidence and faith in Papa, there he stood. He was about twenty feet away, head and shoulders above everyone around him, and intently looking over the crowd. He wore dark trousers and a vest over top of a button-down shirt like Helen had never seen him wear at home. He wore an old-looking homburg hat that Helen did not recognize, but at least he still had the same rich, full mustache. He was certainly Papa, but he looked different. There was something new about him. He looked just the way Helen thought an American should look. She felt proud and hoped he wouldn't be embarrassed by his immigrant daughter.

She jumped up and called out, "Papa!" She grabbed her bag and began running toward him. When he saw her, his face lit up, and he too began to run. They hugged one another. They held each other close. Helen felt tears falling on her face, but she didn't know if they were her own or Papa's. She tried to calm down, so she would not sob uncontrollably.

"Papa, Papa," Helen said in a blubbery voice. "I was so afraid I would never find you." Helen spoke her native Yiddish to her father, and he replied in the same language.

"Ah my little Hinde, my first-born girl. My smart daughter. Here you are in New York. You made it. We did it. You are safe now, you are with me. Were you safe on your trip, nothing bad happened to you?"

"No, Papa, everything was good. I even made a new friend, Rebecca, but she had to go to her family in Texas." Helen felt an enormous relief now that she was with Papa. She noticed that he still smelled like clean soap, just as he did when they had hugged goodbye so many months ago in Panemunė.

"Ah, yes, Texas is far away," Papa said with a big smile. "But you can write to her. The mails are good here." Helen thought how much Papa knew about this country. He even knew where Texas was.

"I am so sorry to be late," Papa said. "You must have been terribly worried. There was a special order at work and even though they had promised I could leave early, when the time came the boss insisted I stay for two hours more than planned. I don't want to lose my job, so I had to stay. I am so glad that you have been alright here in the park. I was so nervous about you."

"Papa, don't worry. I am just fine. I had a nice chat with a lady from Ireland who told me just who to stay away from."

"Here, let me take your bag. I can carry it, and you can enjoy your first look at America. I'm taking you to Aunt Rose's apartment where I've arranged for you to stay with her and her children. They all want to meet you. We found you a job already, so you can pay a little rent, but still save most of your salary for Max to be the next one to come over. Aunt Rose is going to show you how to use a sewing machine."

Helen had seen a sewing machine. There was one in the Breakstone compound in Panemunė, but she had never used it. She was a little afraid of having to learn this new machine, but more than that, she was excited that a new part of her life was starting, new family members, new people, and her first real job with real pay. She was good with her hands and had always done the best sewing of anyone in the compound. Her hand stitches were always even and straight. She didn't quite know how the machine created a row of stitches, but she looked forward to finding out.

"Why won't I live with you?" Helen asked, suddenly tremulous. "Don't you want me to live with you?"

"Of course I do, but I live with a group of single men, men whose wives and families have not come over yet. No girls allowed," Papa said with a big grin. "Once Mama and the other children get here, we will get our own place together. Don't worry, this is all temporary." Helen understood and tried not to let her disappointment show.

Helen and Papa began to walk north through Manhattan. She looked down at the silvery cobblestones that neatly paved all the streets. It was a far cry from the rutted dirt roads of Panemunė. A street sign read, "Water Street." A good name, she thought to herself, looking out over the river on their right. "What river is that, Papa?"

"It's the East River," Papa replied. "Manhattan is an island surrounded by the Hudson on the west and the East River on the east. We are going all the way up to Hester Street to The Lower East Side. I love our neighborhood. It's us Jews and other immigrants all together and everyone is friendly, and everyone helps everyone else. Besides the Jews there are the Italians, and the Irish, and the Germans, people from all over the world. They call it the 'melting pot.' We are all getting started in our new lives here."

Papa put his arm around Helen and pulled her toward him. "I know you'll love it here as much as I do. You'll meet interesting people from all over. Sure, there's rivalry among the different groups, and everyone likes their own people best for socializing. But you won't ever feel the terrible hatred against the Jews here. You won't get the cold shoulder when you go into a shop just because you are Jewish. We can do anything here. We can live where we want, and we can work where we want. There's no army or Cossacks coming to take away all the young boys. We're accepted here, and there are a lot of us. We're all in this New World together. Everyone works hard to make a good life for themselves and their families."

Helen listened closely to Papa, and then squeezed his hand and smiled up at him to show she understood. In the back of her mind she worried about Max and how he was still at risk. She hoped he would be safe for a little while longer, long enough for her and Papa to earn the money to buy his ticket and bring him to safety, but she also knew that she would feel this unease until he and her whole family were safe in New York.

The streets of Lower Manhattan were deserted as the

early evening came on. Work was over for the day, and everyone had already left the neighborhood. They walked past tall brick buildings, some light red brick, some dark red, and a few built with yellow bricks. Many were as high as twenty stories. Helen did not even know such buildings existed. "Does Aunt Rose live twenty stories in the air?"

"No," Papa replied. "Only five stories." Helen felt glad she would not be living up in the sky. She held tightly onto her father's hand. They walked through the narrow streets of what Papa explained was the financial district. The closest experience Helen had ever had was walking through the tall forests near Panemunė. Like the forest trees, these tall buildings blocked the day's sunlight, creating cool shady walkways in between.

After about forty minutes, the cobblestones gave way to a packed dirt street as they entered the Lower East Side.

"This is your new neighborhood," Papa said.

It was the most crowded place Helen had ever seen. The street was completely filled with people strolling about and walking one way and the other. Helen felt tired. She had spent over five hours at Ellis Island, more than an hour in Battery park, and now this walk. It was late in the day. People were hurrying home from work. In every block, there were dozens of vendors with pushcarts and red and white umbrellas advertising something called "Bloomingdale's." The vendors shouted out their wares, fruits, vegetables, everything you could think of. Eggs, watches, candles, matches, potatoes, corn, fish, fabric, and pies. Things Helen had never seen, wooden things, fabric things, foods she had never even imagined.

"This is Hester Street, little Hinde. We will go a block

or two more and you will be at your new home with Aunt Rose. Aunt Rose is your cousin, but we always called her Aunt Rose."

"Papa, please call me Helen now. I want to have a new name. Please introduce me to Aunt Rose as Helen."

"Oh, you're Helen now, are you? You want to give up the name your mother and I gave you when you were born? I don't know if I like that."

"Papa, I love my name Hinde, but today when we arrived in New York, I felt that I needed to start anew, and this new name came to me. Please don't be hurt. I will always be your daughter, and you can call me Hinde anytime. But I want to start my new life as Helen, Helen of New York."

"OK, Helen." Papa seemed to be trying this new name out to see if he liked it. "Yes, I can understand that you want a fresh start. And Helen is a beautiful name. I will try hard to remember to say Helen instead of Hinde. I don't like this change much, but I'm going to believe that you are not turning your back on the old ways. You are thinking Hinde of the old world and Helen of the new, am I right?"

"Yes, Papa," she told him, thinking how he always understood. "I could never turn my back on the old ways. I loved our life in Panemunė before the new tsar made everything so hard for us."

They continued to walk on the packed dirt of Hester Street. Helen drank in the sights of her new home. Vendors lit big torches to illuminate their wares, so the area was glowing with light and excitement. She liked the busyness, the people hurrying by, so different from pokey Panemunė. Excitement bubbled inside her.

Finally, they came to Aunt Rose's. Like all the buildings in the neighborhood, it was five stories and red brick, with about eight stone steps leading up to a center front door and two columns of windows going up to the roof. The street floor housed two apartments with storefront shops, one on either side of the front steps. You had to go down a few steps to enter the shops. On the left was a butcher who sold only chicken. Helen had never seen so many chickens in one place, with more than two dozen of them dangling dead in the window, partially plucked and hung from their scaly legs. The lettering on the glass window said in Hebrew, "Kosher Chicken Market." Painted on the window were also a Jewish Star of David and a picture of a live chicken, in case anyone was still confused. In Panemunė you would never see such a sign prominently displayed. Jews knew better than to make their presence so obvious.

"This store sells children's clothing," Papa explained of the store on the right.

"I can read English, Papa," said Helen. "Children's Clothing and Accessories," Helen read out loud. There were small gloves and hats and other clothing displayed in the window.

Helen took in the store windows and the entire building. She looked up toward the rooftop and saw an exposed, rickety metal stairway hugging the outside of the brick wall and going all the way up to the roof.

"Papa, is that how we have to go up to Aunt Rose's?"

Papa grinned at Helen. "No, my dear. Those stairs are for escaping from a fire. If there were a fire inside, the fire escape would be the only way down. Don't worry. Inside this front door is a normal staircase." Helen shuddered at the idea of a fire in a tall building, something she had never before even thought about. She set the thought aside and followed Papa up the steps.

Papa pushed the large dark wooden door and held it open for her. Suddenly she couldn't see anything, the hallway was so dark after the evening light outside. They paused a moment to allow their eyes to adjust. The hallway had no windows, but soon Helen could see again, enough to reach out for the long wooden bannister leading up the stairs. The ceiling was silver tin embossed with elegant designs. On each side of the stairs hung a painting of roses, which reminded Helen of the beautiful roses she had seen earlier at Battery Park.

"Roses in the park, roses on the walls for Aunt Rose," she said and smiled at Papa. "Who painted these beautiful roses, Papa? I've never seen real paintings like this before. They're so pretty." Papa raised his eyebrows and shrugged to show he had no idea. The beautiful decoration made her happy for this new home, as if she lived in a garden.

Papa said, "Aunt Rose said it was recently all fixed up here. The city is making the landlords keep their places nice for us tenants. I'm happy you like it."

They began to climb the steep stairs. Aunt Rose lived on the top floor. Up and up they went.

"Remember now, Papa, I am Helen from now on," she said more sternly than she meant to.

Papa paused and turned to pat Helen on the shoulder. "My little Helen is here in New York," he said, smiling down at her. Papa joked, "I will try not to miss Hinde, whom I have known since she was born, but who now has been suddenly replaced by this grown-up daughter named Helen." Helen knew Papa was teasing her gently, and the two shared a little smile that lingered.

When they reached the top floor, there was a central hallway with four doors, each to its own apartment. Papa knocked on a door toward the back of the building. Helen counted it up, something she always enjoyed doing: the two stores, then five floors, each with four apartments. Room here for twenty-two families. She imagined owning one of these buildings and sitting around all day as the rent money came in. She wondered what her own rent would be. Would there be anyone in the building her own age? So much to discover.

Aunt Rose opened the door. Helen vaguely remembered her from Panemunė. She was Papa's first cousin, and had come to America eight years ago, when Helen was only eight years old. Aunt Rose looked different now. She was still tall and kind looking, but now she seemed more imposing. Her hair had turned white, and her face was not quite as youthful as it used to be. Even her eyebrows had gone to gray. Yet she still had the same warm and friendly smile. She wore a white apron with more roses embroidered in red stitches on the pockets.

Papa introduced them. "Aunt Rose, I'm sure you remember my eldest daughter." Papa paused a moment, "Helen?"

"I am so pleased to see you again, Aunt Rose," Helen said and gave a small curtsy.

"Come in, come in," answered Aunt Rose in a warm and welcoming voice. "Last time I saw you, you were a little girl. Now you are all grown up. And you were Hinde back then, if I recall. It's Helen, now, is it? That's a good American name. Nothing wrong with that.

"Helen, my dearest cousin, welcome to your new home. The children and I have made a special supper to celebrate your arrival. I want to hear all the news of

Panemunė and most especially about your dear mother, Devorah, and all your brothers and sisters."

Helen could tell right away that Aunt Rose was a generous soul. She had a ready smile and seemed like she would be at ease in any situation. Her gray hair looked pretty piled on top of her head and held in place with tortoise shell combs. Helen had never seen combs in anyone's hair before, and she thought how pretty they were. Aunt Rose wore a green dress, and the dress also had embroidery and a bit of lace. Helen remembered that Aunt Rose made beautiful lace back in Panemunė.

The three of them crowded into the small kitchen where two young children sat at a wooden table. Delicious smells filled the kitchen. "I've made gefilte fish for dinner. My daughter Josie helped me to make it." Helen immediately felt at home as the food was so familiar. Mama would often make gefilte fish for a special occasion.

With a smile, she looked at the two young children. "I am your cousin Helen. What are your names?"

IO

GEFILTE FISH

"I'm Mordecai," said the little boy in English. He stood up from the bench, smiled at Helen, and reached out his hand to her. Helen shook his smaller hand, saying, "I'm pleased to meet you, cousin." Mordecai looked to be twelve or thirteen years old, just Max's age, with dark straight hair and big brown eyes. She wished Max were there with them now, and she felt the worry for him that was always with her now. Mordecai wore pants that were too short, and his knobby knees stuck out. His face was smudged, as if he had been playing outside.

"And I'm Josie," the little girl chimed in. She was clearly younger than her brother, maybe nine or ten. Even at her young age, Josie had a deliberate way of looking at Helen that seemed playful and a bit bold. Helen thought she seemed mature for her age. Josie's face was clean, her smile friendly and open. Her dark-colored dress did not show its spots too much, and you had to look closely to see that her clothes had been mended and made larger more than once. Helen felt a pang of longing for Selma. Would she feel a terrible longing every time she saw someone the same age as one of her siblings?

Helen reminded herself to be grateful for the moment and not think too much about everyone she missed so terribly. Even though she had left home barely a week before, her family and her old life felt years away from here. She slipped onto the bench between her young cousins while Papa and Aunt Rose chatted about New York people and things that Helen wasn't familiar with. They discussed the pushcarts Helen had seen earlier and what new wares they could buy.

"I saw curtains for twenty-five cents that are exactly like the three-dollar curtains in Joe Bloomingdale's store," Aunt Rose said, pointing to the lacy white curtains hung in the window between the kitchen and the front parlor. It seemed strange to Helen to have a window between two rooms of the apartment, but it did allow the outside breezes to flow in from the parlor and cool the heat of the kitchen. Rich cooking smells of garlic, saffron and ginger floated in the air. She was suddenly famished and realized she hadn't eaten since early morning on the ship. The SS *Barbarossa* seemed far in the past already, as she sat in the warm kitchen that would be her home.

"Do you go to school?" she asked her cousins. She was happy for the chance to practice her English.

Mordecai, who was still standing, bounced up and down with enthusiasm as he spoke. "Everybody has to go to school in New York, at least until you're twelve. I like school. I'm going to be an engineer and build bridges over the river, like the Brooklyn Bridge. It's the longest bridge in the whole country. We can walk across it sometime if you want to. It only costs a penny. Anyway, it's summer now and there's no school. In the fall we'll go back to P.S. 188. I'll be in eighth grade. It's the best school in New

York," he said, making a little fist to punch the air as he said the word "best." "I love school because they are going to teach me to be an engineer. Engineers fix problems."

He paused a minute and then said a little more shyly, "You can call me Morty. Everyone does. Morty the Engineer!" he proclaimed with a big smile and a wave of his hand like it was a headline in the paper.

Josie stood up too, standing in place at the table. She chimed in, "I go to P.S. 188, too. I'm only in third grade. I have to write an essay called 'What I Did This Summer.' I'm going to write about how my cousin Helen came to dinner all the way from the old country." Josie pointed up in the air and waved her hand to show that the old country was far, far away. "Cousin Helen, where is the old country? Is everyone there old?"

Aunt Rose leaned over so Josie could not see her face, and caught Helen's eye with a quick wink, hiding a giggle at her daughter's endearing misunderstanding.

Monty and Josie had both been born in Panemunė, but they were young when they came to America and didn't remember. Their father, Aunt Rose's husband, had died young of a bad heart, and she had emigrated not long after, leaving the sad memories behind for a new start.

"No, the old country is where your Mama and my Papa and most of the adults came from. It's not like America," Helen explained. "It's poor and people don't have much to eat or any opportunities." Helen didn't mention to these children the hatred of the Jews or the soldiers who had come to their home. "That's why we came to America, so we can have a better life."

"We have lots to eat," said Morty, spreading his arms wide as if to encompass enormous amounts of food. "We have enough to share with you and Uncle Hymie, like tonight. We are going to have a special meal tonight. Mama made gefilte fish, in your honor."

"Mama let me be a helper," said Josie. "I helped mix up the fish."

Helen had enjoyed gefilte fish at home, but not often, because fish was expensive and the dish was a lot of work to prepare. She felt her growing wave of hunger and looked forward to the meal being served.

Papa came and joined them at the table. He had taken off his snappy hat and jacket, and now he rolled up his shirtsleeves before he sat down. There was just enough room for them all in the tiny kitchen with its two benches pulled up close to the table. Helen and the children sat on one, and Papa and Aunt Rose would sit on the other. Aunt Rose was still busy at the stove, explaining about dinner.

"We got a big pike from the fish man this morning," she explained. "Of course, we make gefilte fish the right way without all that sugar that certain other people use to cover up a fish that is not so fresh. That Galitzianer gefilte fish is not nearly so good as our own Litvak recipe."

Helen had heard about the rivalry between these two distinct groups of Jews back in the old country and now apparently in New York as well. The Litvaks were from Lithuania, and considered themselves more enlightened and modern, respectful of scholarship and education. The Galitzianer Jews came from Galicia, including the Ukraine and other German speaking areas. Litvaks considered the Galitzianer Jews less sophisticated and naively mystical.

Litvaks cooked with chicken fat and garlic and onions and plenty of salt and pepper. Their food had lots of flavor, and it was what Helen and all her family loved. Supposedly Galitzianers put too much sugar in everything, and Helen had heard it said that they were too emotional. Galitzianers thought the Litvaks were too intellectual and not religious enough. It was a long-standing, but somewhat light-hearted, rivalry. Fundamentally, they were all Jews, and that was more important than their differences. But both sides enjoyed a small sense of superiority.

During the six days on the ship, Helen had seen people from many different places. They all had different tastes in food and clothing, in what they thought was important, and in how they practiced their religion. Mama and Papa had taught Helen to be tolerant and to know that nobody had a monopoly on the right way to do things.

Aunt Rose continued about the fish. "First, we carefully took off the skin so that we could stuff everything back into it at the end." Helen swooned a little as wonderful smells accompanied Aunt Rose's explanation. "We removed the fins and all the bones and made a rich broth with it."

Aunt Rose held up a pair of soup spoons. "I used these big *kochleffels* to get the fish onto the platter." Helen knew that *kochleffel* also meant a busybody, or someone who stirs things up and causes trouble. Yiddish was filled with words that had double or triple meanings that were all connected. Exploring words always delighted Helen.

"Removing the skin was hard for us to do properly, wasn't it, Josie?"

Aunt Rose looked on approvingly as Josie nodded and said "We were careful, and we got all the skin off in one piece with no holes in it. We set the head aside and chopped up the fish into little pieces. I chopped up an onion all by myself, and I only cried a little."

Aunt Rose continued, "We added salt and pepper to

the fish mixture. Then ginger and saffron, garlic, fresh butter, black raisins, and finally egg yolk to help it all stay together. Josie mixed those ingredients together all by herself." Aunt Rose beamed proudly at her daughter. "Then we put all this back into the fish skin and neatly fit the head back on. It looked just like it did when it was alive and swimming in the water. Finally, we lowered it into our lovely broth and poached it. Doesn't it look like a big pike having a little rest on the plate before he swims off to have an adventure?"

Aunt Rose had thrown little discs of carrots into the broth. These were the traditional garnish for gefilte fish. She placed the now cooked carrots along the fish's body in a long row like bright coins. She added a little parsley for fresh greenery, artfully hiding where the head did not quite meet the body. She nodded her approval at the fish, as if it had been helpful as well.

Morty got up and gathered dishes and silverware from the simple open shelves above the big sink. He set the table with a place for each person, and he knew to put the knife on the right and the spoon outside. The dishes did not match and were chipped in a few places, but each one was pretty in its own way, and somehow they all went together. Helen imagined that Aunt Rose must have chosen her dishes carefully from yet another pushcart. The cutlery was also a mixture of knives, forks, and spoons from the scattered collections of others.

Everyone was excited about the fish. Aunt Rose placed the platter right in the middle of the table, with one of the large wooden spoons alongside for serving. She sat down and said to everyone, "Let's say a prayer over the food." Everyone bowed their heads and closed their eyes. "Praise be our God, of whose abundance we will eat and by whose goodness we live. And we give thanks for Helen's safe arrival and that she will be living here with us now. Amen."

Helen had never heard a Jewish prayer in English. She was amazed at how simple and short it was. Aunt Rose noticed that Helen's eyes were wide after the prayer. She explained as she served the fish, "We're Reform Jews." Helen didn't say anything, but was all ears. Aunt Rose glanced over to see if she was interested, and Helen bobbed her head and raised her eyebrows so that the explanation would continue. "Reform Jews believe in science and knowledge, and we don't take the Bible literally." Helen's eyes grew a little wider as she remembered Rabbi David in the old country. It was like Aunt Rose knew about that conversation back in Lithuania where Helen had said, "We can still be Jewish and not have to believe in a talking snake."

Helen gave Aunt Rose a big smile, nodding her head up and down to say thank you for the information. She felt a wonderful sense of relief with this glimmer of new understanding. "I'd love to know more about that sometime."

She took a bite of fish and thought to herself, *This is my first bite of food in America.* The gefilte fish tasted the same as it did at home, and she was happy that she didn't have to try anything strange on her first day. The fish melted in her mouth, and she closed her eyes to better savor it.

Little Josie smiled shyly at how much Helen enjoyed the food. "Yum," said Josie, "I think you like this fish. Me, too." Helen nodded back with her mouth full and leaned toward Josie in a friendly way, tilting down her head and leaning her arm against Josie's. Josie smiled up at Helen in reply. Morty smiled at Helen too, still chewing his most recent bite of fish. Soon everyone was smiling at everyone else as they ate. Helen thought it was the best thing she had ever eaten.

"Aunt Rose, you have outdone yourself," Papa announced. "Thank you for preparing a feast for our celebration."

Everyone ate heartily in silence for a little bit until Aunt Rose asked, "So how do you feel about being in America so far?"

"I'm so happy to be here and to see Papa again after the long months we've been apart. It's wonderful to see you again after all these years, Aunt Rose, and to meet my cousins. If Papa and I work hard, soon our whole family will be here, my sister Selma, and my four brothers, and of course, Mama. I miss them all terribly, and that's the one thing that makes me feel sad." Tears gathered in Helen's eyes, even though she had been so happy a moment ago.

"Don't be sad, cousin Helen," said Josie, smoothing her small hand along Helen's arm. "We heard about your family's plan to get everyone here soon. We want to help. Meanwhile, please tell us all about each one of them."

"OK," said Helen, "if you are sure you are interested."

"Very interested," said Morty, and Josie shook her head up and down vigorously in assent.

"Max is the oldest after me. He'll come on the boat soon. He's twelve years old, just about your age, Morty. You can show him around and teach him all about America." Helen felt in her pocket for the dark green picture stone that Max had given her as she left home. It had stayed in her special hidden pocket since then. Whenever she felt bad missing her family, it comforted her to find it in her pocket and hold it tight in the palm of her hand.

"Then comes my sister Selma. Josie, I think you are going to like her very much. She is a little older than you, but not too old to be friends. Finally, the three little boys, Bernard, Milton, and little Julius, who is only six. It will be a good day when they all get here. I want to work hard and earn lots of money to bring them all to America right away."

"We found you an excellent job, so you can start making that money right away," said Aunt Rose. "Your Papa said you can sew and that you want to earn as much as possible."

"Yes," said Helen. "To brag just a little, I did have the smallest and neatest stitches in Panemunė, and I always enjoyed making and mending clothes for the family." Helen paused a minute and looked around the table at everyone. "I'm so glad I'm here. I want to work hard and bring Mama and our entire family here soon. Aunt Rose, I'm grateful to you for letting me stay here with you. Thank you."

"You are very welcome," replied Aunt Rose, and she leaned across the table and squeezed Helen's arm. "We will enjoy one another's company, I am sure."

STITCHES IN TIME

Dinner lasted a long time. First the children fell asleep, and Aunt Rose carried them into the bedroom behind the kitchen. Next, Helen's head began to nod. Images of the long day, of so many people, the sounds of new languages, everything was floating in her mind. Aunt Rose walked her, half-awake, half-asleep, to a sofa in the parlor where she would sleep. Helen was so tired that she barely noticed her surroundings. She had no idea when Papa left.

Early the next morning, Aunt Rose awakened her with a cup of hot tea. "A little *tai* for you, dear," said Aunt Rose. For a moment, Helen didn't know where she was. She looked around for her siblings. She had slept beside them every night of her life until only a week ago.

Within moments, Helen became oriented. She looked up and gave Aunt Rose a sleepy smile. She found comfort waking up to hear the familiar Yiddish word for tea, *tai*. It made things feel more like home. She was used to having tea in the morning. Aunt Rose had brought her a sugar cube as well. Helen held the sugar cube between her teeth as she sipped the warm, comforting drink.

Filtered early morning light came through the parlor windows that faced onto the street. As she stood up and stretched, Helen remembered, with a little clench in her stomach, that today she would start her new job.

"Come and sit with me while I explain what will happen today," Aunt Rose said. Helen followed her into the kitchen where they both sat down at the table. The room was warm from the coal stove where tea water still steamed in its pot.

Aunt Rose lightly clapped her hands together. "Both your Papa and I work in the *schmatta* trade, like most of the Jews in New York. Neither of us knew much about making clothes back in Panemunė, but here in New York the need for garment workers is great. Your Papa is what they call a "Columbus Tailor," someone who came to the New World like Columbus and suddenly found himself making clothes. He works for a *jobber*. The jobber's business is to cut fabric.

"I know Hymie told you about the wonderful new tool he got, the cutting knife. Now he can cut through many pieces of fabric at once. Instead of making only one garment at a time, he can make many identical garments with a single cut." Papa had explained to Helen that clothing produced this way took much less time, was much cheaper to make. The workers who made these clothes could now afford to wear them because they were mass produced. "Your Papa is skilled with the new knife, and suddenly he is in big demand. He can demand higher wages because of his new skill.

"Helen, you have come to New York at exactly the right time. Business is booming here, as it is all over this country." Aunt Rose was excited talking about the clothing business that she clearly enjoyed being a part of. "Let me tell you a little more about how it works and how you fit in.

"Once the fabric is cut, a person called a *schlepper* delivers it to the shop where it gets turned into clothing. The owner of the shop receives the cut fabric. Each shop specializes, maybe in pants or shirts, but always in some particular item of clothing. The shop takes in the piles of cut fabric, and the shop workers sew it all up into clothing. Soon the schlepper comes back to pick up the same fabric, but now as wearable clothing. It all gets delivered to a wholesaler who has all the contacts to sell the clothing.

"I work in a shop nearby, and I found you a job in another shop over on Orchard Street. It's owned by a man named Joe. It's nearby, and they'll teach you how to use the sewing machine. That's how you will fit into the big picture."

"Thank you so much, Aunt Rose. I'm excited to start. A little nervous, but still excited." It would have been more truthful to say that she was terribly nervous. In fact, she felt a bit sick to her stomach thinking about the new job and wondering if she would be able to do what was asked of her. If she failed, the family's whole plan would be in danger. Max, especially, would be in danger.

Helen kept these thoughts to herself. She drank a little more tea and hoped it would calm her stomach. She wanted to understand everything Aunt Rose was explaining, but the jobber and the schlepper ran together in her mind. She tried to look like she was interested and was understanding how it all worked.

Aunt Rose got up and began bustling about, packing up food for each of them to take for lunch. As she worked, she continued, "You'll work in an apartment exactly like this one, three rooms, but in the daytime it's not a home. It's a shop. The whole place is filled with people and sewing machines and ironing boards and piles of fabric and clothing. Deliveries and pickups happen all day. One thing to understand is that, after the workday is over, Joe and his family live in the shop. It overflows with people during the day, but then at night, it's home to Joe and his wife and their two little boys."

Aunt Rose continued, "You'll appreciate working the sewing machines, because they're up front near the windows where there are cool breezes and fresh air. Joe bought a brand-new sewing machine for you to use, a Singer, the best. That's how good business is right now. Everyone is growing and hiring and producing.

"You'll start at five dollars a week, and in time you'll be able to earn up to eight. That's good pay for girls. Men make more, of course. Your father now makes ten dollars a week.

"It will be hot today and for at least another month. Dress as lightly as you can and move slowly because you are not used to this hot weather. It's always cool in Panemunė in the summer, so New York weather may surprise you. Everyone in the shop will be sweating by midday."

Morty came in rubbing his sleepy eyes. He stood close and leaned into his mother. Aunt Rose put her arm around him and smoothed down his hair, which stuck up from the night's sleep. He smiled at Helen. "Good morning, cousin. Will you go to work today?"

"Yes. Will you go to school?"

"Not yet, it's still summer, but soon. I earn money for the family by running errands for the pushcart vendors," Morty said. "The vendors can't leave their carts, but sometimes they need things, so I go for them." He lifted his head and stuck out his chest a bit with sleepy pride. "Josie will stay with the neighbor lady downstairs. She also has an eight-year-old girl." Helen felt touched to hear how everyone was working, how everyone helped everyone else. Her thoughts brought tears to her eyes, but she brushed them away quickly before anyone saw her being so sentimental.

Helen walked down the five flights to use one of the privies in the backyard. As she opened the door to the outside, bad smells overwhelmed her, and she reached up to hold her nose. For privacy, each of the four toilets was in its own rough wooden privy. The entire yard was an unsanitary pit. She was careful where she put her feet, and it reminded her of how she had to watch her step on the ship.

Helen climbed back upstairs and washed herself at the sink like everyone else did. She longed for a real bath, but Aunt Rose said bathing was on Sunday. There was a water pump down near the privies, and she and Aunt Rose would take turns holding up sheets to give privacy to one another. Helen imagined holding up a sheet while holding her nose at the same time.

Helen had one good blouse that Mama had made for her to wear to her new job, whatever it would be. It was a pretty, white blouse with short sleeves, and it was light and cool. She put this on. Although Mama had pressed it, it was wrinkled from being in her bag for so long, but it would have to do. She didn't want to bother Aunt Rose about heating up the little black irons that sat at the back of the kitchen stove.

Morty left, and Rose and Josie and Helen walked downstairs. Rose dropped Josie off with the neighbors.

She confided, "Most of the other mothers put their children to work in the summer to make ends meet, but I can't do it. I want her to have a real childhood and not be burdened yet with work. I don't want her running errands for strangers when she is only eight years old. I would love for her to become a teacher one day, if she would like that. Or a bookkeeper. Her own career."

Helen and Aunt Rose continued down Hester Street. "Now watch where we walk, so you can get back home by yourself this evening. We try to get home before sunset, especially on *Shabbat*, but you never know if you will have to stay late at work. We do our best."

Helen paid attention. She noticed there was trash on the streets and sidewalks that she hadn't seen in the dusk of evening yesterday. Only a few short blocks from Aunt Rose's, they turned onto Orchard Street. As on Hester Street, there were many pushcarts hawking their wares. The vendors were already doing business at this early hour. You could buy a chicken or a tablecloth or a lamp before work. Helen thought of the quiet roads and the narrow paths through the trees in Panemunė. Orchard Street was busy and noisy and full of activity. Helen thought there must be hundreds of pushcarts just on this street.

They entered a building and climbed up to the fifth floor. They went into one of the front apartments where the door was held open with a brick. As Helen entered the apartment, a cacophony of sounds affronted her. There were several conversations going on all at once over the sound of several whirring machines coming from the front parlor.

"Hello Joe. This is my niece Helen." Aunt Rose pushed Helen forward slightly toward the heavy man who sat at the kitchen table drinking tea and writing in a green ledger book. He pushed his glasses up on his forehead and squinted at Helen.

"How do you do, sir," Helen said.

"So, you are my new sewing girl," Joe replied, looking at her doubtfully. "We require that you work hard here," he said gruffly. "We make knee pants. Nothing but knee pants. For all the young boys in America. Knickerbockers they call them, because they come from New York. All those old Dutchmen who founded New York City, they wore knee-breeches. They were the original knickerbock-ers." He peered at Helen and his voice changed to a warn-ing tone as he said, "We make the best knee pants in New York, and if your stitching is not excellent you will be let go on the spot. There are lots of girls in New York who want this job."

Helen's stomach did a flip at the thought of losing her job before she had even started. She heard a ringing in her ears and was afraid she might need to sit down, but she took a deep breath and got herself under control.

"Yes sir, I will work hard to make good knickerbockers for you." Helen tried to sound as bright and cooperative as she could, but she didn't quite dare to meet his eyes.

"Get started then," he concluded. "The girls will show you what to do." He waved his hand toward the front room where Helen could see three sewing machines. Then he pulled his glasses down from his forehead and returned to his ledger book.

Aunt Rose ushered Helen into the parlor. Helen was hit with layers of smells, the smell of the dye in the fabric, the smell of too many people in one room, the smell of hot irons on fabric. Three men with ironing boards stood at

the back. Two girls sat at sewing machines in front of the
windows. There was also an empty chair before a third
sewing machine that Helen figured would be hers. Green
fabric was strewn everywhere. A boy carried stacks of cut
green fabric to the sewing machine girls, and then carried
partly sewn green pants back to the pressers. Two tod-
dlers slept on the couch, almost disappearing into the
piles of fabric, both partly sewn and unsewn. Helen wondered if they spent all their days like this. Where was their
mother?

Knee pants in every state of assembly covered two
long tables that ran the length of the room. The sewing
machines, two going at once, created a high-pitched sound
that reverberated in her head.

Joe came in from the kitchen. The two sewing girls
bent more deeply over their machines to show how hard
they were working. Joe reached down and checked on his
young sons asleep on the couch, pulling a light blanket
over one child's shoulders. Helen realized Joe and his family really did live here in this apartment, as Aunt Rose had
said.

"Helen, you gotta buy your own tools." Joe had come
over and now held out a roll of leather. "Everything you
need is in here, your cutting knife, needles for hand stitching, a thimble, and a spool of green thread. I'll deduct the
cost from your first pay. Everyone gets paid on Fridays,
that's tomorrow. So, your first day's work will cover the
tools. You'll get your first full pay next Friday." Aunt Rose
had warned her about this and mentioned that Joe would
make a nice profit by selling her the tools. Helen knew
that the job was valuable, and that this was a small price
to pay. Aunt Rose said that Joe was not nearly as oppor-

tunistic as many shop owners were, some of whom made as much as 500 percent profit on the tools.

Joe pointed over to the empty machine. "You sit there," he said. He turned to the young woman at the next machine. "That's Esther over there, and next to you is Kathleen. She'll teach you how to sew with the new machine." Esther ignored them both, but Kathleen stopped her work and looked up with a smile. Helen smiled back, glad to see a friendly face.

Aunt Rose came in saying "I have to go to my own job now. See you tonight, Helen, and have a good first day." And she was gone just like that.

"Give me a minute to finish what I am doing," said Kathleen. "Then I will show you everything you need to know."

As Kathleen lowered her head to her work, Esther, sitting at the sewing machine on the far side of Kathleen, raised her head from her work and gave Helen what could only be a sneering look, wrinkling her nose and upper lip as if Helen were a bad smell. Helen shrank from the hostility and froze in place. The girl tossed her head, then looked back down at her work, smiling to herself as if she had enjoyed making Helen feel bad. Helen was shocked but managed to calm herself down. She quickly realized it was Esther who had a problem rather than herself. After a few minutes she set the unpleasant event aside.

Kathleen finished what she was doing, and once again looked up and gave Helen her full attention. Helen was mesmerized by her red hair and green eyes. She had never seen anyone with this coloring before. No one in Lithuania had red hair. Helen tried hard not to stare in amazement. Here she was, sitting in this crowded room with all these unknown people, next to a young woman with red hair and green eyes. She took a deep breath.

"Don't worry," said Kathleen, "I'll show you everything. It's not hard. This is a brand-new Singer, the 'Singer Sixty-Six.' It's the best, and you will love it. Look at the beautiful lotus flower decals on the front." Helen did love the look of the machine. It was sleek and black with golden scrollwork everywhere it fit. The design included a stylized lotus plant and even a sphinx.

So far everyone at Joe's spoke English all the time, and Helen wasn't having any trouble understanding. Kathleen did not seem to have any particular accent as she spoke.

"This is the treadle." Kathleen pointed down to the lacy iron platform near the floor. "Put your right foot at the back of the treadle and your left foot at the front." Helen complied, carefully wiggling her legs under the machine and her feet into place. "You make the machine go by pumping the treadle bar alternately with your right and then your left foot, kind of a rocking motion. That turns this wheel, up here on the right, and it makes the needle go up and down. Let's practice with some scrap fabric."

Kathleen picked up a strip of green fabric off the floor. Helen noticed Kathleen's arms were completely green up to the elbows from dye rubbing off the fabric. She stole a quick look around and saw that everyone's arms were green. She was glad her blouse was short sleeved, or it would have been ruined.

"Take the little black cutting tool out of your tool kit," Kathleen advised. "It is quite sharp, and very useful. You'll need it to cut the threads at both ends of every seam. Joe wants us to do quality work, so we never leave loose threads sticking out." Helen rolled open the tool kit and placed the sharp tool next to the machine. "We each mark our own tools so there is no confusion about who owns what. You don't want to have to buy more tools because someone took yours by mistake." Kathleen held up her own cutting tool which had a white ribbon tied to it. "Use these green scraps to mark yours, no one is using green yet. Now let's start sewing."

There was green thread already in the machine. "This is not that hard. Put the fabric here under the needle and lower the pressure foot to hold it." Kathleen showed Helen on her own machine and Helen followed on the new Sixty-Six. "Lower the needle into the fabric first, by turning this wheel toward you. Then sew a line of stitches by pumping the treadle bar back and forth." Kathleen demonstrated. "You stop the machine by stopping the wheel with your hand."

Helen did as she was instructed and was amazed to see a perfect row of stitches appear on the cloth. She stopped pumping with her feet to finish the row, but she forgot to stop the wheel with her hand. "Oh no," she exclaimed as her neat row of stiches went on for a several inches more than she had planned.

"Don't worry, you're getting it. Try it again," Kathleen said encouragingly. Helen made a new row of stitches and stopped them right where she wanted. Kathleen continued, "Now, let's try turning a corner. With the needle down into the fabric, lift the pressure foot up and turn the fabric ninety degrees. Put the foot back down and sew in a different direction." The machine made another beautiful row of stitches, although this time Helen accidentally jerked the fabric too early, and her stiches went veering off at a zigzag.

"That's okay," said Kathleen. "You'll get used to it. Sew some more rows until you can keep them straight, and you feel confident that you can stop stitching exactly where you want to. Then we'll try a pair of knee pants." Helen practiced and practiced. At the end of half an hour she could sew a straight row and stop it right where she wanted. She could turn a sharp corner and continue to stitch in a new direction. She was proud of herself.

Kathleen looked over and nodded. "I think you are ready to try the real thing. Before we do that, let me show you how to thread the machine," Kathleen said. Deftly, she pulled the entire spool of green thread off the machine. She showed Helen how to loop the tread around this hook and under that lever and finally through the eye of the needle. Helen was good at this kind of thing. She could thread the machine properly after a couple of tries. Kathleen also showed her how to work with the bobbin thread that came up under the needle. Helen quickly grasped that the thread from the needle locked with the thread from the bobbin and that was how stitches got made.

Picking the top layer from a stack of pre-cut fabric on the floor, Kathleen showed Helen which seams to sew first, joining the front and the back at the legs and crotch. As soon as Helen sewed these seams, one of the boys immediately snatched the fabric away from her and took it over to the presser. In moments, the pants were back with warm, flat seams, and Kathleen showed her what to do next.

By the end of the day Helen had made eight pairs of good-looking knee pants. They had pockets and hand-sewn button holes. She already knew how to make good button holes; she had learned that from Mama years ago, and she had only messed up one today. Kathleen showed her how to fix the mistake. Helen thought that Kathleen had made twice as many pairs as she had, but she was still happy with her progress.

As she tidied up her work area for the night, Helen reflected on her first day of work. She had stitched pieces of cloth together to make something new, something that didn't exist before today. Only a pair of knickerbockers, but soon they would belong to someone, to a young boy. He would be from a family that could afford to buy new clothing for the children, no hand-me-downs for him. Maybe he would pick out the dark green color because he liked it, and he might have a matching sweater to wear.

Life was like that, Helen thought. Separate pieces were always rearranging and fitting together into something new. Today she lived with Aunt Rose. Tonight, she would have dinner, and Papa would be there. But now she missed her little house in Panemunė. She missed Mama and her sister and brothers. All this was new, pieces of life stitching themselves together into new and ever-changing patterns.

Helen said good night to everyone and walked down the stairs to the street. The evening was coming on, and the sky had only begun to fade into darkness. For as far as she could see, the street was aglow with the light of thousands of torches. Pushcart business was good in the evening, and owners mounted torches alongside the goods. The torch fires burned brightly, creating a fairytale view of the street as darkness came on.

Papa had told Helen there were an amazing twenty-five thousand pushcarts lining the crowded streets of the Lower East Side. And why not? There were pushcarts all over Europe, so it was a familiar way to make a living or to shop. All you needed was to rent a cart and find something to sell, and, quick as that, you were in business for yourself. Pushcart operators came to work at dawn. They rented a cart for twenty-five cents a day from the stable that Aunt Rose had pointed out, over on Sheriff Street.

Things to sell could be purchased from wholesalers. It was at least a subsistence living to start, but there was also a chance of future prosperity. Who knew what wonderful goods the operator would discover, and what great profits might lie ahead? And who knew what bargains customers like Helen could find? You could buy a bandanna for two cents or a quart of mixed fruits for a penny. Everything you needed was right outside your own door.

Helen was too tired to pay much attention to the last few blocks back to Aunt Rose's apartment. As she walked, she noticed that the pretty white blouse Mama had made for her was smudged with green here and there. She hoped she could scrub it clean tonight. She took a deep breath as she turned onto Orchard Street. Any big city grime or trash was hidden in the low light, and the street was a vision, the firelight of the torches softening everything. Helen smiled to herself as she thought that she had truly arrived in the promised land. This cheered her up quite a bit, and she paused to drink in the lovely sight. She wished there were some way to share this moment with Mama. She wondered what everyone was doing at home. The sadness of missing her family crept further into her heart.

The next day, Kathleen invited Helen to take their thirty-minute midday break together. They went down to the stoop outside to eat the lunches they had brought and to breathe the outside air that was so refreshing after the hot workrooms. Aunt Rose had packed a serving of leftover gefilte fish and carrots from the welcome dinner, everything carefully wrapped in a small cloth kitchen towel. The two girls sat side by side on the marble steps together. Helen enjoyed eating outside and watching the busy pushcart world go by.

As Helen had guessed, Kathleen was Irish. Her family had come over and she was born soon after, so she was a citizen. Helen hadn't thought about citizenship before. For the first time, she thought how she, too, might one day become a United States citizen. Mama would never believe Helen had an Irish friend. With red hair!

Kathleen mentioned that on Friday nights, workers from all the nearby shops like Joe's went out together to Katz's Deli for dinner. It was a friendly place, Kathleen explained. Others who were their own age would come by, young people who worked the same schedules and who lived in the surrounding apartments. She hoped Helen would join them.

Helen wasn't sure what Katz's Deli was, but she was sure she wanted to go. Whatever it was, she hoped it would not be costly. And she was a little nervous about meeting people her own age socially. Would they like her, or would they find her too much of an immigrant who didn't understand New York ways? Would they find that off-putting? She set her worries aside, happy to have a new job and a new friend in America.

KATZ'S DELI

Helen sat by the parlor window gazing down five stories to the street below. The sky was starting to turn light, and already she could see people walking with purpose toward whatever the day's business might be. This was New York. Nobody wasted time, and the street was always busy. Helen had been in the city for an entire week now. She missed her mother, and especially Mama's way of knowing what to do in every situation. There were so many questions she would have loved to ask her. Although Papa was reliable and the strong head of the family, Mama was the foundation. Mama understood the nuances of every situation. Helen took a deep breath and then heard herself sigh. Mama was too far away.

Still, it was exciting to be in New York. She loved the busy, noisy city, so different from quiet Panemunė with its wide, slow river. Many of the people she met here had not been in New York for long. They still remembered what it was like to be fresh off the boat. People wanted to be helpful. If she got lost, someone would stop what they were doing and help her find her way. When Aunt Rose asked her to pick up garlic on the way home one day, Helen had trouble finding the spice pushcart. The very first person she asked for directions insisted on walking with her to make sure she found it. Morty and Josie were always eager to tag along when they could, providing constant informative babble. She loved the children already, and they reminded her of her brothers and sister back home.

She had worked all week sewing at Joe's. She and Kathleen were becoming closer, chatting amicably over their work, then walking down the stairs together at lunch time to sit on the stoop, sharing impressions and stories of the people they worked with and the city they lived in.

As she walked to work, she skipped a step. She was thinking about how today was her first payday. Friday. She knew exactly what she wanted to buy, a new blouse. It was a problem having only one blouse for work, because it meant washing it each night, and then it had to be ironed every morning. Aunt Rose did not appreciate Helen taking up time and space in the kitchen ironing, at the very moment when everyone was getting ready for their day. To not be in the way, Helen would get up extra early and start the coal fire, both to help Aunt Rose and to get the two flat irons hot. She knew from the old country that when you ironed clothes, you had to use two irons. The first one would cool off quickly, and you then could switch to the second one. You kept alternating, and one of the irons was always hot enough to smooth out wrinkles.

Every evening for a week now, she had walked home, passing through the pushcart vendors, but only yesterday had she gathered up the courage to stop at a few clothing carts. She went from one cart to another until she found a cart that had women's clothing that she liked. There it was, the perfect blouse. White with a hint of pink, a small bit of lace down the front. Nothing too fussy, nothing that could get caught in her work by accident. It looked like it would fit her perfectly, and it was only five cents. Aunt Rose had said that was a fair price. Helen knew that Aunt Rose would appreciate her not ironing so much during busy mornings. With two blouses, she need iron only every other day, and she could do it at night if she waited until everyone had retired.

At work, Helen and Kathleen sewed away at the piles of green fabric while talking about their plans for that night after work. They were planning to join the gang at Katz's Deli. "I'm looking forward to it," Helen volunteered. Then she asked, "I know Katz's is a restaurant, but why do they call it a deli?"

Kathleen looked surprised for a moment, but then she smiled in an understanding way and said, "Of course, sweetie, how could you know?" Helen liked it when Kathleen used friendly endearments like "sweetie."

Kathleen had a good ear for languages and loved to describe how American words had come to be. Helen, eager to learn all the unfamiliar new words, was interested in Kathleen's little lectures. It was helpful to have an explanation of how a word came to be. It made it less strange and more "her own." It was all part of learning to navigate this New World.

For example, Kathleen had explained, "A greenhorn is someone new to America. They don't know how things work yet. They dress funny like they are still in the old country. The women wear *schmattas* on their heads. New Yorkers don't do that. Of course, the word 'greenhorn' comes from a young male deer whose antlers are still covered with green fuzz." Helen had seen young male deer in Panemunė, their horns still green, so this made perfect sense.

Helen knew she was a greenhorn, and she knew that her clothes looked like they came from a faraway European village. But she didn't take offense because she and Kathleen both knew that clothes were not the most important thing. It was more important to learn new things. That's what was going to make her an eventual modern New Yorker.

Kathleen explained, "Katz's Delicatessen is on Houston Street, only a few blocks away. It's owned by the Katz family. It's a wonderful place to go for pastrami and corned beef and all the great Jewish foods. It's not kosher, but that's okay with you, right?"

Helen nodded that it was fine with her. "We're modern women," she said. After her conversation with the Rabbi back in Panemunė about taking every word of the Bible literally, there was no way she was going to be a stickler for every Jewish rite and ritual.

Kathleen went on, "My favorite Jewish food is a big dill pickle, but Friday night is frankfurters and beans. It's a tradition. Everybody from work goes, and it's inexpensive, only five cents, so we can all afford it once a week on payday."

"So, what's a delicatessen?" Helen asked.

"You know how the most expensive and finest quality food is called a *delicacy*? These are our delicacies, so we go to a 'delicatessen.' Essen means 'to eat' in German. So, we will go and eat delicacies." Once again Kathleen was explaining the words and ideas of this New World, and Helen was happy to add to her growing vocabulary.

Frankfurters and pastrami and corned beef were apparently Jewish favorites in New York. Helen had never heard of any of them. She was happy to understand what a delicatessen was, and she looked forward to discovering frankfurters and pastrami soon.

Another purchase Helen hoped to make was a small notebook and a yellow Dixon pencil. She could keep them in her pocket and take them with her everywhere and not worry about leaking ink. She could sharpen the pencil with a small paring knife. Aunt Rose kept her paring knife sharp, taking all the household knives down to the sharpening pushcart whenever it was needed. The pencil would be for writing down all the new English words and American ideas. Helen was learning so many new things, and she didn't want to forget any of it. One vendor had a small notebook with a brown marble-looking cover that Helen coveted. It was seven cents. She could get a pencil with an eraser from the same vendor for another two cents. She realized that the notebook and pencil would have to wait until next week, because one purchase a week was all she was going to allow herself.

Since coming to America, it was Papa's evening ritual to have dinner with family at Aunt Rose's. He often brought treats for Josie and Morty, or a fish or a nice cut of meat. He didn't cook, but he certainly did contribute. The night before, Thursday night, Helen had told Papa and Aunt Rose about Kathleen's invitation to Katz's Deli. She wanted to know if they thought it would be all right for her to go there with the others from work, especially since it was Friday night, *Shabbat*.

"So long as you are careful, you should go," said Papa. "You must stay with your friends from work, and not speak with strangers, especially men. Just the group from Joe's and their friends. Of course, you need to make friends in America, but you also need to be careful in a big city. Katz's is lots of fun. I have been there often with the other men from where I live."

Aunt Rose smiled and nodded her head in agreement. She addressed Helen's concern about it being Friday night. "Don't worry about it being *Shabbat*. You and I can go to temple early Saturday morning if we want." Aunt Rose embraced the new Reform Judaism and wasn't worried about Helen missing an occasional Friday night.

Helen confessed how she felt torn inside spending even the smallest amount of money. She wanted nothing in this world the way she wanted to get Max's ticket purchased as soon as possible. Papa and Aunt Rose assured her that spending five cents from time to time would not slow them down.

That night, after dinner was cleared away, they all discussed what Helen would do with her paychecks. "You will need a little money for yourself. You work hard. You will need a few personal things," Papa said. "How about you give two and a half dollars of your weekly five dollar pay to Aunt Rose to help with room and board. She should not be burdened with paying for your food and other expenses.

"Then give two dollars to me to save for Max to come to America. This will be the third Atlantic crossing for our family. I can save six dollars each week, so together we will save a total of eight dollars every week. We have your fifteen dollars from the pocket money that Mama gave you before your journey. That gives us a good start. We will have enough to bring Max over in only two months! That's before the end of this year. Won't it be wonderful to have him here with us?" Papa got a faraway look in his eye at the thought of his oldest son. Helen knew that Papa had a special place in his heart for Max and could hardly bear to think of him being in danger.

The fare was thirty dollars. They would need to save twice that much to cover all the expenses of his trip, including pocket money for him. Helen felt excited when she thought about Max being here soon. It was the only thought that soothed her anxiety and her loneliness for the rest of the family. They wouldn't be here for months yet, maybe years. Once Max was here, she could believe that the whole family would be here eventually, too.

"And Morty," Papa went on, now addressing the young boy. "You and Max are close in age, so we will be relying on you to show him around." Morty nodded, glowing with pride.

"I'm going to take Max for a walk across the Brooklyn Bridge," Morty said. "He'll be so impressed. You can look down between the boards of the sidewalk and see the East River far below."

"Morty, guess what Max's real name is? He's Mordecai, just like you are. You are practically brothers already," said Papa. "But like you, no one calls him Mordecai. Today we have simple names, like Morty and Max, not the hard to pronounce names of the past."

Helen sat back and took in the idea that Max would be coming soon. The thought spread comfort and ease through her body. She relaxed into it as she pictured him sitting here at the table with them, bantering with Morty, smiling at Josie. Of course, she longed to see Mama. But Mama was not in danger like Max was. Max was the priority.

"Our budget leaves you fifty cents a week to do with as you please," Aunt Rose pointed out. This felt like a lot of money to Helen. She would never spend it all, she thought. She would save every penny she possibly could, for Max.

On the Lower East Side of New York, she rarely encountered any unpleasantness about being Jewish. She had heard it was not that way in other neighborhoods, and that she needed to be careful if she left these nearby streets.

She remembered that day at the bakery in Panemunė, the disapproving look on the face of the baker's wife. There were so many Jewish people on the Lower East Side. Everyone was an immigrant, either Jewish or Irish or German or from some other country, but they were almost all newly arrived. Everyone was discovering together what it meant to be American. Some people didn't like Jews in New York, but Helen didn't encounter them often.

Work had been going well. Helen felt close to Kathleen and was happy to have found a friend. The other people in the shop were polite, except for Esther, the third sewing girl, the one who had sneered at her on her first day. Esther had yet to say a nice word and took every opportunity to express her disdain of Helen. Helen didn't understand what Esther's problem was, and she tried not to let it bother her. Who knew what troubles that girl had in her life outside of work? Troubles could make a person act cold and scornful.

People came in and out of the shop all day, schleppers and jobbers and other people who had business with Joe. Helen could see into the kitchen from the parlor where she worked. A few times, she had seen a handsome young man come in to talk with Joe. Beside his blond hair and blue eyes, Helen noticed how strong looking he was, not bulky but very athletic. He always brought a bolt of fabric to discuss with Joe, probably hoping to sell it to him. During his most recent visit, Helen had gently kicked Kathleen under the table and gestured toward the young man without looking in his direction. Kathleen got the message and managed to take a good look at him without being noticed.

"Do you think he could be Jewish?" Helen asked in a quiet voice, so no one could hear them.

"Absolutely, he could be," Kathleen whispered back. "Some of the German Jews have his handsome coloring. My boyfriend is Irish like me, but today, many girls have boyfriends who are not from the same background. So even if he isn't Jewish, you could still go out with him."

Helen noticed whenever the blond fellow came by. He did look German, and lots of New York Germans were also Jewish. Maybe his name was something funny like Otto or Helmut. That would be all right, she could adjust to a funny German name. She hoped he was Jewish. The idea of dating someone who wasn't Jewish just didn't feel right. Helen was pretty sure she was going to be a Reform Jew as she learned more about what that meant. But whatever kind, she was Jewish through and through. She wanted a Jewish husband and a Jewish family. If the blond man wasn't Jewish, then that would be the end it. Of course, she was just as glad that she didn't know yet. One day, she might even have blond children.

Finally, work was over. Joe, the boss, had come around and tried to be a little private, leaning over and whispering as he counted out the cash due each person. He gave

Helen her first pay, five amazing one-dollar bills, then moved on to the next person.

Helen looked closely at the American bills. They were dark and greenish. An eagle with wings spread wide stood atop an American flag. Beneath the bird it said, "Payable to the Bearer One Silver Dollar on Demand." People had confidence in the paper because they could take it to the bank and change it for real silver anytime. Helen put the bills deep into her hidden pocket, right next to the special stone from Max that she always kept with her.

Kathleen and Helen dusted off their Singer sewing machines, covering them with spare pieces of cloth. They happily left Joe's sweaty parlor. Kathleen said, "Tomorrow will be your first day off." Everyone in New York seemed to work a nine-hour day. Because Jews observed *Shabbat* on Saturday, and Christians had their sabbath on Sunday, everyone at Joe's worked a five-day week. Most people had to work on Saturday, so Helen felt lucky.

The two girls walked down the five flights to the street. The Lower East Side was a homogeneous neighborhood, and each street looked a lot like the ones next to it. Row upon row of five-story brick buildings, each building with two small businesses on the first floor, one on either side of the front stoop, a few steps down from the street. Each business with a big glass window with signs and wares displayed. Looking up at the red brick front, there were two windows facing the street on each floor. A fire escape up the front completed the picture. Helen imagined all the people behind those windows, sitting together after the long day's work, talking, making dinner. She had heard that these apartments might house ten or even fifteen people in the three small rooms. She felt lucky that only the four of them lived at Aunt Rose's.

The two girls arrived at Katz's. There were large plate glass windows along the street, all beaded up with steamy moisture. Inside, the floor was white tiles with little black diamonds and long rows of marble-topped tables and dark bentwood chairs. It was humid and warm in Katz's but not uncomfortable. All manner of wonderful food aromas filled the air.

Kathleen led Helen over to a table where Helen was happy to recognize a girl she had seen come into Joe's shop, and also a schlepper who came each day to deliver fabric and take away the knickerbocker pants. There were lots of other people at the table, too, but it felt good to know someone besides Kathleen. Of course, the third sewing girl, Esther, had not joined them. She didn't seem to have any friends, and she disappeared without a word each day as soon as work ended.

Everyone was enjoying themselves and digging into large plates of steaming hot baked beans with a sausage in a bun on the side. Kathleen had explained that the sausages were called frankfurters, or "franks," because they had originated in the city of Frankfurt in Germany. The franks were served in a long bun. Helen hadn't expected them to be piled high with sauerkraut, but it looked delicious. The smell alone was making her mouth water.

Kathleen said hello to everyone, and then, "You all know Helen, the new sewing girl. She's joining us tonight for the first time." Everyone smiled and was friendly. Kathleen and Helen walked over to the frank and beans station and got their own piled-high plates.

"The franks are kosher, so don't worry. They're all-beef franks," Kathleen said.

"Oh, thanks for letting me know, that's very helpful," Helen replied. She had been wondering if she was about to eat pork and was relieved that was not the case. She wondered if Reform Jews ate pork. She was hungry, and she couldn't wait to try this new food.

Near the station was a big golden cash register. Helen exchanged one of her dollar bills for a pile of change that she was too embarrassed to count. She knew that the franks and beans were only five cents, so she figured she must have ninety-five cents in change in her pocket now. She loved counting the money in her pocket, and she was determined to keep close track of her spending and put aside more savings than Papa even expected.

The two girls made their way back to the table and sat down. Helen watched Kathleen pick up the bun with the frankfurter in it, and bite into the end. Helen did the same, as if she ate this kind of food all the time. She inhaled the warm fragrant aromas and took another big bite. Heaven. She tried the beans and was pleasantly surprised at their dark sweetness.

Kathleen said, "Sometimes they call these franks *hot-dogs* after the little sausage shaped dogs." Helen laughed, remembering those very dogs waddling around on their leashes at Battery Park.

Another girl sat across from Helen. Helen had noticed her coming in to see Joe from time to time. She leaned over and said with a smile, "I'm Margaret. Your name is Helen?"

"Yes," Helen replied. "I'm the new girl."

"I work for one of the fabric houses, and I come around to see Joe from time to time to arrange fabric deliveries to him. I noticed you, and I noticed that you seem to be catching on fast," said Margaret. "That's great. Joe is quite demanding. He's let people go before their first week was up if they were too slow or too clumsy. I think he's happy with you."

The schlepper was sitting next to Margaret and listening. "I'm Lewis," he said. "Pleased to meet you, Helen. I work for the same company as Margaret, getting the fabric over to Joe so you can sew it up. I can tell you are quick and good with the sewing machine. I dropped off a lot of fabric and picked up a lot of knickerbockers from you this week. Joe always likes a good worker. You'll be fine."

Helen felt a wave of relief wash over her as she thanked Margaret and Lewis for their kind words. She felt more secure, knowing they thought Joe liked her and was happy with her work. Lewis and Margaret seemed so friendly and kind. Helen was happy to make new friends.

A few days later Helen and Kathleen were chatting together over their work, and Kathleen said something funny. Both girls tried to stifle their laughter so as not to appear to be shirking their work. But suddenly Esther, the grumpy third sewing machine girl, pushed back her chair with a loud scrape of the floor, pushed herself up, and trounced back to the kitchen where the boss Joe was sitting as usual. Kathleen and Helen fell completely silent, both trying to see what was happening as they also tried to look like they were working hard. Esther leaned over Joe and said loudly for everyone to hear, "I am very sorry, but it is difficult to work with so much chattering and gossip and laughing going on from those two." Esther pointed towards Kathleen and Helen.

Joe motioned for Esther to sit down and discuss things. Some time went by before Esther returned to her machine. A little while later, Joe came over and told Helen and Kathleen to come into the kitchen and sit down. He remained standing and said sternly, "You two are not here to have a good time. I am paying you good money to do an important job and to keep your attention on your work. There will be no more of your gossip and laughing, do you understand? This is your only warning!"

Both girls nodded and stood up, scurrying back to their places and burying themselves in piles of work for the rest of the day. Helen could see Esther stealing a glance at her from time to time with a satisfied smile on her face and a small toss of her head that no one could see but Helen.

13

MAX

Helen never bought the notebook and yellow pencil. She never bought the brown leather shoes with the shiny buckles that had caught her eye along the walk to work. She passed by all the carts with clothes that would help her look less like a greenhorn and more like a modern American woman. She wanted all these things, but she couldn't bear such indulgences until Max was on a ship headed west. If she had bought them, she would have been reminded of Max's danger every time she saw them. Before anything else, Max had to be safe.

With Papa and Helen both working hard, both sharing the urgency to bring Max to America, they saved every penny they could, even more than the agreed upon amounts. It had been three weeks now. She and Papa had written to Max to let him know the time was coming soon and to prepare himself. They hoped that hearing this would lift his spirits and help to allay his fears. Helen could still see the look in his eyes when she lifted the floorboards and found him shivering there. She longed for him to be safe.

After about three weeks of more savings, they sat at Aunt Rose's table and counted up their money. They had saved fifteen dollars from their wages. They also had Helen's fifteen dollars from what Mama had given her to take on the boat. That meant they had the thirty dollars for Max's ticket. In six weeks they would have sixty dollars, enough to cover not only the ocean ticket for Max, but also the travel expenses for Mama to take him to Bremerhaven and see him aboard the boat. There would even be enough for Max to have emergency pocket money, in case of trouble.

Before the end of this year, Max would get on the boat and come to America, just as Helen had. Max was only twelve, but he was adventuresome and brave, and Helen believed he could do it. Once he arrived, there would be three of them working, saving more and more each week to bring over the rest of the family. Selma was the next oldest, but she was only eleven. She was still young and unsure of herself. She wasn't bold like Max. She could not come alone; she would have to come with Mama.

In fact, Mama and the four younger children would all need to come at once. Bernard was the next oldest boy, and he was only nine but nearing ten. There was time before he would be in danger from the draft, a little more than two years until he would be twelve. There was time to save money for passage for them all.

Helen thought through the finances. Besides Selma and Bernard, there were the other two little boys, Milton and Julius. Plus Mama herself. So, they would need to buy five tickets to bring them all over at once. One hundred and fifty dollars for five tickets. This seemed an insurmountable sum. Helen thought about how long it would be before she saw her mother again. She longed to feel one of Mama's warm hugs and to hear her no-nonsense practicality when difficult situations arose. Helen had always relied on Mama, and she missed her deeply.

She took a deep breath. Mama had taught her how to stop when she began to get overwhelmed with feelings. Sit up straight, take a deep breath, know that it will pass. Mama was wise about working with the mind. She taught Helen that her state of mind was under her own control, that she did not have to live in fear.

Helen started with the simple thought, *we can do this.* Once Max comes, there will be three of us working. We don't need as much emergency money for a whole group as we did for Max and me to come over individually. Probably three hundred dollars would get them all here. With only three wage earners saving a total of ten dollars a week, it would be more than eight months, almost a year, before they could all come.

A year was a year. Helen and Papa and soon Max would figure it out. They would save even more money. Every time Helen wore her new blouse, she felt a little bit bad, because what she most wanted in this world was to have Mama and the family here.

The weeks marched by. Helen went to work at Joe's five days a week throughout the rest of summer and fall. She fell naturally into a comfortable routine: coffee with Aunt Rose first thing every day, good hot coffee with hot milk. You could buy a cup of coffee from a coffee stand in the neighborhood for a penny. It was good, but it would never be as good as Aunt Rose's coffee. Aunt Rose bought a pound bag of vacuum-packed coffee. Everyone agreed this was the best and most modern coffee. Helen had had tea every morning in the old country, but now she had converted to coffee. She enjoyed her conversations with Aunt Rose each morning. It wasn't the same as Mama, but Aunt Rose was also wise and Helen could confide in her. Aunt Rose was sympathetic and gave good advice about difficult situations, such as what had happened with Esther.

"Pay no attention to her, Helen," Aunt Rose had spoken strongly. "This is someone who is disturbed. We don't know why. Maybe something bad happened, and this is only a temporary bad time in her life, or maybe she will cause trouble forever. You must bring some compassion to your feelings for her. I know this is difficult because she has been so mean and tried so hard to make trouble for you. But the best thing will be if you find it in your heart to understand her. She is the one in pain, much more than she causes you and Kathleen."

Helen was struck by Aunt Rose's gentle advice. She realized the she would only spite herself if she walked around angry and hurt at work. She would have to bring her own kindness and understanding to bear. Esther would probably never know, but Helen would be much calmer and feel much better if she could understand instead of just react.

Aunt Rose continued. "You and Kathleen cannot appear to have fun at work. Save it for your lunch time or after work." Helen knew Aunt Rose was right about the entire situation and took her advice to heart. She made plans to share this with Kathleen one day when they were out on their own. She was sure Kathleen would agree.

The fall in New York was cool. Breezes blew up and down the short streets and the longer avenues. It was a special time for sunsets, the sky turning luminous shades of pale pink and aqua. As she left work each night, Helen looked far down the avenues that ran west to the Hudson. She would see a rectangle of sky between the tall brick buildings. Sometimes she would stop and watch as the rectangle turned silvery pink or blue and the clouds above the Hudson River lit up with glorious colors. Helen had found her new home. She knew that she would never want to live anywhere but New York.

One Sunday in September, she walked with Papa and Aunt Rose and the children across Manhattan to the west side. They found a patch of grass for a picnic along the river. Helen had not realized how broad the Hudson was, more than a mile wide. Compared to the lazy Nemunas in Panemunė, this river was a mighty torrent rushing to the sea. New York would be a great city one day, was already becoming one, due in large part to the river and its expansive natural harbor. As the evening slowly gathered around the family picnic, the sky lit up above the tall cliffs of the New Jersey Palisades. Streaks of gold above the high rock walls were mirrored in the river. Helen felt like she was in a magical setting.

Every Friday, she went with her friends from work to Katz's. Sometimes she went to the Saturday morning services with Aunt Rose at the People of Kindness Synagogue on Norfolk Street, only a few blocks away. The synagogue was not Reform, but it wasn't completely traditional, either. It had been founded by German Jews who had arrived in New York half a century ago. They were much more liberal than most Middle Eastern Jews. Helen liked going, but she didn't go every single week. Some Saturday mornings it seemed a great luxury to just do nothing, or to help with shopping and cooking.

When she did go, it was comforting to sit in *schul* and enjoy *Shabbat* with the traditional words and music, as if it were the old days sitting next to Mama. The main space of the temple was beautiful, amazingly designed to replicate the Sistine Chapel in Rome. Rabbi David in Panemunė had once shown the class pictures of the Sistine Chapel, so Helen especially enjoyed this synagogue.

The atmosphere was easy going. Just like in Panemunė, women sat in a separate area, with a screen between them and the men. In Reform synagogues, everyone sat together, and Helen thought the separation of women was insulting. But she loved the warmth of the services. Everyone was relaxed and comfortable, and the children were allowed to run around and play and be natural. It was a relaxed place to spend a few hours on Saturday morning, even though for Helen it was not about worship, and even though she did not like having to sit separately with the women. Still, the peace and ease and familiarity fed her soul.

September turned to October and the weather cooled marvelously. No longer was it hot working at Joe's. Now breezes flowed through the window next to her sewing machine. At Aunt Rose's, a similar window between the parlor and the kitchen kept evenings cool and comfortable in all three rooms of the apartment. Morty and Josie were back in school, full of interesting information every night at dinner. Last week Morty had told them all about the tallest building in the world, the new City Hall just finished in Philadelphia. He had explained how the tallest buildings had always been churches, but this was a government office building. Josie taught Helen how to sing the Star-Spangled Banner and say the Pledge of Allegiance, like a real American.

Late one Saturday afternoon, Helen heard Papa knocking at the door. She let him in and gave him a big hug, happy to see him because she had missed him the night before, having been at Katz's with all her friends from work. Aunt Rose had a pot of chicken soup simmering on the stove, and the apartment smelled wonderful. Dinner would be good tonight. Aunt Rose had gotten the chicken from the Kosher poultry store downstairs and mentioned that the owner was always nice and friendly. Josie and Morty were still outside playing.

Papa sat down on the long bench at the wooden table. Helen brought over the teapot and the big can of tea leaves. She made Papa his favorite, strong black tea. They both watched the steam rising as Helen poured boiling water into the pot and then covered it to brew for a few minutes.

Papa reached into his pockets. Helen's eyes grew wide as Papa laid a stack of dollars on the table. It was more than two inches high, all in rumpled bills. Papa said with a big smile, "This is what we have saved, my Hinde. Finally, we have enough. Max is one boy the Russian army is not getting their hands on."

"We have sixty dollars?" she asked. It had so long been a dream that it hardly seemed possible that it was real. But there, for both to see, was her brother Max's safe passage.

"Yes, we have sixty dollars!" Papa proudly exclaimed. "I will buy a ticket on Monday and send Mama all the information. Then we will wire the rest of the money. Let's write a letter together."

Papa took out a pencil and a piece of stationery that he had carefully brought tucked into a book. Helen remembered when the letter had arrived, finally announcing it was time for her come to America. She knew Max would be as excited as she had been. He would be so eager to start on his adventure, he would probably rip open the thin blue aerogramme.

Dear Devorah, my beloved wife, Papa began. Helen imagined the journey. Max and Mama riding in the Troika, taking the ferry to Kaunas, getting on the train. She knew Max would be thrilled with the entire adventure, the long train ride to Bremen, and finally boarding the ship in Bremerhaven. She hoped that he, too, would make a friend for the journey.

Helen missed Rebecca, her good friend from the boat. She had written and mailed a letter during the summer. After a few weeks, Rebecca had written back. She wrote how happy she was to be reunited with her family. They lived in the city of Houston, and there were lots of Jews there and many synagogues. Some people in Texas didn't like Jews, so it could sometimes be like the old country, with people treating them badly in the shops and on the streets. There was even an organization called the Ku Klux Klan that hated Jews as well as anyone who wasn't white, but Rebecca's family was determined to stay put.

Everyone saved so they could buy their own land and raise horses on their own ranch. The two girls wrote about visiting one another, perhaps in a few years. Helen hoped Rebecca would come to New York so that she would not have to go to Texas. She had had quite enough of people who treated Jews badly.

Helen continued to think about Max. Perhaps he dreamed of being a cowboy in the New World, of living in the Wild West like Rebecca's family. She pictured his sturdy body, no doubt taller now. Mama's last letter said that Max was so tall now that she had to look up to him. He could no longer pass for an eleven-year-old. It was not good that he was getting so big so fast in Panemunė, but it would be good on the journey. Helen told Papa that she thought Max would do fine in the rough world of men's steerage that she had watched from afar.

"Max knows how to take care of himself, Papa."

"Yes, he always has," Papa replied. "Even when he was a little boy in school, the bullies never bothered him. Our Max is tough. He will be fine."

He was young and healthy like she was. He would have no trouble at Ellis Island.

Papa continued to write. Max would come over on the ship SS *Kaiserin Maria Theresa* in late October. "I'm happy we could buy a ticket for early November. Crossing the North Atlantic in late November can get rough," Papa explained.

On November 8, 1900, Max's ship came in. Helen and Papa finished work a little early and rushed down to Battery Park. They were both wearing heavy woolen overcoats against the newly arrived winter weather. Helen had found her coat at a pushcart for only two dollars. She hadn't been able to save as much that week, but you couldn't live in New York without a winter coat. It had not turned icy cold yet, but everyone said it would soon.

At first, they didn't see Max anywhere. They combed the entire park until they were sure he wasn't there yet. They were glad they had gotten to the park before him, so he didn't have to wait and wonder if they would come. They walked over to where the ferries from Ellis Island landed and waited there. Soon they spotted a boat coming in. As it pulled up to the shore, they could see Max, waving wildly at the railings. He couldn't see them yet. He was just waving to all his new countrymen. Papa and Helen waved back and shouted, but no one could make out a word in the noisy jumble of languages. They watched Max waiting his turn at the gangplank. Soon he walked down and put his foot onto American soil for the first time.

Helen watched his face, his expression serious. She remembered her own first moment in America, and she knew how full Max's heart was. She was excited to watch him repeating her own ceremonious step onto the American earth, and she felt a surge of love for this strong and gentle boy, her brother.

Helen ran up to him yelling "Max, Max! It's me." He looked up and saw her coming, His face broke into a wide smile. He opened his arms to hug his sister. Her name was all he said. "Hinde. Hinde." Papa came up behind Helen and ruffled Max's hair and hugged both of his children. Max hugged Papa back, now with tears in his eyes. "Papa, Papa. It's really you, finally."

"You made it, my boy," said Papa. "My oldest son is in America now, along with my oldest daughter. Today I am a happy man."

Max grinned. He was much taller than Helen remembered, and he looked more grown up. He still looked strong, and even more lanky and long-limbed than before. His hair was cut short, no doubt by Mama before he left home. He still had his beautiful boyish grin that melted Helen's heart the way it always had.

The three of them walked north. They walked along Water Street, through the financial district with its tall buildings and colonnaded marble banks. The area was mostly deserted, with just a few stragglers coming out from work late in the day; bankers and business men wearing dark suits, overcoats, and stylish bowler hats.

Max had a coat, but it was thin brown wool, practically threadbare. It was too small for him, torn and patched. Helen realized how her perceptions had changed now that she was a New Yorker. Max looked like he had just stepped off the boat. As he literally had. These days, Helen could immediately tell the difference between a seasoned New Yorker and a new immigrant. It wasn't just how they looked. It was also about a certain confidence that came with time.

Helen never looked down on the new arrivals, and she didn't worry about Max. She knew that he would find his way. He would fit in, find friends, build a life, and be happy here. Helen had no doubt about it. She felt like she was seeing the future, and it was a good future. Now they had to get everyone else over here to live out the rest of her family's dreams.

Max talked about the trip and the bad storm they had been through, similar to what Helen had endured. Like Helen, he was young, and he wasn't hurt, only a bruise or two that bothered him for a day.

Papa explained that Helen lived with Aunt Rose, and

that Max would live with him and the other men who had no families in America yet. Helen was happy Max had arrived. Now he would settle in. No more terror that the soldiers could arrive at any moment and destroy his life. He was safe. An unexpected surge of victory filled her, as she pictured the Russian soldier who had so contemptuously thrown her chicken soup on the floor so many months ago. *Who's the winner, now?* she asked the soldier in her mind.

Soon they came to the Lower East Side and climbed the stairs to Aunt Rose's apartment. Aunt Rose opened the door wide and embraced Max. She put him at arm's length with her hands firmly on his shoulders, her eyes on his eyes. "Let me look at you! You've gotten so big. I remember when you were a little boy in Panemunė."

She stepped aside and swept her arm into the room to welcome him. "You are always welcome here," she said. "Let this be your second home."

Aunt Rose introduced Morty and Josie, who sat at the table. Morty stood up and came over. He was not as tall as Max and had to look up to make eye contact. He extended his hand to welcome Max in a grown-up way. Josie smiled shyly at her tall, handsome cousin.

Aunt Rose had made gefilte fish again, for the first time since Helen had arrived, exactly three months ago. Helen loved seeing the beautiful golden coins of carrots lining the back of the realistic fish. Perhaps this would be the special 'new arrivals meal,' to be served once again when the rest of the family arrived from the old country. Helen imagined that day when Mama and all the other children would squeeze around this table for gefilte fish.

"Max will live with me," Papa said. "Aunt Rose has

graciously invited us for dinner every night. Max and I will bring lots of good things for us to eat together."

Papa went on, "Max, Aunt Rose has even found you a job. Did you see the Kosher Chicken Shop on the first floor of this building? With the sign in Hebrew? Aunt Rose always buys her chickens there, and she is friends with the owner, Mr. Bloomberg. He's a good man, and his business has grown fast so that now he needs a helper. We told him about you, and he would like to hire you. You'll learn all about chickens: how to prepare them and how to sell them. You'll make five dollars a week, good pay in New York for a twelve-year-old boy. That's what Helen makes.

"But Max, this is important. Once the whole family is here, you must go back to school. A good education will help you to have a good life. You must promise me that you will return to your studies. This is important to me, but for now, we will all work."

"I'm happy to do anything to help the rest of our family get here soon. Yes, Papa, I promise to return to school once the family is here," Max said.

"And who's Helen?" he asked with a confused expression on his face. Everyone laughed as they realized that Helen had not told Max her new name yet. She explained how she had changed her name when she saw the Statue of Liberty.

Max replied, "I can understand that. This morning, everyone on the boat laughed and danced with joy that our journey was complete. When they saw the copper lady, her golden glow in the sunlight, everyone suddenly got quiet," Max explained. "Then, after a bit, the beautiful moment was over, and everyone erupted back into noise and happy song. What a wonderful day I have had. I will never, ever forget today."

Papa leaned over and squeezed Max's arm. Helen, who sat next to Max on the bench, leaned in to him and turned her face to hide in his shirt for a moment. She took a big breath of Max. He smelled of the ocean, the boat, and the journey. And deep, deep behind, there was just a hint that lingered of Panemunė, of home, of Mama and the family. Helen breathed in deeply.

Aunt Rose began to cut the fish into portions. "Your cousin Morty and you have the same name," she said to Max. "Morty's real name is the same as yours, Mordecai." Max and Morty exchanged smiles. They were exactly the same age, and now they found out they even had the same name.

As boys do, they took measure of one another. Max was taller, but Morty was more filled out. Helen thought perhaps Max had lost weight on the ship. And she knew that food was more plentiful in New York than it had ever been in Panemunė. She remembered how she was always hungry in the old country, and how it seemed Max could never get enough to eat. Helen thought how Morty knew the city and the ways of the New World that Max needed to learn. She was happy to see them talking together.

"I'll show you all around New York," Morty said. "You don't start work until Monday, so we can explore. You'll know your way around by the time you go to work Monday morning."

"And my real name is Josephine," said Josie. "Welcome to New York, Max." Josie smiled at the older boy and then served everyone gefilte fish, starting with the guest of honor.

"Mama makes this dish sometimes back at home. It's my favorite dish, so thank you very much for making it,"

Max volunteered to Aunt Rose and Josie. They both beamed back at him. Aunt Rose's food went a long way toward making a new arrival feel comfortable in a foreign land.

That night after Papa and Max had left and everyone had gone to bed, Helen lay in the darkness. She thought back over the last months, remembering her constant fear that the army might return and take her brother away. The weight of worry that she had been carrying was like a heavy stone in her heart. Tears welled up in her eyes and began to run down her face as she felt the weight she had been bearing. All these months, she had kept her attention on saving money, never letting herself feel the full impact of what it would mean to lose her brother. For the first time, she let the tears fall freely, and with each tear, a little more of the heaviness was lifted. In its place came a sweet relief. Eventually she was smiling through her tears.

Helen fell into a peaceful sleep.

THE SAVING YEARS

The bitter winds blew right through Helen's thin winter coat. She shivered and wrapped her babushka more tightly around her ears, hoping the blizzard would not blow her over. At least her feet were warm. Lewis from work had given her a pair of shiny, black leather, fur-lined boots. He had moved into his own apartment with other young men from work, and the expensive women's boots had been left by the previous tenant. Lewis didn't have a sister or a girlfriend, so Helen was the lucky beneficiary. She felt like the girl in the fairy tale whose foot fit into the glass slipper. In the old country, the girl was called *Ashenputtel*, but here they called her *Cinderella*. The beautiful boots were beyond anything Helen could afford.

Max appeared to be thriving in New York. Helen could see that he shared her determination to bring over the rest of the family as soon as possible.

It was unusual for a twelve-year-old to be earning five dollars a week, but Max was a hard worker. The chicken store owner, Mr. Bloomberg, liked Max. Mr. Bloomberg was getting older and was relieved to employ this strong young man whom he could trust. Every Friday he paid Max with five new dollar bills like it was a celebration for them both.

Max spoke of his boss with genuine affection, saying how smart he was and how good at business. Mr. Bloomberg taught him to notice what the other merchants did and whether their tactics were successful or not. If something worked for a competitor, then they would try it, too.

One day Mr. Bloomberg sent Max to buy live chickens from the ferry boat that docked on the Hudson River. It carried chickens that had been sent by train from the Midwest. There was no way for trains to cross the river into Manhattan, so everything that came in by train had to be ferried over by boat. Previously, they had bought chickens from a middle man, but Mr. Bloomberg found out that prices were lower if you met the boat and bought direct. He trusted Max with the money to buy the chickens, over ten dollars.

Max's chest filled and his chin raised up as he told Helen about his trip to the boat. The first venture was so successful that every week now, Mr. Bloomberg gave Max ten dollars to buy chickens. The chickens were alive and in cages, so Mr. Bloomberg rented a pushcart for the afternoon to bring them back to the shop. Max said he liked steering the laden cart through the city. He liked being a part of New York's busy street life, passing through all the neighborhoods between the chicken shop and the docks. Helen thought Max already seemed to know more about the city than she did, and that he loved New York as much as she did. Max did mention that there were a lot of tough-looking boys and men at the docks and in the parts of the city he had to pass through.

The demand for chickens in New York was huge, and business was growing fast. Newly arrived immigrants couldn't afford beef, but chickens were cheap. Max told Helen that there seemed to be a kosher butcher shop on every corner of the city.

Here on Hester Street, the chicken business was booming. Even in his first months on the job, Max saw that growth was so fast they could hardly keep up with the demand. Papa talked about starting his own chicken business, once Mama was here and settled.

Sometimes the owner left Max alone in charge of the store. Max loved being left in charge. He got to act like a real grown-up, taking care of the customers who walked in. He would point out the different sized chickens, recommending which was the best buy for the size of the customer's family.

Part of Max's job was to kill the chickens and then pluck them and dress them and hang them in the shop window. The chickens had to be killed and cleaned in accordance with Jewish law so that they would be kosher. Mr. Bloomberg had trained Max how to do it. The first rule was to make it as easy as possible for the chickens. Everything needed to be done fast and away from the other chickens, so they didn't get agitated. The killed chickens had to be carefully cleaned, all the innards carefully removed, and the blood drained out. The last step was to rinse the chicken in clean water several times. Once all the chickens were properly prepared, Max hung them in the window to look as appealing as a dead chicken could look. The idea was that a passerby might think how a nice fresh chicken would be perfect for dinner.

$\rightleftharpoons$

$\mathcal{O}ne$ night at dinner, Max complained about having to kill the chickens. "I like the little guys," he said. "I try to make it go fast so it's over before they know what happened."

Papa looked at his son for a moment. Anyone could see that Max was troubled at having to kill dozens of these poor creatures each week. Max was a sensitive soul, and Papa always wanted to protect his children from hard realities. Helen knew that Papa was torn that Max was working instead of being in school.

"What don't you like about killing the chickens, son?" he asked kindly.

Max slumped down a bit and looked at his plate. "I don't know. I like the chickens. Mama used to kill a chicken every few weeks. But one chicken is different from dozens of chickens. It's the worst thing I have to do."

Papa sighed. "I'm sorry this is so hard Max. I wish it weren't. A twelve-year-old boy shouldn't have to do a job like this. You should be learning and doing homework. I am so happy that you are here and finally safe, but things are still not what they should be for you."

Papa continued, "I want you to know how proud I am of you that you don't like killing the chickens. It shows me once again that you are kind-hearted, my son Max. Once Mama is here, we will send you back to school so that you don't have to ever kill a chicken again."

Aunt Rose added, "Once you are back in school, you will learn things. Maybe you can be a doctor and help people to live longer and healthier lives. Then the little chickens will have given their lives to help you on your way."

Morty piped up. "Max, once I'm a high-paid engineer, I will help you go to school. And you, Mama, I will support you completely. You can plan on being a lady of leisure and drinking coffee in restaurants for five cents a cup. You can buy beautiful dresses and hats, and you can be friends with the Astors and the Vanderbilts." The family all laughed warmly at Morty's planned generosity and his devotion to his mother. Helen reached out and ruffled his hair.

Everyone knew about the Astors. They were one of the world's richest families. They had been the "New York Landlords" since the 1700s. Astor Place was named for them, just a little north of this neighborhood. The Astors and Vanderbilts and other well-known New York families had all lived on Astor Place until not so long ago. Recently, they all moved north to the newly fashionable Murray Hill area. Helen had seen the big mansions where these families used to live. She and everyone else in her family walked all over Manhattan, especially Morty and Max who loved to explore together and knew the city better than any of them.

Morty picked up the conversation with his own difficulties. "School is hard, too. I have to do really hard homework every night. I need to get perfect grades, so I can get into college and be a top-notch engineer. I'm going to get accepted to City College of New York. It's the first free college in America."

Even Josie chimed in. "I'm going to college too, to Hunter College. It's the second free college in the country, and it's only for girls." Helen could only marvel at the advantages these children would have in life with a college education. One day she would have her own children, and she vowed to herself that they would all go to college and be successful. Engineers. At least the boys.

Would the girls go to college, too? Helen spent just a moment imagining herself at college, of all things. She loved school, learning about history, hearing new ideas and old wisdom. She loved imagining such a life, but she knew it was not possible for her to fulfill such dreams. One day she would have children, and they would get to live out these dreams, and that was enough.

Every Sunday, Max and Helen and Papa sat together and added up how much they had saved, and how much they still needed to bring over the family. Every weekday, Helen went to work at Joe's, Max went to Mr. Bloomberg's chicken store, and Papa went to work cutting fabric. They all got paid on Friday.

On Sunday night, Papa and Max brought all their money over to Aunt Rose's. Helen would bring out her salary. Before dinner, the three of them would gather at Aunt Rose's table and count out their savings together. They added in their share from the new week's pay. When they were done, they knew just how long it would be before Mama and the other children would arrive. Some weeks, Aunt Rose would put in a dollar, if she could afford it. Even Morty and Josie would add small change left over from their allowances. Each week Papa wrote a family letter to Mama and the other children.

Helen and Papa had to start all over again from zero after they bought Max's ticket early last October. It had left them with nothing. The two of them had saved a little in early November before Max arrived. Now they had three salaries and together they could save ten dollars a week. By December they had forty dollars, and by New Year's Eve, 1901, they had eighty. By June first they had two hundred and eighty dollars. Papa thought they needed to have three hundred dollars to buy the five pre-paid tickets and pay for the ferry and rail fares for the five members of their family who would be coming.

Furthermore, money for the ticket wasn't enough. The reunited family needed a place to live. Papa wanted to have another two hundred, so they could rent their own place and have food and money when the family arrived, once they were all together again.

Helen figured out it would take the three of them another six or seven months to save all this money. They would reach their goal early in 1902. Helen would be eighteen years old by then. It seemed so far away that there were moments when Helen despaired of ever seeing her little sister Selma again, the three small boys, and Mama. How much she missed Mama.

Yet missing them gave her energy and determination. Every day, she went to work with the knowledge that she was adding a little more money to their savings, that she was bringing her family a little closer. She never stopped thinking about this.

At work one day, Helen and Kathleen were sitting on the front stoop having lunch. Helen was thinking about Esther, the third sewing machine girl. Helen had thought a lot about the incident where Esther had reported them to Joe, and Joe had warned them strongly about having a good time at work. Esther's actions could have gotten them both fired. Helen was careful around Esther now, and she and Kathleen never laughed or talked louder than a whisper.

Shortly after it happened, Helen had asked Kathleen why she thought that Esther was so unfriendly, why she always scowled and wanted to get other people in trouble. Kathleen had told Helen a terrible story. "Esther is very unhappy. It has nothing to do with you or with any of us. She was engaged to be married to a nice boy. He was Jewish like her, and he worked as a courier, delivering important packages around the city. But he was killed in a terrible way. He was in another part of the city, not our Lower East Side, and he was attacked and beaten to death right in the street. There were some people who saw, and they said his attackers called him a 'Dirty Jew.' He always wore the little round hat that Jewish men wear, so that must be how they knew he was Jewish. Esther has been miserable since then, and she heartlessly tries to make everyone else miserable too."

Helen had been shocked at this story. She couldn't imagine how someone could live through such a terrible thing. She had thought so much about it frequently ever since hearing the story. She said to Kathleen, "You know, I think Esther has lost faith in the human race."

"Yes, I think you are right," said Kathleen. "She never says a nice word to anyone and keeps to herself completely. I've tried to be nice to her, but it's no use. It's not the first time she has tried to get someone in trouble with Joe. Before you came to work, she reported one of the schleppers for being too 'friendly.' I think he was interested in her, but she wasn't having it. But I never dreamed she would try to hurt us. Live and learn," Kathleen said philosophically.

Whenever Helen thought about Esther's experience, she couldn't help but think about Max and how he was travelling around the city for work, picking up the live chickens at the ferry boat dock each week. She decided she would tell him the story of Esther's fiancé. It might make him more cautious as he went into strange neighborhoods. She reassured herself that Max did not wear what Kathleen called the "little round Jewish hat," a *yarmulke*. She let herself relax, hoping that her brother, being less conspicuously Jewish, would be safer.

Finally, by the late spring of 1902, Papa, Helen, and Max had saved over five hundred dollars. It had taken the three of them more than a year of saving, but they had done it. They were all getting nervous because Bernard was almost twelve years of age. The pressure to draft him and take him away would start soon. They needed to get the whole family out of Lithuania fast. They had saved the money, and it was time.

One night in June, Papa brought out a fresh piece of the blue aerogramme paper. Together they all wrote a letter to Mama telling her to come and bring all the children. Papa had booked five tickets on the SS *Kaiser Wilhelm II* to arrive in New York on October 29, 1902. This would give Mama plenty of time to prepare, to sell anything she could before leaving, and to make arrangements for herself and her children to depart. He wired another hundred dollars to Mama for all the other expenses she would have getting to America.

This schedule gave Helen, Max, and Papa time to get everything set up for the family's arrival. They looked for an apartment that would suit them all. By mid-summer, they found a modest apartment on Delancey Street. It was a ten-minute walk from Aunt Rose and a short walk to work for all of them. They would be in the back of the building, on the fourth floor, away from the street and all the noises of the Lower East Side pushcarts and street life.

The building had two flushing toilet rooms in the hall outside the apartment. All four apartments on the floor would share the new toilet rooms. They were now the law, and landlords had to comply and add them to their buildings. To Helen, the thought of not having to go all the way down to a backyard toilet was amazing. A luxury. One day, soon after they had rented the apartment, she went into the toilet room and closed the door. She stood watching as she flushed the toilet four times in a row, just to watch the water swirl around and disappear and fill back up again. No doubt the Astors had many toilet rooms conveniently placed all over their mansions, but to Helen, this was magic.

They would move into the new apartment on October 1, so they would have a whole month to find furniture and make curtains and buy food. By the time Mama arrived, it would be a real home.

October came quickly. It was time to buy furniture. They needed a kitchen table and a bed for the little back bedroom where Mama and Papa would sleep. They needed a trunk for the parlor where they could store all the bedding during the day. Maybe a sofa and one or two chairs if they could find them. All six children would stay together in the front parlor each night. If they bought soft bedding to put on the floor, it could all be put in the trunk during the day, and the parlor would be available for sitting and reading and conversation.

It had been more than two years since Helen had waved goodbye to Mama in Bremerhaven. Soon they would be together again in their own home.

For the entire month of October, 1902, Helen, Max and Papa scoured the pushcarts for good furniture of the right size and shape for their new home. They found a sturdy kitchen table with two long benches. They found two smaller armchairs for the parents to sit at each end. Six small blankets could be folded up and tucked away into a trunk. They found a wooden poster bed complete with mattress and bed sheets and a blanket for Mama and Papa. It would just fit into the tiny bedroom at the back of the apartment.

One evening after work, Helen wandered through the furniture pushcarts. Bright strips of brass caught her eye, and she realized they were bound around a shining wooden chest that might have belonged to a pirate. A big lock secured whatever treasure might have once been inside. There was even a large decorative key with delicate brass scrollwork. This was the perfect trunk for the parlor. It was flat on top, so it could double as a table or as seating, and the children could fold up their blankets and put them away for the day. Helen told the vendor she would be back the next day and gave him a small payment to hold the chest.

Papa had a friend with a cart who offered to come along and help. That Saturday morning, everyone gathered around, including Morty who was getting stronger and could help lift heavy pieces, and Josie who wanted to help. They went from pushcart to pushcart, bargaining for their final purchases. Once a deal had been struck, Max, Morty, Papa, and his friend loaded the furniture into the cart.

When they came to the pirate chest, everyone was intrigued and wanted to imagine its history. Max said he was sure it had been filled with gold and precious gems and had been recently recovered from the bottom of the sea. Morty swung an imaginary cutlass over his head, shouting "Avast Ye Mateys." Morty and Max leapt around in a mock pirate duel.

Helen bought a blanket for each child, heavy enough for winter. She found lacy fabric for curtains for the parlor and simple cotton for a tablecloth for the kitchen. Joe had told her she could stay late after work one day and sew up some personal items.

Helen discovered a pushcart that sold dishes. She found a set of eight plates with a blue and white willow pattern that she knew Mama would love. In the old country, they had never had anything so pretty. She found mismatched knives and forks and spoons. Anything else, she would pick up during the weeks before Mama arrived.

It took until late that night to get everything all the way up to the fourth floor. Aunt Rose came over to pick up Josie and Morty. Helen gave each of them a tearful hug, realizing that for the first time in America, she would not sleep in Aunt Rose's parlor, would not wake up to Aunt Rose's coffee. Helen reached out for Aunt Rose's hands, and she thanked her for everything.

"We'll miss you," said Morty.

"Yes," said Josie. "We'll miss you very much."

"We'll see Helen all the time. She'll visit us, and we'll come here all the time," Aunt Rose added, nodding her head to reassure her children that things would not change too much.

"Helen, I have loved having you stay with us. I have

enjoyed having another working girl around, and we have had so many good times. I know I'll miss your living with us, so just expect us to be frequent guests at the Chaim Breakstone apartment." Everyone hugged goodnight, and Aunt Rose and the children departed. Then, it was just Helen, Max, and Papa.

Papa looked exhausted with all the activities of the day. He retired to the little bedroom behind the kitchen, where he could crawl into his big new bed. Helen and Max pulled out their blankets in the parlor. It was the first night in their own home in America, and they all slept soundly. They were ready for Mama and the children.

MAMA

OCTOBER 29, 1902

Helen awakened to gentle morning light that filtered through the lace curtains. It was just dawn as she opened her eyes to this day for which she had waited so long. She pulled her warm blanket close around and stole a moment to just feel her happiness. Today was the day she and Papa and Max had worked for. She held her breath as she imagined how they would soon be walking to the park to meet the ferry from Ellis Island.

This morning the SS *Kaiser Wilhelm II* would arrive in New York Harbor. It was the newest model of steamship afloat, even newer than Helen's ship, the SS *Barbarossa*. It held the record for the fastest Atlantic crossing ever, only five days. Papa had a knack, it seemed, for booking passage on the fastest ships.

All she had thought about for the last week was Mama. Mama leaving Panemunė and travelling on the train with the four children. Mama boarding the ship. Mama in steerage, keeping the family close, keeping the family safe. Mama.

Helen ached to see Mama, to hear her wise and calm voice, to feel the comfort and safety of her strong arms. Helen imagined her young siblings awakening now for the last day of their journey, going out on deck, taking in the sight of the beautiful harbor and the powerful copper lady who welcomed them. She imagined them sleeping all together in this room, this very night.

Even though it was a Thursday, Helen's boss Joe had given her the day off. As gruff as he was, he understood the importance of family. Papa and Max had also gotten the day off. Like a precious fabric that had been torn apart, the ragged edges of their family would be rejoined, mended, and stitched back into a single piece.

Light was now streaming in as Helen threw off her blanket and jumped up. She was ready for the day. She tiptoed out to the toilet room, opening and closing doors quietly to not awaken anyone. She went to the kitchen to wash at the big sink, then returned to the parlor and found light clothes to wear. She had a blue skirt with a matching blue blouse she had been saving for the day. Practical, no ruffles or lace, pretty and clean. The blouse had a print of little birds and was lightweight for a warm day.

New York had been having what everyone called Indian summer, a week or two of warm days before the real winter set in. In the old country, it had been called "Old Woman's Summer," but it was the same thing. Whatever you called it, the weather was glorious, a perfect temperature, clear skies and gentle breezes. Mama would see New York at its best.

Because there were no closets in the apartment, Helen stored her clothes flat with her blankets under her mattress to keep them pressed and neat. Max did the same and so did Papa. She hung her nightgown from a wall sconce near the front window to let the morning air blow it fresh once again.

Helen started a fire in the big kitchen stove, then put on water for coffee. She sliced bread for toast and brought out the newly purchased bag of vacuum-packed coffee, measuring enough for three. Max was only fourteen, and there was a bottle of milk for him. Papa said Max could have mostly milk with just a little coffee. People worried that coffee was bad for you and that it stunted children's growth, but Max was already almost as tall as Papa. Helen had tasted Postum, the coffee substitute that was so popular. It tasted more like dishwater than coffee. She would make her own pot of real coffee.

Once it was ready, she poured herself a cup and sat down and held it in her hands, breathing in the warm steam and the aroma. She looked across the table, this table where the family would soon unite. She was glad they had found a table big enough for all eight of them: three kids on each side bench and Mama and Papa in the armchairs. In Panemunė, the table had always been the heart of their house, the place where everyone gathered whenever something important came up. Helen knew this table would be that table.

Helen imagined how Mama would sit here. This would be her chair, and from now on, Helen would always leave the armchair for Mama. They had found three little chairs for the parlor that could be squeezed in around the table in case of guests.

Helen picked up one of the two special china cups she had found last week. They were for sale on the sidewalk outside a house on Astor Place. The residents were moving, and their son was selling off their possessions. Each of the cups had flowers painted on the side, a gold rim, and a matching saucer. They weren't in perfect shape, a few chips here and there, but they had cost next to nothing, and they seemed like treasures in their new home.

She sipped her coffee from this new cup, then set it down on the matching saucer. The other matching cup and saucer were of course for Mama. The once fine china spoke of elegant days past. She imagined herself sitting at a table in a mansion like the Astors', sipping her coffee from these cups, brand new and perfect. Breakfast would be served on imaginary matching plates. She took another sip.

Now that the whole family would be together again, they would all work to help one another. Helen expanded her little dream of the mansion to include the entire family sitting at the fine table, everyone sipping from perfect cups.

Helen brought Papa's and Max's cups down from the shelf. Papa's was large and brown. Max was a boy, and of course had more important things on his mind than cups. He wouldn't notice what cup he was using. Each of the little boys had their own cup, and the cup she had chosen for Selma had little flowers on it and almost matched Helen's and Mama's. Helen knew that Selma would notice and appreciate the similarity. She leaned back in the armchair and closed her eyes and smiled.

Soon Max and Papa were up and dressed, joining Helen at the table. Both wore fresh white shirts and trousers with light jackets. Papa looked especially dapper today. She noticed a look on his face, a dreamy look that she had not seen before. He had to be thinking about Mama. He wore a new straw boater hat, like what everyone in New York was wearing, having set aside his heavier homburg until the weather turned cold again. Max had a plaid wool cap like all the young men wore.

Soon they set off for Battery Park. Helen realized this was Papa's third trip to gather the members of his family. He had met her more than two years ago, and then Max a few months later. This would be the third and last time. Helen had no living grandparents, both Mama's and Papa's parents having passed away in previous years. Today when they returned to their new home, the entire family would be here in New York. As they had longed for, planned and worked hard for, the dream was coming true.

Helen remembered how happy she had been when Max arrived at the park, and she felt her heart swell with anticipation. They arrived at Battery Park early. They could see a large liner in the harbor, and Papa was sure it was the SS *Kaiser Wilhelm II*. He wasn't happy about the name of the boat, because Kaiser Wilhelm was the Emperor of Germany and a man whom nobody respected and who was a well-known anti-Semite. Papa had talked about it a few days earlier. Still, Helen thought that a boat was a boat, and a fast boat was best.

For two hours, they sat on the benches under the shade trees in the park, watching people, checking traffic on the river every few minutes. Max described how the children had looked when he left home, how big each of them had been. They all knew that things have changed by now.

Finally, they could see the ferry coming toward them from Ellis Island, belching smoke and making loud noises.

As the ferry came closer, they could see the crowd on deck. They strained to make out any familiar faces.

"Max, Papa, look!" Helen could not hold still. Her feet were shifting back and forth under her, her arms were waving and flying, her face upturned to see the passengers. "There she is!" Helen could just make out Mama. She didn't see any children and suddenly felt a small panic as she remembered the grueling tests of Ellis Island. Had everyone made it?

Mama was scanning the shore, but she was still too far away to identify anyone in the huge crowd. Helen sighed with relief when she saw that Mama held hands with two children on each side. Everyone was accounted for. They were all hanging onto one another for dear life in the crush and excitement.

Deckhands jumped off the boat onto the dock and tied up the ferry with big ropes. They dragged out the heavy gangplank and attached it in place. Passengers began to disembark. The noise of so many people speaking in different languages filled the air, punctuated with cries and laughter as families recognized one another. Suddenly, for Helen, all sound stopped as she saw Mama at the top of the gangplank. Mama carried a big hand-stitched bag like the one Helen had carried. She imagined Mama with the children in steerage. How happy they would be to leave behind the terrible smells and the rough seas and the inconvenience of lugging that bag around everywhere.

Helen shaded her eyes as she looked up to watch Mama. She counted each of her siblings one by one as they appeared on the gangplank. Once they were all moving forward, Mama followed. At the moment of stepping onto the soil of New York, Helen saw Mama pause and look down at her foot as it touched the new country. Helen had done the same, as had Max, and she guessed that Papa had as well. Marking the very moment of arrival. So many immigrants must have done this before them. So many would do the same in the future.

The four younger children ran ashore. Papa walked toward them all. Then Mama looked up and saw him. Helen watched as they locked eyes and stood frozen, gazing at one another. Mama had tears in her eyes, and Helen was surprised that Papa did as well. They began to glide slowly toward one another, their arms outstretched, moving down the ribbon of excitement that flowed between them. As they met in an embrace, Mama buried her face in the warmth and safety of Papa's large chest. They had been apart for more than two years. He tenderly pushed her back just a moment to gaze upon the face he had missed so terribly. Gently, he kissed Mama on the lips.

All six children stood frozen as they watched their parents. Never before had they seen their parents kiss on the lips or act so romantic. *I'll remember this moment for the rest of my life*, thought Helen. Now there were eight people with tears in their eyes.

Helen recognized her sister Selma, inches taller than she remembered. "Selma, Selma, it's me, dear sister." Selma looked up and realized it was Helen. She reached out to hug and hold her only sister.

"I've missed you so much, Hinde," said Selma. "Let's never be apart again."

Max ran to the three little boys. "It's me, Max. Welcome to America." All six children were grinning and crying and hugging at the same time.

Mama and Papa walked toward their children, arm in

arm. Suddenly Mama saw Helen, and more tears came to her eyes as she stretched out her arms. Helen also burst into a new round of crying as she once again felt the warmth of Mama's love. Papa and Max knelt down with Selma and the three little boys and hugged them and talked to them and welcomed them.

All around the Breakstone family, there in Battery Park, other families were having similar experiences of reunion, of remembering, of love. The faces were different, the languages were not the same, but the love was the same in every family group. Helen took a moment to look around her and feel the power of these renewed connections. Nothing had been certain for a long time. No one had been sure they would be reunited. But now they were.

Soon the eight of them, arm in arm, began the long walk uptown. Papa led them along Water Street, north through the financial district. Prosperous men, most of them wearing boater hats like Papa's, crowded the streets. Papa was smiling at everyone, talking to each child in turn, holding hands and leading the way. Helen had never seen him look so happy. In that moment, she realized that he and Mama had carried the burden of worry even more deeply than she had, and seeing them reunited and still so in love, she understood some of what they had sacrificed to save their family.

Everyone was chattering and asking questions. In Panemunė, the family had always spoken Yiddish, but Helen could tell that all of them had been working hard on their English and wanted to try out their new phrases and words as much as possible. She watched as Mama leaned her head back to see the tops of the tall buildings. Mama spoke, saying in Yiddish, "These buildings are so grand.

I've never seen buildings so elegant and beautiful." On either side, Mama held the hands of the two smallest boys, Milton and Julius, now so big at ages eight and ten. She let go of Milton for a moment to point upward so that the children would not miss seeing the wonder of the skyscrapers. Then she took hold of Milton's hand again immediately. Helen remembered how Mama was always connected to her children, watching that they were safe, showing them important things, making sure they understood the world they lived in. Helen broke into a big smile. This was the Mama she had missed for so long.

Julius looked up at the tall buildings, taller, Helen knew, than anything he had ever seen in his young life. "Do the buildings fall down on people?" he asked, holding onto one of Mama's legs and hiding in her skirts.

"Don't worry," Papa said, scooping the little boy into his arms. "None of the buildings has ever fallen on anyone. You are safe with me, my cautious little man." Julius started for a moment, as if he didn't remember Papa all that well. Then he leaned back and looked Papa in the eye quite carefully for a moment, making sure it was a good thing to be picked up by this "Papa" person. Apparently, Papa passed the test, because Julius then giggled and snuggled his head into Papa's chest. After a moment, the little boy turned back to face the world from this new and safe vantage point. He wasn't quite the same little chubby bundle he had been when Helen last saw him. Like every one of them, the youngest child was taller and older, but nonetheless enjoying his Papa treating him like the baby.

Helen held hands with Selma, now twelve. She looked more womanly, less like a little girl. She was still delicate and as beautiful as Helen remembered. Helen leaned over and hugged her, and they smiled at one another. Selma looked at Helen admiringly.

The children had a million questions about their new lives. They wanted to know where they were going to live, if they would go to school or perhaps they could get a job and be a real grown-up? Was it cold like home in New York, and would there be snow? Were they rich people now? Or still poor people, not that they minded.

Soon they came to their own building on Delancey Street. Everyone went up the outdoor steps and into the dark hallway.

"It's five flights of stairs up," said Max.

"We are going to live up in the air," said Selma, obviously excited at the thought.

When they finally arrived at the top, Papa went first, and everyone followed. He opened the door with a flourish, sweeping his arm to invite everyone into their three little rooms. Helen had worked hard to make everything perfect for this day. The lace curtains blew in the gentle October breeze, in from the outside and then through the window from the parlor to the kitchen. The air was fresh and cooling in every room. The new cloth was spotless on the kitchen table. Everything was thoughtfully placed. Helen had made up Papa and Mama's bed with the blanket carefully placed and looking comfortable. They had even found pillows for the parents' bed on a pushcart that sold inexpensive bedding.

Mama smiled and laughed and danced around. She swung her arm out to encompass everything in the room. "All this is ours?" She turned to Papa and raised her shoulders and her hands in the air with the question. Papa nodded and smiled at her. Max said, "Mama, sometimes fifteen or twenty people will live in an apartment this size. We are lucky to have this all to ourselves." The three-room apartment was bigger than their one room in Panemunė.

As Mama had got off the boat, Helen had noticed that she had changed. Her hair was gray around the temples now, and even her eyebrows had flecks of gray. Was she shorter, Helen wondered? A little bit slower? Mama looked worn. Helen knew it was from the worry and weighty responsibilities of caring for all the children since she and Papa had left. But she was still Mama, smart and observant.

Helen took all the children into the parlor and showed them how they would arrange the blankets to sleep and how they could put everything in the pirate's chest in the daytime. She remembered how they had all slept near one another in Panemunė. Once again, she would feel the comfort of sleeping near her brothers and sisters.

All of them went back into the kitchen, and everyone sat down at the big wooden table. Mama and Papa at either end as planned—Mama at the end near the sink and the stove, Papa's back toward the tiny bedroom. Three children sat on each of the long benches at either side of the table.

Bernard was soon to be twelve, and here he was now, safe with no danger from the Russian draft. Helen stopped a moment to drink it in. Her entire family was sitting around this kitchen table. In America.

Helen got up and began to pass out cups of water from the kitchen tap. She watched each person's face as she handed them the cup she had found and planned for them. Good utilitarian cups for the boys. Selma's flowery cup, no gold trim but it did have a butterfly and a bee. Selma reached for the cup and beamed back at Helen with shining eyes. Of course, Mama's special cup to match Helen's, with the gold rim and only a few chips. Mama looked at the cup and then looked up at Helen with a question on her face.

"This precious china is ours?" she asked.

"Yes Mama, someone was selling it off and I happened to walk by."

Mama took a sip of her water, holding the cup by the delicate handle. She smiled up at Helen, enjoying the beauty as much as Helen knew she would.

"Aunt Rose has been wonderful," Papa told Mama. "She is coming over tonight with her special welcoming dish, gefilte fish, enough for all of us. She will bring Morty and Josie, and we will squeeze in the three extra chairs from the parlor. This wonderful table takes up most of the kitchen, and it is big enough for all of us to sit together."

Meanwhile everyone was hungry for a midday meal. Helen had prepared a big pot of beef stew with wide egg noodles the night before. She also had rye bread from one of the pushcarts in the street outside and real butter. Helen showed Selma where things were in the kitchen, and the two girls set the table with the blue willow china. They ladled out soup into eight bowls and set them on the table and gave everyone a big spoon.

Everyone ate as if they hadn't eaten in a week. As a treat for the little ones, and to celebrate the day, Helen brought out a box of tiny "Barnum's Animals," a new kind of cracker that was popular. The package was decorated like a wagon in a circus train, fierce animals in cages on all sides of the box. The box had a white, flat string attached so you could hang it up on your Christmas tree.

Helen knew about Christmas trees, but of course Jewish families didn't have them. The little boys had fun biting the heads off the lions and bears and staging fights between the elephants and the tigers. Helen also brought out a roll of a new candy called Necco Wafers. Everyone picked the pastel color they liked best and enjoyed the chalky, powdery sweetness.

Mama pronounced the meal delicious. "Hinde, you have become an even better cook since you came to America."

Helen replied, "Yes, Mama. Slowly over time I have learned so many things. This beef stew recipe is from my Irish friend Kathleen. Maybe we can have her over to dinner soon, I want to introduce her to you. She has red hair. It's a little strange at first, but you get used to it. And everyone, I'm not Hinde anymore. Please call me Helen. This is my new name in America."

Mama lifted her eyes to Helen's slowly, taking in the idea of Helen's having changed her name. "I will need to get used to that," Mama said, frowning and shaking her head from side to side.

"Me too," added Selma. "I'll get used to having a big sister named 'Helen.' Maybe I should change my name to Clytemnestra?" Selma was showing off, demonstrating that she knew Helen and Clytemnestra were sisters in Greek mythology. Rabbi David had taught them many things. Selma had always liked to do whatever her older sister did. This apparently had not changed.

"Selma is a perfectly good name, young lady," Mama retorted. "One daughter with a new name is quite enough for now, thank you very much. I am not sure I can remember to call you by this new name, Hinde." Mama sounded a little cross with the idea of her daughter having a new name. "You have always been Hinde. We named you Hinde when you were born. How can you suddenly be someone else?"

Papa chimed in. "Yes, our Hinde is now Helen. She has worked hard to help make this day come true, so I am happy to honor her choice of a new name."

Helen glowed with Papa's compliment, and Max held up his cup and proposed a toast. "To Helen of New York, my amazing sister!"

Mama sighed. Her voice softened. "I see I am outnumbered. And Hymie, when you put it that way, maybe I can try to remember this new name of Helen." Mama raised her cup along with everyone else. "To Helen, then."

"To Helen," the whole family repeated, and all cups were raised on high.

16

ROBERT

A few wonderful weeks went by, and everyone in the family was enjoying being reunited. One morning Helen woke up before everyone else. As she blinked the sleep from her eyes, she realized how relaxed she felt. She noticed her breathing was deep and full. She had held onto one worry or another for her family's safety for so long. She smiled as she pulled the covers around herself and curled into the coziness of her blankets for just a moment more. She thought of meeting the boat, of seeing Mama again for the first time in years. She felt so much relief now that they were all here, all safe, her family all together at last. She peeked open her eyes to see the children sleeping on the floor all around her. Nothing would ever separate them again. Everything was going to be all right.

Helen thought of Max. Now that the family was together again, Papa dearly wanted Max to complete his education. The plan was for him to return to school the next fall. Max had worked hard, alongside Helen and Papa, to help bring everyone over from the old country. He had only been twelve years old when he arrived, but he had fulfilled his part like an adult. Now it was time for him to have less responsibility, to study and to prepare for his own life.

Max had always loved school. He would go back to the grade where he had left off in Lithuania. Even though he would be older than his classmates, he was smart and would progress quickly. Helen thought it would not be long before he enrolled in one of New York City's free colleges.

Max loved his job working at the kosher chicken store. Every night around the family dinner table he told stories of his best moments at work. Mr. Bloomberg trusted him to take care of any aspect of the business. Max was still going out every Monday with the rented pushcart to buy chickens from the ferry boat over at the Hudson River docks. Helen and Mama worried about Max going so far from home, outside of their relatively safe, mostly Jewish neighborhood. But Mr. Bloomberg had complete faith in Max, and Max loved being in charge like a real grown-up. He was still making five dollars a week, and Papa had bragged to everyone about how Max had contributed to reuniting the family by working hard and taking on grown-up responsibilities. Now the family would be able to save money. In time, they might move to Brooklyn where there were grass and trees, where it was peaceful and quiet. The subway would get you back into Manhattan in only twenty minutes.

Later that evening, around six o'clock, Helen was home from work helping Mama with dinner. Papa was sitting in his comfortable chair at the table enjoying a cup of tea that Helen had brought him. The younger children were all enrolled in the neighborhood elementary school, and they had strewn the table with their pencils and papers, their English readers and arithmetic books. Each one worked to finish the day's homework. Papa was enjoying helping everyone at once.

"Max is late getting home today," Mama said to Helen.

"It was his day to meet the ferry and buy the chickens," Helen replied. "Perhaps the ferry boat came in late." Just then, someone knocked on the door. Helen opened it to see Mr. Bloomberg, wringing his hands and looking worried.

"Max has not yet returned from buying the chickens," he said, coming in past Helen to speak with Papa. "He left the store at around noon, and he is always back by now. Something may have happened." Mr. Bloomberg was tall and had a long face with drooping eyes. His hair was gray, and he wore a heavy gray wool coat. He looked terribly worried.

Papa stood up. Mama stopped cooking and came over. "Mr. Bloomberg, thank you for coming here to let us know. Chaim, you must go and look for our son. It's not like him to be late. Something may have happened to him."

Papa agreed. "Yes, of course. I will go immediately. Mr. Bloomberg, can you tell me how to get to the ferry boat?"

"It's on the Hudson, just above Canal Street. It's the ferry that comes over from the train station in Jersey City. Lots of people are usually waiting there for it to arrive. Look how dark it's getting outside. We should leave right away."

Just then the door to the apartment opened, and everyone turned to see who it was. A tall, sandy-haired young man stood in the doorway. He was holding onto Max, his arm around him, helping him to walk and stay upright. Both of them looked disheveled. Max's shirt tails hung out, and his pants were ripped and bloody. He had a black eye and was leaning heavily on the stranger for support. His nose was bleeding down his face and onto the front of his shirt. The blond man's upper arm and entire sleeve were soaked red. His shirt was also ripped and filthy with streaks of dirt.

"Oy vey," gasped Mama, running to her son.

"What has happened?" Papa cried. Papa put his arms around Max to take some of the weight from the stranger, then Mama led them both over to Papa's chair where they helped Max to sit down.

"Please, sir, sit down," Helen said as she gestured for the stranger to sit in Mama's chair.

All the younger children crowded close together on the far bench, eyes wide and mouths agape as they stared at their older brother, bruised and bloodied. Little Julius started to cry. Helen reached over to pat him on the back. "It's alright little one. Max is home now. He's going to be all right."

The stranger spoke up. "Your son was attacked by a group of hoodlums near the river. They looked older than him, a rough group. They must have known he was Jewish because they kept calling him names like 'dirty kike' and 'filthy hebe.' They looked young, but they were big guys, and strong. I was afraid they were going to hurt him badly."

"Thank goodness you were there," said Helen. She immediately thought of poor Esther. But Max was here, and it looked like he was not hurt too badly. Helen imagined how it could have been different, and a shudder went up her spine.

"I just happened to meet the same ferry as Max, picking up some fabric that had been shipped to me. I couldn't just stand by and let these ruffians attack him. I saw them come up from behind, then begin to taunt him. There were three of them, and one of them hit him on the back of the head, and then they all started beating him. They knocked him down, and they were kicking him, so I ran over and jumped into the fight."

"Not everyone would have done that," said Papa. "It was a brave thing to do."

The man nodded at Papa, then continued. "I held them off long enough for him to get up again so the two of us could fight together. One of them grabbed some money from Max's pocket, and then they ran off. They must have watched him when he came in the week before and known he had money. I think that is what they were after. But we gave them as good as we got. I think they might be hurt worse than we are." The stranger grinned, but no one else was laughing. Max lifted his head for the first time. "I am so sorry. They took the money, the ten dollars. I tried to hide it, but they knew which pocket it was in. They must have seen me last week."

"Max, don't worry about the money. We will be fine without it," said Mr. Bloomberg. "I am just grateful you are not hurt any worse. Just concentrate on getting better. You are a good boy, and you put up a good fight."

"I will take Max to get cleaned up," said Mama. She handed the stranger a clean towel. "Here, wrap this around your arm to help stop the bleeding."

Max lifted his head and spoke for the first time, his

voice cracking and dry. "Everyone, don't worry. I will be okay." He lifted his head and tried to smile. Papa helped Max stand up, and the two of them went into the front room. Mama followed, then Papa returned, closing the door.

"I believe we will both recover," said the stranger. "Neither of us is hurt too badly."

Papa spoke to him gently. "What's your name?" he asked.

"Robert Fein. I live nearby. I work in the garment industry here on the Lower East Side." He looked up at Helen and said, "I think I have seen you at Joe's?"

With a jolt, Helen recognized him. This was the handsome blond man she had seen come into Joe's many times. She hadn't recognized him with his bloody face and torn clothing.

"Oh yes!" she said. "Now I recognize you. You bring fabrics in for Joe to look at all the time." This was the one about whom Kathleen had said that he might well be Jewish. Helen felt aflutter as she realized who this was.

"Right," he replied, smiling at Helen.

"Thanks be to God that you came along when you did," said Papa, walking over, reaching down and grasping the man's hand and shaking it over and over as he looked deeply into his eyes. "You probably saved my son's life. How can we ever repay you?"

"I feel terrible," said Mr. Bloomberg before anyone else could speak. "I should never have sent such a young boy out on this errand."

"No, no," Papa interrupted. "Max was happy to go to buy the chickens. He was proud that you trusted him with the money, and that you rented the pushcart for him. He loves working for you. Please don't blame yourself. Blame those anti-Semitic ruffians who attacked Max."

"I think the money is gone," said Robert. "But the pushcart is downstairs. I laid Max on it to bring him home. He could hardly walk."

"The money is not important, only that no one is hurt," said Mr. Bloomberg. "Thank you for bringing back the pushcart, and I'm glad it helped to get Max home safely."

"Mr. Bloomberg, stay with us for dinner."

"No, no, thank you very much, but my family will wonder where I am. I am so sorry Max had this terrible experience, but I am happy he is home safe and is going to be alright." Mr. Bloomberg shook Papa's hand, put on his hat and went towards the door.

Papa spoke up, "Mr. Bloomberg, you must come back and have dinner with us soon. Something like this makes us all more like family, pulling together to be sure everyone is all right."

Mr. Bloomberg turned back and said, "Thank you very much, Mr. Breakstone. I would be honored." He turned again, went through the door, and was gone.

Helen grabbed a second towel and brought it over to Robert. She peered at him shyly as the towel turned red from the scrapes and cuts on his arm. When he thanked her and handed back the towel, she crouched down before him. He was still seated in Mama's chair, and now she was near to eye level with him. "You saved my brother," she said in a quiet voice. "He could have been killed. How can we ever thank you?"

Robert turned to look at Helen. "I only did what anyone would do. I just hope he is not hurt too badly." Helen returned his gaze, appreciating his modesty. She felt conflicted feelings with Max beat up and bruised, and this handsome man she had been thinking about suddenly here in their home.

Helen looked up to see Papa watching her with a wary frown. Mama returned, and noticing the moment between her daughter and the stranger, smiled quietly. "Max is cleaned up, and he's going to rest for a while," she said. She turned to the stranger. "I believe Max will recover quickly from this attack," she said. "But only because you came along and were brave enough to jump into the fray."

"Devorah, this young man is Robert Fein. He works in the *schmatta* trade like we do," Papa said to Mama.

Mama replied directly to Robert. "Young man, you must stay for dinner, and we must all get to know you better," she said, smiling at him, welcoming him to stay. "Let me have that bloody towel. You take this clean one for your arm. Please, come and clean up at the sink, then you must stay so that we can all get to know you."

"Thank you," Robert replied. "I should be happy to sit for a little while before I venture back out onto the streets, and I would like to get to know your family."

Robert smiled down at Helen, and Helen smiled back.

17

ATTRACTION

The next day, Helen sat at her machine. The clacking away of all three machines had become normal to her after all this time working at Joe's. She no longer noticed the thick smell of fabric dye that filled the air. She found herself slipping into a familiar trance-like state, one seam after another, one garment after another.

Suddenly, Helen snapped back from her trance as she heard the same voice she had heard just the night before. She managed to casually look over her shoulder into the kitchen, and there he was with Joe. Robert was here. She saw that his eye was even blacker than it had been last night.

By then everyone at work had heard the story. It had even grown a bit in the retelling. Robert had now rescued Max from five very large men with iron pipes, rather than the actual three boys without weapons. Helen told Kathleen first thing before work started, and Kathleen had told the whole shop.

While Kathleen related the story, Helen noticed that Esther had gone white. She was staring at Kathleen, transfixed by the story of the anti-Semitic attack on Max. Suddenly her eyes had gotten a glassy look, and she had sat down immediately and buried her face in her work, sewing furiously even though no one else was working yet. Esther never looked up, and Helen could hardly imagine her feelings. The attack on Max had to remind her of the fatal attack on her fiancé. Esther didn't want anyone to see her feelings. In spite of how mean she had been, Helen felt sad to realize Esther's lonely pain. And lucky that Max was going to recover. After a little time went by, Esther got up and told Joe she was feeling sick. Joe let her go home.

An hour or two later, Robert walked in. Everyone stopped what they were doing. One person began to clap, and soon everyone stood up and joined in, most of all Helen. Robert was the hero of the day. He laughed and waved at everyone, then pushed his hair off his forehead, looked down at the floor, and shuffled his feet a bit.

After shouting their congratulations to Robert, everyone went back to work. Robert had brought some fabric for Joe to see. When their business was concluded, he asked Joe if he might speak to Helen. Helen could hear this quiet conversation, and her heart gave a small flutter that he wanted to speak with her again.

"Make it quick, Robert. She has a lot of work to do today," Joe replied with a wink, smiling at Robert with renewed respect.

Robert walked into the front room and made his way over to Helen. She had been watching everything from the corner of her eye, but now looked up as if surprised to see Robert had come into the front room to see her.

"How are you?" he asked. "And how is Max?"

"Max is good, I am happy to report." Helen looked up and gave Robert a big smile. "When he woke up this morning, he seemed to be his normal self. In a day or two he will be good as new."

Robert was happy to hear it. "I often go to meet that ferry to pick up fabric. Please tell Max that from now on, he is not to go there alone. We can go together and both feel safer."

"That is very kind. I know it will make my parents feel much better to know you and Max will go together. We have felt so safe since we came to America. We forgot that anti-Semitism is not only in the old country. We have learned that we have to be vigilant here, too."

"It's true," Robert said. "Sadly true."

Then Robert changed the subject. "I know that your group here goes to Katz's Deli on Friday nights. Would it be alright if I came along this week?"

Kathleen had been sewing furiously, not looking up even once as they talked. It was as if she were in another world, but Helen knew she was listening to every word. Helen noticed a slight smile playing around her lips, but turned back to Robert immediately.

"Of course," Helen replied. "Please come and join us! I'll look forward to seeing you there." Helen felt heat rise to her cheeks as she considered the idea that this handsome man whom she had been fantasizing about from afar might be thinking about her as well.

Friday night finally arrived. Both girls were happy to wrap up the work week and to spend an enjoyable hour or two with friends. They covered their sewing machines with large scraps of cloth and walked down the five flights to the street. They chatted as they walked, about the week's work, about the other people in the shop, about their boss Joe. They agreed that Joe was gruff but essentially treated them well. They laughed and decided that "his bark was worse than his bite." This expression was always used about the famous and well-liked New York State Governor Theodore Roosevelt, and the girls enjoyed it being true of Joe as well. Behind his exterior, Joe had turned out to be a fair and kind boss.

Soon they could see the steamy glass windows of Katz's up ahead. They entered the deli and walked across the black and white tile floor to the table where their friends were gathered. Helen looked around to see if Robert was there. She could see Lewis and Margaret, both of whom Helen enjoyed. They hadn't become close friends, but they were friendly and welcoming. From time to time they would chat at work, or they would join Kathleen and Helen for lunch. Helen always felt gratitude toward Lewis for giving her the wonderful winter boots.

The two girls approached the cash register and paid for their franks and beans. They carried their trays back to the table, sat down, and happily began to eat. Helen popped a bite of frankfurter into her mouth. It was every bit as delicious as it had been the first time, although this time her mind was on other things. She couldn't stop thinking about whether or not Robert would show up, whether or not he wanted to see her. Helen chatted with Kathleen who was sitting on her left.

"I don't think he is going to show up," Helen pouted.

"Just give him a little more time," Kathleen assured her. "He'll probably be here soon."

Helen started tapping her fingers on the table a few times, then craned her neck to look around the restaurant.

Just then, a strong and friendly voice from the right came from behind her, "I'm so glad you are still here. I was delayed at work and couldn't come earlier."

Helen picked up her napkin and dabbed at each corner of her mouth. "I'm so happy to see you again, Robert," Helen said nervously. As she turned to face him, her elbow collided with her glass of water, still full, creating a little tidal wave across the table onto her skirt and worst of all, onto the front of Robert's shirt and pants.

Helen looked up, her eyes filled with horror. Robert's mouth dropped open, and his eyebrows raised as he let out a small yelp. For a moment, they both looked at one another, frozen in time. Then Robert threw back his head in a boisterous laugh that filled the entire room. Helen sat still, at first confused, watching him, but after a moment, she, too, began to laugh. Pretty soon, everyone at the table was laughing as they mopped and brushed the water onto the tiled floor.

Helen and Robert laughed so hard they had tears in the eyes. After the deluge, everyone was in a light mood.

Lewis piped up, "Did you hear the one about the Jewish girl who spilled a glass of water?" Everyone laughed again at the joke. After all the laughter, the warmth of friendship made conversation relaxed and easy. Robert sat down next to Helen, and everyone chatted together and enjoyed the evening. Finally, it was time to go.

"Let me walk you home," said Robert. Helen smiled and nodded.

As they walked down the street, Helen said, "I don't know how our family is ever going to repay you for saving Max from those hoodlums."

"Don't worry about repaying me, Helen. I am very happy that we met at long last, even if it was terrible circumstances that brought us together. I have noticed you at Joe's for a long time." Helen smiled, and then looked down shyly to escape his steady gaze.

"You know, I'm in the *schmatta* trade, too. A friend and I started our own company. We pre-shrink woolen cloth before it comes to you."

"That's so impressive, your own business," Helen said admiringly. "What do you call your company?"

"Merit National Shrinking Works," Robert replied proudly. "We are going to be the number one shrinking company in the whole country, so we chose a name that sounded like we already are."

Helen smiled at the audacious name of his business. "You're thinking big, I see." Helen watched Robert as he spoke. His beautiful big blue eyes sparkled as he spoke; one lock of his blond hair fell over his forehead. He kept brushing it away with his hand, but it kept falling back in a way she found most appealing, like he was both a small boy and a man at the same time. She felt a warm feeling inside, walking next to Robert with both of them speaking so comfortably.

"How did you ever come to own your own business?" Helen asked.

"I came here seven years ago from Amsterdam, with my mother and my younger brother, Abe. We're originally from Germany. We had two family friends here, the two Maxes. Max Schneider and Max Mendelsohn. They got me a job for the shrinker where they worked, and that was good for a few years. Eventually, we all thought we could do better work and charge less if we started our own shrinking business. We didn't want to compete with our boss, who had taught us everything, so we were not sure how it would work out."

Robert explained how the three of them, himself and the two Maxes, had worked hard to save money. "We were fortunate when the boss announced that he wanted to retire and sell us the business. We had all saved, so we were able to buy the business from him right away. We renamed it and have been working hard ever since."

"You've been here seven years!" Helen exclaimed. "I came from Lithuania, and I've only been here three years. My Papa came first, and my Mama arrived only a month ago with all the rest of the family. You met my four brothers and my one little sister, but I'm the oldest, so I came to America first."

"That must feel wonderful for you all to be together again," said Robert. Helen nodded in agreement. She could feel that Robert understood how important it was to her that her whole family was finally together. Robert continued, "I'm happy to have my younger brother, Abe, close by. He lives in Brooklyn now, and he works making carnival games for the big amusement parks at Coney Island. You'll meet him soon."

"I would like that," Helen replied, noticing that he had suggested they would have plans together in the future, and hoping he was being genuine. "How old are you?" she asked him.

"Twenty-one," Robert replied. "But I started working early. I was in the Merchant Marine when I was young."

"You have seen the world. Was it wonderful to travel?"

"It was," he replied. "I was the cabin boy on my first ship, and we travelled through the Suez Canal. From there we went on to China. Later I went to Africa and South America. I've seen people of every color and on every continent. I've seen people living in grass houses and houses made of sticks on stilts over water and houses made of palm tree leaves and every other kind of house there is. I love coming back here because New York is the best place in the world."

Helen felt drawn to him, even though she did not have much experience talking with young men socially. She realized that Robert was a man, making his own way in the world. He was more mature than Leonard back in the old country, who was, she realized, the last boy who had paid attention to her. She had thought of him from time to time, hoping he was safe in the rising tide of anti-Semitism that she and her family had fled. Whenever he came to mind, she would always send up a small prayer for him and his family. She wasn't sure prayers worked, but they couldn't hurt.

Meanwhile she was enjoying Robert's attention. "I know the city pretty well, Helen," Robert said. "Maybe we can go out on the town together next weekend, and I could show you around the city?"

"I'd like that," Helen nodded her reply. She could not resist a small flutter of her eyelashes as she looked up at him.

He smiled an even larger smile than before. Helen smiled back.

18

FIRST DATE

Helen walked into Joe's bright and early on Monday morning. Kathleen didn't waste any time. "You certainly caught Robert's attention Friday night. I know you like him." Kathleen kept her voice low so that everyone in the room would not know Helen's business, at least not immediately.

"Yes, I do like him," Helen said, sitting down at her machine and getting settled for a new week of sewing. She too kept her voice low. "He's nice. Friendly. He cares what I think about things. And he's polite, too."

"And handsome," whispered Kathleen with a big smile. "Let's not forget that!"

"There's no denying that," said Helen, smiling back.

"Did he ask you out?"

"Yes, we are going out a week from Friday. Robert has a business trip this week, so he asked if we could get together the following weekend. He says it's fun to ride on the Staten Island Ferry, so that is what we're going to do."

"The ferry boat is lots of fun. You'll get to see the Statue of Liberty up close again." Kathleen held Helen's gaze to show she remembered the importance of this event. Helen had shared the story of her moment entering New York Harbor and first seeing the statue from the deck of the ship after the long journey from Europe. Kathleen had been born in New York, so she hadn't realized the power of that first sight of Liberty.

Helen could not stop thinking about the upcoming date. Her mind kept drifting over imaginary details, what she would do to look pretty, and hoping that he would admire her. She played imaginary conversations in her mind that they might have. Robert would say something intelligent and wise, and she would reply cleverly, but not too cleverly. She didn't want to be a showoff.

She had never been on a date before. Over the weekend she had asked Papa and Mama if it was all right for her to go, and they had both agreed that yes, she should go and enjoy herself. Of course, he must come to their home first and be properly introduced. Even though they had already met him as a hero for rescuing their son, they had not yet met him as a suitor for their daughter. They had to make sure he was a suitable young man to take their precious daughter on a date. And they must have a chaperone. When Aunt Rose heard about the date, she offered to be the chaperone. She would bring Morty and Josie over to stay with Helen's family for the evening.

Over the weekend, Helen worked on Saturday because Joe needed extra sewing done. He paid an extra dollar and a half to everyone who came in, so Helen had a little extra money to prepare for her date.

Now that the whole family was safe in New York, and there was no reason to save as furiously for ocean liner tickets, things had become easier financially. Papa was working, and already, Mama had started to take in hand sewing. Word spread quickly about her talented stitching. Within days, people were bringing their mending and unfinished sewing projects.

There was enough money to pay the rent and keep everyone fed and happy. Selma was going to school, as were the three younger boys. With all the children out of the house, Mama had time for herself, to relax while doing her sewing projects, and to consider what she wanted to do next in life. Helen had been spending every available moment at home, just to be in the same room with Mama. Max was planning to go back to school in time, but for the moment he was still working with Mr. Bloomberg at the chicken store. Helen sometimes dreamed of going back to school herself, but it wasn't customary for girls to continue on in school. Boys could use the education to become professionals, but there were few opportunities for women.

On Sunday after the extra work day, Helen had an entire day to herself. She visited Aunt Rose in the mid-morning, sharing a slow and leisurely cup of coffee in her kitchen. It was a pleasure to visit this apartment where she had lived and felt so welcome for all those months, and to enjoy a bit of quiet.

"Don't worry about me being in the way on your date," Aunt Rose said. "I'll bring my knitting and that will keep me busy. You two will have plenty of privacy to talk together without me butting in."

"You would never be in the way," Helen replied, but she secretly appreciated knowing that Aunt Rose would give them room to get to know one another better.

⇌

Later, Helen wandered among the thousands of pushcarts outside on the street. She decided she needed something new to wear on her first date. She tried to act nonchalant and not too interested in anything because she had discovered this was the best way to get a fair price. If you were too eager the pushcart man would charge you all he could. If you acted like you weren't all that interested, the price might come down.

Months ago, Helen had purchased a black A-line skirt. She thought it would look nice with a high-necked blouse. These blouses were popular now, and they had lots of applique details around the neckline. Helen knew the style would suit her full figure.

She wandered down Orchard Street looking from cart to cart. Soon she spotted a pushcart that had several blouses of the style she was looking for, in white and pastel colors. All were long sleeved and high necked with lace and gathering and applique that made the blouses look quite elegant.

The pushcart man noticed Helen eyeing his wares. "Any one of these for just twenty-five cents," he said. Helen knew he was inflating the price. She slowly went through all the blouses that were neatly folded on his cart.

"How about this one, it's not as lacy," she said offhandedly pulling a simple but lovely pale blue blouse out of the big pile. It still had the high neck and the embroidery but wasn't as elaborate as most.

"Oh, that's only fifteen cents," he said.

"How about ten?" she offered.

"Make it twelve and it's yours."

She reached into a deep pocket and brought out two shiny nickels and two shiny pennies. The man wrapped the blouse in clean white paper and handed it over.

Normally, Helen enjoyed her work. It was always fun to make things that had not existed before you started. Even if they were only knickerbockers. Helen was Joe's number two sewing girl, producing more items per hour than anyone else in the shop, save Kathleen. This week they were sewing a plaid wool, and Helen wondered if the fabric had been pre-shrunk by Merit National Shrinking Works. Her thoughts somehow always found their way back to Robert.

She and Kathleen were always careful now around Esther, never giving her any opportunity to complain to Joe again. They continued to enjoy their lunches together on the stoop each day. Kathleen had confided that she too was interested in a certain boy. His name was Kevin, and he wanted to be a policeman. Helen had a hard time understanding how a policeman could be a friend, much less a boyfriend. The closest thing she could imagine was Russian soldiers coming into the compound to see if there were any young Jewish boys to carry away into the army.

"It's not like that," Kathleen assured her. "In New York, the policemen watch out for us. It's not like it was for you in the old country. When Teddy Roosevelt was Chief of Police in New York, he cleaned up all the corruption at the NYPD. Still, I'm worried because being a policeman is a dangerous job. I'm proud of him that he wants to help people, but I get scared something bad might happen to him."

Helen tried to understand that a policeman could want to help people. The idea of a benevolent government worker was too foreign. She would have to ask Papa and Aunt Rose about what Kathleen was saying.

Helen had truly become a New Yorker, and sometimes she had felt safer seeing a policeman nearby at night or when she was in another part of the city for some reason. What with a job that she liked, and her wonderful family now reunited, she had never been so happy. She had a reliable base from which to go forth and explore what she wanted her life to be. It was an adventure, and there were lots of things to try, with so many cultures, and languages, and customs all converging outside her door. Now, suddenly, there was Robert. The thought of his blue eyes made her swoon a little inside.

Helen reminded herself that she was not going to allow giddy emotions to be in charge and make important decisions. She wanted to be with someone with whom she had lots in common, someone who thought like she did, who wanted a family and a stable life.

The week passed quickly. Friday was a beautiful day, not so hot as it had been. At closing time, Kathleen gave her a hug and said, "Have a wonderful time." Helen tried not to hurry as she made her way home. As she entered the apartment, there were the other seven family members sitting at the kitchen table waiting for Robert. They looked more like a jury than a family.

Everyone was curious about this Robert person. She went into the parlor and changed into her new blouse. Mama came along behind her and fixed her hair so that it looked perfect. The two came back into the kitchen.

"You look beautiful, my daughter," Papa said to Helen when she entered the room.

"You do," agreed Selma. "So pretty."

Before Helen could say thank you for the compliments, there was a knock at the apartment front door. Helen walked through the little bedroom, which was how you had to enter the apartment. Throughout the Lower East

Side, entry to the rear apartments on each floor was through the small bedroom behind the kitchen. It wasn't ideal for an entryway, but that's the way it was, and Mama had made sure everything was tidy. Helen stopped for just a moment before opening the door, taking a deep breath. Then she opened the door to see Robert standing there, about to enter her home.

"Come in, please," Helen said, stepping back and sweeping her arm toward the kitchen. She felt her heart beating faster than usual. Robert looked as good as he always did. He, too, had dressed up for the occasion. He wore a suit of dark blue wool, no doubt shrunk by The Merit National Shrinking Works. The suit brought out his blue eyes. He held a small bouquet of flowers.

"For you," he said, extending them toward her.

"Oh! So pretty," Helen said with true surprise. In all her imagining of this moment, she had not once included flowers, the first she had ever received. She reached out to accept the small bouquet, inhaling the fragrance of the ivory rose tucked among cheerful daisies.

"This is so thoughtful of you," she said.

"You look nice tonight, Helen," Robert said with a grin.

"And you look handsome," Helen replied.

She paused to share the moment with him, then continued, "Before we go out, please come into the kitchen and meet everyone. And my Aunt Rose will be our chaperone." Robert did not display surprise that they would be chaperoned. It was how things were done.

Helen led Robert into the kitchen. "Mama and Papa, you both have met Robert." As Helen turned toward the sink to put the flowers into a glass of water, Mama came forward and held out her hand to Robert. "Welcome again,

Robert," Mama said. "We are happy to see you under more peaceful circumstances."

"Thank you, Mrs. Breakstone," Robert replied politely. "I'm very pleased to see you all again."

Papa joined in, standing up and extending his arm to shake hands with Robert.

Robert took a few steps toward Papa, and the two men shook hands and exchanged a steady look.

"Your eye is still a little bruised from that day," Mama noticed. "We are all so grateful to you for being the hero who saved our Max."

"I only did what anyone would do," Robert replied modestly. "And my eye is almost all better now. I've brought you a little gift," he said, holding out a paper bag.

Mama said thank you and peered inside. "Oh, candy for everyone, how very nice of you. We will enjoy this later tonight."

"And this is our Aunt Rose," said Helen. "She is our cousin, but we have always called her our aunt because we are so close."

"Very nice to finally meet the hero who saved my nephew," Aunt Rose said with a big smile.

"And you as well," replied Robert, gently shaking the older woman's hand.

Helen came back from the sink and put the flowers in the center of the table. Helen introduced her siblings. As she did, each of them came forward and shook hands with Robert. "These are my three younger brothers, Bernard, Milton, and little Julius."

"I'm not little anymore, Helen. I'm in school and everything," said Julius, marching up to Robert and extending his hand like a grown-up gentleman.

"It's true, you are not so little anymore. You are get-ting to be a real grown-up," said Papa.

"I never would have thought of you as 'little,'" said Robert, likely winning Julius as a friend for life.

They all sat down at the table. Papa addressed Robert. "I understand you are going for a ride on the ferry tonight. It should be beautiful with the statue all lit up. The water will be calm, as there hasn't been any wind at all today."

"I promise to get the ladies home before it's late." He smiled at Aunt Rose, who glowed at being called a lady.

"By ten-thirty, at the latest, please," Papa said.

"I promise," said Robert.

"Have a fun time," said Mama.

Aunt Rose and the couple said good night to everyone and went on their way.

19

STATEN ISLAND FERRY

Robert, Helen, and Aunt Rose walked down the steps. On the sidewalk, Robert moved to the outside, closer to the curb. He extended his arm for Helen. The sidewalks were wide, and he extended his other arm to Aunt Rose.

"The Staten Island Ferry leaves from Battery Park. Shall we walk?"

"Yes, it will be pretty at this time of evening. Battery Park is one place in New York I know well," Helen answered. She told him of her three encounters with Battery Park, each a happy tale of reunion.

Robert picked right up where she left off. "We came through Battery Park as well, my mother, my younger brother Abe, and me. This was before Ellis Island opened. Back then, immigration was in Castle Garden, right in Battery Park. You saw the round fort there?"

Helen nodded and pictured a younger Robert waiting on long lines outside Castle Garden.

"Where is your mother now?" Aunt Rose asked.

"I live with her on Clinton Street," he replied. "My father passed away before we came to America, but my mother keeps busy helping out at my company every day, Merit National Shrinking Works. Keeps all the books. She's my biggest supporter."

Helen liked that Robert honored his mother. Men who had good relationships with their mothers tended to like women more in general. "It's important to have someone who believes in you," she said.

Robert turned to look at her as they kept walking. "So true," he agreed. He squeezed her arm close to himself as he gazed down at her. He looked at her so directly and brought her arm in so close to himself that it made Helen feel a little light-headed.

Robert turned to Aunt Rose. "A beautiful night to be out and about, isn't it?"

"It certainly is," she replied, smiling at his good manners for including her.

The three of them ambled toward the ferry. Helen enjoyed his deftness as he guided them. She could tell he was a man of strong character, like her father. Like Max would be. She liked the feel of his hand on her arm. She appreciated how he involved Aunt Rose in the conversation. Again, she thought, *this is not a boy. This is a man.* His sense of being in command was attractive to her.

All this from a walk down the street, Helen thought, though she knew she was right about this man.

They walked toward the East River, past all the apartment buildings, the windows alight with families settling in for a Friday night. Helen thought warmly of *Shabbat* and how many of these families might be observant Jews lighting the candles now at sundown. While Helen had no longing to be lighting candles, she still felt a warm spot in her heart for the family rituals of Judaism. They provided a reason for everyone to gather and enjoy a simple moment of peace together. A Reformed Jew. She could light the candles or not, and her God wouldn't get upset about it.

Helen and Robert chatted about their week as they walked.

"I was working hard all week to get a new contract with a big woolen manufacturer. Wool has to be shrunk before you can sew it, and at Merit, we have the machines and expertise to do the best job. When we started the business, we managed to get used equipment, but now we have the best. No other shrinker can compete with the excellent work we do."

Helen pictured an imaginary shrinking machine. She had no idea what one looked like, but she pictured a complicated metal box with many dials and knobs and settings, maybe with steam coming out of the top. Maybe woolen fabric passed through from the top and came out the bottom. She thought of the many yards of fabric that had passed through her hands to make knickerbockers, and wondered if Robert's hands had touched the same cloth. Perhaps they'd been connected before they even knew one another. Perhaps the very threads . . . perhaps the two of them were already stitched together.

"I hope this big outfit in South Carolina will have us shrink their entire line. I took the ferry boat to New Jersey, then got on a train to travel south. Once I arrived, I met with a major textile company called Milliken." Helen saw that Robert made sure to turn toward Aunt Rose from time to time, to keep her included in the conversation. "If we get the contract, Merit National Shrinking Works won't be a small-time shrinker anymore. We're going to be one of the big players in the growing shrinking world." Robert looked at her with a twinkle in his eye as he said "growing, shrinking."

Though Robert spoke with pride about his business, Helen never felt he was bragging. She laughed at the phrase he had used. "I'm trying to picture your growing shrinking world."

She thought how many worlds like Robert's there were, growing, shrinking, staying the same, each of them impossibly important to those who moved within. She thought of her own little world of sewing at Joe's. Mama's world arriving in New York with all the young children, reunited with her husband. The worlds of the pushcart vendors, the world of Max as he sold chickens around the city. Worlds that touched one another. Worlds that were sometimes worlds apart.

"I hope you get the contract," she said. "I'd pray for you, but I don't pray much anymore."

"Me neither." Robert picked right up on the subject of religion. "I'm Jewish and proud to be Jewish, but to me the Bible offers a lot of fairy stories, not literal events. I believe in science. Engineers will change our world, you watch."

"I agree," said Helen, both relieved and delighted to hear that they were in accord on the important subject of religion.

Aunt Rose said, "We Reform Jews believe that the Bible can help people to treat one another kindly and behave in a good way. I don't worry about whether or not the stories are true." Helen had thought this was Aunt Rose's opinion and was glad to hear her speak it aloud.

Helen told Robert more about Mama having recently arrived and how the whole family was finally reunited.

Robert's expression matched her words—his eyes sad when she spoke of missing her mother for so long, then sparkling with joy as she told of their reunion. He smiled with admiration when Helen told of Aunt Rose's generosity, opening her home and heart when Helen first arrived. Again, he pulled her arm toward him just a bit, to show that he understood how important this was to her.

"I can tell you are a determined person who makes a plan that is important and then doesn't waver until it is complete. I admire that," Robert said. Helen warmed with the thought that he understood, and glowed with his compliment to her character.

The fall was coming on, and the days were shorter. There was still plenty of light left to see everything as they walked, but sunset colored the sky a golden pink that soon illuminated everything. The light fit Helen's mood perfectly. When they got to Tompkins Street, they turned to walk along the East River. A few small boats sailed up and down in the calm waters, reflecting the last of the pink sky.

"The river looks beautiful," Aunt Rose observed. Both Helen and Robert concurred.

They walked toward the Brooklyn Bridge, which Cousin Morty had extolled and admired as a great feat of engineering.

Robert also admired it. "They finished this bridge a few years before I arrived in New York, twenty years ago. Before then, the only way to get to Brooklyn was by boat."

Helen looked up at the massive stone towers and the delicate tracery of the cables, draped like spider webs and glowing in the last rays of sunshine. It was darker and damper under the overpass, but the sunset light showered them again as they emerged.

"It's the longest bridge in the world," Robert said proudly. "Back then, people were scared the bridge would collapse. But one day the great New Yorker P.T. Barnum led a parade of twenty-one elephants over the bridge. That showed everyone how much weight it could support, and from then on, no one questioned that bridge. Barnum's biggest elephant, Jumbo, led the way. The *New York Times* said that it was like Noah's Ark had emptied itself over Brooklyn."

"Who's P.T. Barnum?" Helen asked.

"He runs 'The Greatest Show on Earth.' It's a circus. After that stunt with the elephants, everyone in New York came to see Barnum's circus. Once the circus comes back to America, I'll take you, so you can see the elephants and the trapeze artists," Robert said.

Elephants and trapeze artists! Helen had never seen any such thing. She felt honored that Robert wanted to share enjoyable experiences with her. She did not usually allow herself to consider promises that might be empty, but from Robert, the words felt genuine. She looked back up at the bridge and smiled to herself as she imagined those twenty-one elephants marching along. "I think I can see Jumbo up there now," she said.

"Me too," Aunt Rose chimed in with a giggle.

Robert laughed and shaded his eyes with his hand, the better to see Jumbo. "I believe you are right. I think I see him, too."

As they walked through the financial district, Helen remembered her first day in New York, how she and Papa had walked this way. The buildings still seemed impossibly high.

Soon they were at Battery Park at the very spot where

she had waited for Mama. Robert bought three ferry boat tickets at a kiosk for a penny each. As they waited in line, she reached over and squeezed Aunt Rose's arm. The two women shared the moment together. Robert was looking around at everything. Helen liked that he was always curious and interested in his surroundings.

The boat arrived, blowing a loud horn and smelling harshly of burning coal. Water sloshed up onto the dock, and two ferrymen jumped onto the pier and made the boat fast. Robert gestured for Aunt Rose to go up the gangplank first, and then Helen so that he could bring up the rear and be sure everyone was doing all right. Right away, Helen felt the boat lurch under her feet, and she reached forward to steady Aunt Rose. At the same time, she felt Robert reach out to hold onto her. She remembered the sea legs that she had developed on her ocean crossing. A little lurch from a small boat wouldn't have bothered her then, but it was pleasing now to have someone strong to hold onto her.

They made their way up a staircase to the ferry's upper level, taking seats outside on a long wooden bench that was worn shiny from years of service. Helen worried that her hair would be blown all about in the strong breeze, but Mama had arranged it so that invisible pins held it in place despite the wind.

Aunt Rose took out her knitting and started to work on it. "Don't mind me," she said. "If I concentrate, I will be very close to finishing this beautiful red sweater for Josie. You two just go on and enjoy yourselves." Robert gave Aunt Rose a smile, and Helen leaned over and put her head on Aunt Roses' shoulder for just a moment to express her gratitude.

Their seats faced out into the harbor. The ferry blew its belching horn, and they were off. They moved at a sharp clip across the water, turning golden now as the sun finally went down behind New Jersey. Soon the big brick building at Ellis Island was gliding by. Helen shuddered as she recalled how frightened she had been that she might be turned away. "Were you worried when you came through immigration?" she asked Robert.

"Oh yes, like everyone. More worried for my mother, who had a bad cold. In fact, she was detained for a day, one of the worst days of my life, worrying that they would put her back on the boat and send her back to Europe. Luckily, her cold went away, and they let her enter the country."

"That sounds terrible. I was so afraid of that happening to me. I'm so glad it worked out for you and your mother."

"Me, too," Robert replied. "Me, too," he repeated, wearing a wistful look of reminiscence.

As the ferry moved out into the harbor, Robert closed his eyes for a moment.

"Are you remembering something from your trip to America?" Helen asked.

"I was just remembering the time that I spent at sea when I was younger." Robert had mentioned being in the Merchant Marine. "I loved being at sea. Seeing the world was a great adventure."

Robert went on. "My mother and brother and I left Germany to get away from the growing anti-Semitism. We liked Holland. People are far more open-minded there. We stayed a few years, and my mother rented a house and took in boarders to make ends meet. My brother helped her, so she didn't need me as much. We lived near the docks, and I watched the ships every day. Finally, when I was eight years old, my mother allowed me to join up as a cabin boy. My first trip was through the Suez Canal."

"Tell me all about it." Helen had not enjoyed her one ocean voyage. It was hard for her to imagine anyone enjoying being at sea.

"My favorite thing, no matter where in the world we were, was to look at water stretching away forever in every direction, like I was standing in the center of a great circle of ocean. I loved that feeling, with the power of the boat churning along, taking us anywhere we wanted to go."

The two of them looked out the window at the copper lady that Helen had loved so much, now aglow with the last light of the day. It was in the presence of Lady Liberty that she had decided to take her new name. Just as she thought of that, the lady turned bright gold with the last rays of sunset.

"She was a gift from France, did you know that?" Robert asked.

Helen had heard this from her friend Rebecca. "Yes, I knew that. I think the French love the idea of Liberty as much as we Americans do," she said. Helen heard herself saying *we Americans*.

"Yes. We Americans!" Robert repeated with enthusiasm, lifting his arm just like the statue, launching the phrase out into the air, then swinging his arm around to encompass everyone on the ferry and everyone who lived on every shore around them.

Helen turned back to look at Manhattan Island. Darkness was setting in and the greenery of the park was gone, the large buildings of the financial district only vague outlines. She could see the silhouette of the Brooklyn Bridge on the right side of the island, the East River on the right and the Hudson on the left. Small and large boats of every shape and size plied the waters in the tableau of near darkness. Helen realized Robert was watching her watch New York, and she looked up at him shyly.

"It's our home," he said. He reached out and found her hand, discreetly holding it with both of his, a bit away from Aunt Rose's view. "Even though we've both travelled the world, who could want anything more than to be a real American in New York?"

20

CONEY ISLAND

The idea of spending an entire day at the beach had never occurred to Helen. In Lithuania, people regarded beaches as dangerous, storm-tossed places where the wreck of an ancient ship might wash ashore at any moment, complete with the emaciated ghosts of long-lost sailors. But it was hot in Manhattan in August of 1903, and the idea excited her. There were tales of beautiful white sand beaches and cool ocean breezes no matter how hot it was in the city. Icy blue water and clear skies forever. Helen longed to see a fresh and natural landscape. In New York, you could hardly find a patch of dirt or a tree.

Several people from their Katz's Deli crowd, including Kathleen and Kevin, were going the following Saturday, to spend the entire day. Robert asked Helen if she would go with him. Amazingly, for only five cents each, they could take the subway all the way to Coney Island and arrive in only an hour and a half. The trains returned to the city for the same low price. You only needed to be careful that you didn't miss the last train at nine o'clock.

With a mischievous sparkle in her eye, Kathleen had told Helen that if you missed the last train, you had to sleep on the sand. She said it was fun, and she had heard that people built a fire and enjoyed the night. Robert said they should bring a blanket to spread out on the sand, and he also asked if Helen wouldn't mind making a picnic lunch.

Kathleen invited Helen to stay over with her that evening. Mama and Papa approved, as Kathleen lived with three other girls, two of them Jewish and known to Aunt Rose as nice girls.

Lunch and transportation were easy to handle, but Helen was in a panic about what to wear. "Kathleen, what about bathing costumes? Do you have one? Where do I get one?" Helen had a barrage of nervous questions for her friend.

"Don't worry," Kathleen replied, putting on her most worldly face. "I know where the special pushcart is."

After work, the two girls went down Hester Street, weaving their way through the thousands of vendors. Without Kathleen, Helen realized, she would never have been able to find this particular pushcart. Finally, they arrived. Like all pushcarts, this one was a long, wooden table with high edges that kept things from falling off. The rough wood was piled high with every style, fashion, and color of bathing suit.

"Look at this one. It's like a sailor outfit. And it's only one dollar." Kathleen held up a black woolen middy blouse with a short skirt and leggings attached. It had white trim around a big square collar. "Or stripes." Helen looked aghast as Kathleen picked up a black and white striped woolen suit with barely any sleeves at all and cut so the wearer's legs and arms would show.

Helen held up the middy blouse suit for a better look. "It's like a wool dress," she observed, holding the garment up to herself and spreading it out. "But the leggings only come down to my knees."

Both girls were wearing the floor-length skirts that were considered customary, modest attire. In the city, no one showed their ankles, and there was even a ridiculous story that some particularly prudish Victorians covered the legs of tables because they were too much like women's legs.

Kathleen said, "I read last week about Annette Kellermann planning to swim the English Channel. That picture of her famous one-piece bathing suit was the talk of the town. She exposes her entire body and isn't embarrassed in the slightest. I think it's wonderful."

Helen had seen the photo in the *New York Times*. "Don't even think about that. There is no way I am going to appear in a Kellermann in front of Robert and the entire world. This little sailor suit with the black stockings under it will be the most daring thing I have ever worn in my entire life."

"Me, too, in all honesty," said Kathleen. "Be sure to put it on under your regular clothing in the morning. Even though it will be bulky on the way there, you will be happier when it comes time to change. You won't have to worry about taking off all your clothes in public."

"Oh, Kathleen, I'm so glad you said that. I would never have thought of it. You always watch out for me."

Kathleen's face transformed into a big smile. "You are most welcome. You will look terrific in that suit, don't worry. And I bet you will love the beach."

Helen couldn't think of anything beyond the fact that

she would be baring her legs, in short stockings, in front of Robert and everyone. Then again, Helen knew she had nice legs, and it gave her a little thrill to think that Robert might like seeing them. Everyone has advantages, she thought. Some girls have a pretty face, some girls have a pretty figure, some girls are smart and sassy, and some girls are so worldly and sophisticated that nobody can resist them. Helen thought of herself as having a nice figure, shiny hair, and being smart and sassy enough.

Saturday morning arrived, and Helen pulled on her new black wool swim stockings and swimsuit. Mama looked askance. "Helen, you are going to wear that in public?"

"Mama, don't worry, I am going to put regular clothes over it. Everyone who goes to the beach wears swimming costumes now. There will be hundreds of girls there dressed just like me."

Mama didn't look happy, but she managed to let it go with a harrumph. Helen smiled to herself when she heard Mama muttering something under her breath about respectable women.

Mama also fussed that they needed to invite Robert to dinner again. He had come to dinner every other week, but it was time again. Robert had asked Helen to go out every weekend. Robert was always polite to Aunt Rose, their constant chaperone, and he and Helen both took every opportunity to include her and to make sure she was never left out. Helen was glad that Robert had the means to pay for both her and for Aunt Rose wherever they went.

Robert was inventive in thinking up interesting places to show off New York. One Sunday, they had taken a picnic over to the Hudson and dined on a blanket and then walked north along the river. Another time, they had gone uptown to see the arch at Washington Square. Helen had learned that it was built to honor the 100th anniversary of George Washington's becoming America's first president. Another time they had walked even farther north to Madison Square Park where Helen had been amazed to see electric lights illuminating the darkness.

One Saturday night, Robert took her out to dinner at Pete's Tavern, and Helen tried Italian food for the first time. Except for Katz's Deli, Helen had never been in a restaurant. Kathleen had reassured her and gave her advice, such as putting her napkin in her lap immediately, and not ordering spaghetti because it was too hard to eat, and you could easily splash spaghetti sauce all over your clothes.

The night before the beach day, Mama had helped make a picnic lunch for two. She made tongue sandwiches, a favorite of Helen's, with mustard and grated horseradish, with potato salad on the side and gingersnaps for dessert. Helen had bought a small wicker picnic hamper, and she and Mama packed all the food, then covered it all with a red-and-white-checkered cloth.

When Robert came to pick up Helen that Saturday morning, he came in and spent a little time with the family as had become his custom. Robert and Mama and Aunt Rose sat together at the table and chatted while Helen gathered her things and was soon ready to go. It was Helen's great joy that Robert liked her family and the feeling was mutual. There would be no future with a man who did not fit in with her family.

"You two," Mama addressed Helen and Robert. "We are only allowing you to go without Aunt Rose as your chaperone this time, because you are going with the big Katz's Deli group." Helen and Robert exchanged a glance, and Helen blushed, knowing that Mama was telling them, without saying it directly, that she expected them to behave properly while they were together unchaperoned. To remain chaste. "Aunt Rose and I will go downstairs to see you off and say hello to your friends."

The four of them headed down the stairs. As soon as they stepped outside, they saw Kathleen and Kevin walking down the street toward them, right on time. Kathleen had been over for dinner a few weeks ago, and the whole family had taken to her. Helen waved excitedly, and then jumped off the stoop to join them.

Everyone was introduced to everyone else. Helen was curious about Kevin. He had blue eyes, straight dark hair worn longer than usual, and an attractive face. His cheekbones were high, and his jawline was straight. He was shorter than Robert, but he looked strong, like he could handle himself in any situation. Helen thought he looked a little forbidding until he gave a friendly smile that made his face light up. He put out his hand toward Robert, and he and Robert shook and exchanged pleasantries.

Kevin held out his hand to Helen as well. "Kathleen talks about you all the time. I am so happy to meet you," he said.

"We had better be going if we are going to spend the day at the beach." said Robert. "Let's go." Helen held out the picnic basket for him to inspect and carry. "You can't look inside yet, it's all a surprise for later."

The two couples walked to the subway stop. It was

hard to talk over the noise of the crowded train. Robert took advantage of the crowded seats to sit close to Helen. She enjoyed the warm feel of him closer than ever before. She wondered if he was wearing a swimming costume under his clothes, too. Helen imagined Robert would look quite fine in it. It was comforting to know that she wouldn't be the only one exposed today.

Finally, the train arrived at Coney Island. As they approached the sand, Robert said, "Close your eyes and I'll lead you." Robert held on as they walked onto the beach. "Okay, you can look now."

Helen kept holding onto him as she opened her eyes. It was just like Robert had said, blue skies forever, swooping seagulls, and little white clouds floating by. The ocean was calm and blue with small white waves rolling in. As for the white sand, the beach was so crowded with people that she could barely see any sand at all.

Those in the Katz's Deli group who had been here before knew how crowded it was going to be, and everyone had made precise plans about which steps to take onto the sand, and what direction to walk in to find one another. Helen could see Lewis and Margaret and the rest of the Katz's Deli gang.

They spread out their blankets and used their shoes to anchor the corners. Helen had never felt sand on her bare feet before. This sand was warm, fine, and golden. She stood for a moment and curled her toes around the grainy substance a few times. She grinned at how much she liked this new feeling.

Then came the moment of truth. Helen thought to herself, *I am going to take off my clothes and sit down on this blanket.* And she did. Robert watched her quite openly, and Kevin stole a peek or two, but his attention was soon diverted to Kathleen, who followed Helen's lead. Once Helen was sitting down in her woolen suit on the blanket, stockinged legs spread out in front of her for all the world to see, Robert tore his eyes away and took off his own shirt and trousers.

He wore a striped bathing costume and looked as good as Helen had imagined, with his broad shoulders and his nicely muscled arms and legs. He sat down next to Helen and shot her a big grin.

"Want to go in the water?"

"Yes!" Helen jumped up, and Robert reached out his hand to her. Together, they ran down the beach to the water's edge. They stopped together and watched gentle little waves curling up onto the dry sand, wetting it to a darker color and packing it down firmly. Helen lifted her eyes and saw the waves coming in, one after another. Not too big, nothing that would knock her down.

Helen had never been in the ocean before. In summertime, she had waded up to her knees in Lithuania's Nemunas River when it was hot. She had sailed across this forbidding Atlantic Ocean to come to America, never once imagining swimming in it. But this was a different ocean; this was an ocean for fun.

They continued to hold hands, walking forward side by side until the water was up to their ankles. Helen enjoyed the endlessly changing patterns that the wind sketched on the blue water. Each new part of her body that was immersed in the water felt cold for a few moments, but that passed quickly, and then she was ready to walk farther in. Soon the water reached her waist.

"That'll be fine for now," she said as she stopped moving forward. Robert grinned and reached down and splashed her with a big sweep of his arm through the water. "Oh no, you devil," she exclaimed, backing away from him and splashing him back. "Stop that immediately." Mama had again done her hair up, and she knew the splashing water was going to leave it a shambles if Robert kept this up.

He did, and she soon forgot all about her hair as great waves of foaming white water splashed back and forth between them. As they twisted and turned to avoid the water, they both fell over and were soon soaking wet from head to foot. They laughed and splashed, enjoying the coolness and the brilliance of the water droplets as they sprayed one another. Helen's hair went all straight, but she didn't care. Robert started to walk out farther, but Helen called him back, afraid to let the water come up any higher than her knees because she didn't know how to swim. Robert came back. He reached down and found her hand. Together they stood side by side, looking out over the water as far as the eye could see.

The two couples took turns going into the water and then drying off on the blankets in the hot sun. After a couple of hours, they opened their picnic baskets and shared what they had brought. Everyone loved Mama's feast. Kathleen had brought ham sandwiches. Helen had never eaten ham because Jews didn't eat pork products. It wasn't that she kept strictly Kosher, but ham wasn't a food that had ever been set before her. Kathleen offered her a bite, and she tasted it and thought it was good. Robert tried the ham too, explaining he had eaten it in Amsterdam where it was a local favorite. Helen didn't ask for another bite, and she thought if someone served it to her again, she would eat it. But probably she would never make it herself. She was used to what she was used to.

After lunch, the four packed up everything and walked along the street through Coney Island, looking for fun activities. There were several big amusement parks as they walked along. At Luna Park, there were wooden streets to walk down as you chose what rides you wanted to go on. You could ride an elephant. You could visit Lilliputia, a miniature village populated by little people. Kathleen and Kevin decided to take a gondola ride through the canals of Venice. They waved from their boat as they disappeared around a curve.

After the gondola ride, a man in a Middle Eastern outfit and a turban came along leading a camel. "You would like a ride?" he asked.

"Yes, how much?" Robert replied excitedly.

"Only seven cents for both you and the lady."

Helen looked closely at the camel. It smelled like the horse stables in Panemunė and had an arrogant expression on its face. But she could see that Robert was dying to climb on, so she nodded her head and agreed to the ride.

Robert climbed up as if he were getting on a horse and immediately looked like he had ridden camels all his life. The man in the turban produced a small footstool and Helen climbed up behind Robert. She kept her arms tightly around Robert's waist as the man led them down the streets of Luna Park. Helen enjoyed the camel ride. A beautiful carpet served as the saddle. Robert was full of questions for the camel owner about what the animal ate and how little water it could get by with.

After the camel ride, they all walked along until they came to Steeplechase Park. The men each purchased two twenty-five cent tickets, good for every one of the park's twenty-five different rides. They all rode the Steeplechase horses around a circular steel track. This ride was meant to simulate the horse races. Kevin told them that Coney Island was the race track capital of the whole country.

Kathleen suggested they all go on the Trip to the Moon, a rocket ride where you could see images of Niagara Falls and the Earth itself out the window. She and Robert sat together on the seats for two. Once you arrived on the moon, you could walk around its papier mâché lunar surface. Beautiful dancing Moon Maidens performed, and finally everyone exited through a Mooncalf's mouth, whatever a Mooncalf was. Helen just knew she was having fun.

By this time, a few hours had passed, and they were hungry again. They all went to Feltman's on the boardwalk and tried the Coney Island Red Hots, a hot sausage on a warm bun, similar to Katz's franks. At Katz's you got your food on a plate, but here having it on a bun meant you didn't even need a napkin. Everyone ate standing up or even walking around. Helen wondered if she was eating pork again, but the hot dog was so delicious she decided it had to be all-beef.

The four wandered through Feltman's beer gardens, around all the amazing rides, and through the Tyrolean village as they ate. Helen thought Katz's hotdogs were better. She missed the sweet taste of beans that were such a good accompaniment.

Finally, they ended up back at the beach, where they spread out their blankets and lay down on the warm sand. They all fell asleep as the sun was setting.

When Helen and Kathleen woke up, it was already eight o'clock in the evening.

"The last train is in just an hour," Helen whispered to Kathleen, careful to speak in a low voice so the men didn't wake up.

"I think we should miss the train because we all over-slept," replied Kathleen with an impish grin.

"I think so, too," replied Helen. She felt a bit nervous about doing something so forbidden, but everything just seemed to be flowing in that direction. And it was exciting. Helen knew that Mama and Papa weren't expecting her to come home, as she had arranged to stay at Kathleen's. Kathleen's roommates wouldn't worry. They knew the group was at Coney Island, and might choose to stay the night on the beach as many people did. It wasn't like she was going to do anything scandalous or unladylike. How different was it for the four of them to be on the beach in the dark than it was for them to be on the beach in the daytime?

Of course, never in her life had she done anything like this. Part of her felt it was wrong to lie to her parents and to stay out all night with a man she was only dating. But another part of her wanted to have an adventure, wanted to be a modern woman who was independent and knew how to have fun without anyone getting hurt. She was conflicted, but the part that was happy about missing the train was the winner.

It was after nine when the men finally woke up. Kathleen and Helen pretended to be waking up, too. They rubbed their eyes and acted sleepy.

"Oh dear," said Robert. "We missed the last train. Your parents will be terribly worried."

"No, it's alright," Helen said. She explained to Robert that her plan had been to stay at Kathleen's that night. Robert looked relieved. Helen thought how Robert and Kevin had no inkling of the planning the girls had done. *Girls need to have their secrets,* she thought.

"I'm so glad. I don't want to get on the wrong side of your parents."

"That's not likely. They think the world of you. You saved their first-born son from who-knows-what fate, not to mention how nice and polite and caring you are." Of course, it was true. Both Papa and Mama had been impressed with Robert, to the point where Papa had almost stopped scowling when Robert and Helen sat near to one another or spoke privately together. "In fact, they want you to come to dinner again next Saturday. Would you like to?"

"Absolutely," Robert replied.

It was a magical night. The moon was full. There were so many stars in the sky, it was like the skies of Panemunė. In Manhattan there were so many street lights that the stars were barely visible.

The two young couples enjoyed their freedom. For Helen, it was the first time she had ever spent the entire night outside. The men gathered driftwood from the beach and built a large fire. Kevin and Kathleen went back into the town of Coney Island and brought back cookies and cake. The four of them stayed up past midnight, talking about life in New York and sharing their hopes and dreams. Finally, around two in the morning, they all fell asleep, Kathleen and Kevin on one blanket, and Helen and Robert on the other.

Helen was the first one awake. While everyone else slept, she wrapped herself in her towel. The beach was completely deserted in the early morning light, but Helen wasn't taking any chances that someone might come along. She pulled off her sandy swimsuit and tried to brush off the sand, all the while staying covered with the towel. Finally, she got her regular clothes back on. She cleaned her teeth with ocean water, not sure it was improving anything, but it was the best she could do. With her fingers, she combed her hair into some semblance of grooming. She walked into town and found a little shop open that sold coffee in special Dixie cups for hot drinks, and warm bagels with cream cheese. She decided to splurge and bring back an early morning treat for everyone. The store people packed everything into a big paper bag and Helen carried it all back to the blanket. Kathleen and Kevin were still asleep, but Robert was just opening his eyes.

"Coffee and a bagel?" Helen offered.

Robert sat up with a questioning look on his face, as Helen took a paper cup and a bagel out of the bag for him.

"All the comforts of home," she added, handing him the Dixie cup and the warm bagel wrapped in paper.

Robert took the breakfast, and then put it down on the blanket for a moment, as he pulled Helen toward him. "You are amazing. What a beautiful night. Thank you."

Robert's arms were around her. He pulled her close. Helen tilted back her head and closed her eyes and enjoyed the first kiss of her life with the man she loved.

21

WORRIES

The next day around noontime, Helen opened the apartment door as quietly as she could, hoping to tiptoe past Mama and Papa and slip into the parlor without anyone asking any questions. She should have known better. There was Mama sitting at the kitchen table embroidering. Mama had decided to make a tablecloth like one she had to leave behind in the old country. She had found a piece of beautiful white linen and was stitching a traditional Lithuanian border, a wide row of complicated red geometric shapes, around the edges. Mama looked up.

"Did you have an enjoyable time at Coney Island?" she asked in Yiddish. Mama raised her eyebrows and lifted her empty palms into the air with the question. The family often spoke Yiddish when there was no one else around.

"Perfect, Mama. It was beautiful at the beach. We must take the whole family one day. They have an amusement park with rides and special shows. The sand is white, and the ocean is so blue and calm."

Mama smiled. "And Robert Fein? Did you and he have a good time?"

"Always, Mama." Helen's gaze moved into the distance. "We always have a good time together. He is so kind and thoughtful."

"And did you invite him to dinner again soon?" Mama asked.

"Yes, Mama, and he will come. You can plan on it."

"What kind of a name is Fein?" Mama asked. "I hadn't thought about that."

Helen was relieved the conversation was turning away from the previous evening's activities. "It's a good German name, Mama. 'Fein' means the same as 'fine' in English. It means elegant and handsome and genteel. It suits him."

"It will be good for our family to spend lots of time with Robert," said Mama firmly. "We all want to get to know him very well."

In the early days of their courtship, Helen had been worried about Robert getting to know the family. The thought of the entire family, little kids and all, looking him over, judging whether he measured up to the family's standards of who would be good enough for her. She had worried that the little kids would say all the wrong things, and she would be embarrassed. And Papa. Could anyone be good enough for his oldest daughter?

But it had all been easier than she had imagined.

She came back to the present. "Mama, I'm happy he is coming to dinner these days, and that he enjoys spending time with the whole family. I know that as time goes by, you are going to like him even more than you do now, so I'm not worried about it at all."

"I'm so glad you are happy to have him join us for family occasions," said Mama. "This next time I'm going to prepare all my best dishes." Mama was a great cook; Helen knew food was an area she need not worry over. What she could worry over was Papa or Mama changing their mind and deciding they didn't like Robert. What if somehow Robert said the wrong thing? Helen had never seen Robert say the wrong thing anywhere, but it's something that could always happen. What if the little kids blurted out some terrible thing about Germans or people with blond hair? The most memorable blonds they had known were Russian soldiers.

And what about problems from the other direction? What if Robert decided her family wasn't American enough, was too much a whole family of greenhorns? Mama and the younger kids had only been in New York for a short time. They were learning fast, but they still didn't understand all the ways of this New World. And what if the younger boys made inappropriate remarks? Sometimes they could enjoy being a bit bratty.

What if Robert begged off and made some excuse that he couldn't come? Would that mean that he had never been serious about her, that he was just having a good time? Helen felt her heart sink at the thought of losing him. She was working herself into an unfamiliar state of frenzy, thinking about all the things that could go wrong.

This would be the crossroads. Either he was serious and wanted a wife and a family, or he was having a good time and wasn't the strong character she believed he was. Helen tossed her head at her own silliness.

Monday arrived. Helen sat in front of her window at Joe's, stitching navy-blue woolen knickerbockers. Most Mondays meant a new color and a new fabric. Her work area already had a fine fuzz coating everything, and little snippets of navy-blue thread covered the floor around her.

Her hands and lower arms were already turning dark, as was the apron she had learned to wear to protect her clothing. Just as she ran out of bobbin and had to concentrate on winding a new one, in walked Robert. He carried a large bolt of maroon wool in a beautiful herringbone pattern. Helen strained to listen to his conversation with Joe in the kitchen.

"Very nice goods." Joe held the fabric up and ran his hand over it. "This could make some nice knickerbockers."

"That's why I thought of you, Joe. Merit National Shrinking Works always saves the best just for you," Robert said. The two men smiled at one another, and Joe reached in his pocket to pay Robert for the material.

Robert stood up and accepted Joe's payment. They shook hands. Then Robert craned his neck to see into the parlor.

"I'll just say hello to Helen, if that's okay," he said.

"Don't keep her long," replied Joe sternly. "We've got a lot to do today." Robert nodded to Joe and moved into the parlor and up to Helen's machine by the front window. Helen had completely given up trying to rewind the bobbin. Her hands shook with nerves.

"Hi Robert." Helen stopped sewing and stood up. "Can we go out into the hallway and talk for a moment?" Helen forgot to smile at Robert. Her heart was beating fast as she led him out into the hallway at the top of the stairs. She had worked herself into a state thinking about everything that could go wrong between them.

"Robert, you are still coming to the family dinner this Saturday night," Helen said, not quite daring to look him in the eye. "You remember I mentioned it to you at the beach?" She willed herself to stop talking and not fill the empty space between the two of them.

"Oh," Robert said. He seemed taken by surprise. "Well . . ." he said. Then he seemed to square his shoulders. He put his strong hand under Helen's chin, lifting her face so she had to look him in the eye. "As I said at the beach, I would love to accept your family's invitation." He spoke a bit formally and clearly, so that his words hung in the air between them.

She looked into Robert's blue eyes and saw his steady gaze. He had a small smile on his face, which she took to mean he understood all the deeper meaning of this conversation and best of all, that he was happy about it. It was everything Helen hadn't even known how to hope for.

"Come over around five thirty or so. Mama's such a good cook. It's going to be a great meal. My little brothers and my sister enjoy your company so much. You'll have lots of time to be with all of us."

"That sounds wonderful. I'm going to look forward to it. You must meet my mother sometime soon as well," he replied.

Helen flashed on an imaginary meeting with Robert's mother. She decided to leave that alone for now. She had enough on her mind. Robert leaned over and brushed his face against Helen's hair. Helen was glad they were alone in the hallway.

"See you Saturday," he said as he turned and skipped down the stairs.

"See you Saturday," Helen answered. Robert gave her one last smile before he disappeared around the landing and onto the floors below.

22

DINNER

Helen woke up early on Saturday, remembering that she wanted to help Mama get everything ready for the dinner. Joe had asked her to put in a few extra hours of work this morning. Since it paid extra, Helen was glad to do it, and it would take her mind off the evening for a while.

Mama had made morning coffee, and Helen poured the dark, steaming liquid into each of their delicate teacups.

"You finished the tablecloth!" Helen exclaimed. Mama had spread the tablecloth over two chairs to show off the fine stitching. She had done her work in the Eastern European style, geometric, only red thread on a white cotton background. She had sewn little squares half an inch wide that zigged and zagged around slightly larger diamonds. The embroidered shapes marched all around the edge of the large cloth. Helen realized that Mama must miss the old country. "It is beautiful. Just like a tablecloth in Lithuania. Can we use it tonight?"

The sight of the tablecloth brought an unexpected

wistfulness to Helen. She realized that she, too, missed Panemunė, the peacefulness of it, something hard to find in New York. She pictured the lazy Nemunas River that meandered and curved its gentle way along the edge of Panemunė. If it had not been for the rising feelings against the Jews, the family would have spent safe and happy lives along that river. But it was not to be; hatred had propelled so many people to leave their homelands and start anew. Helen knew she was lucky to have come to a place that she loved as much as the old.

"Of course. We will set a fine table with the willow china and now this new tablecloth. I'm going to make roast chicken." Helen gave Mama a big hug and a smile. Things were so very different here, but they were good.

Mama said, "Max's boss saved two big hens for us. There will be plenty to eat for everyone. Mr. Bloomberg loves Max so much, he gave us the chickens."

Mr. Bloomberg lived in the back of the store downstairs with his family. He was so grateful to Max and of course felt bad about Max getting hurt while working for him. He was always sending Max home with free chickens, things that hadn't sold and needed to be eaten or they would go bad.

Helen said, "Joe says I won't be too long today. I can come back early and help get things ready. I'm going to wear the new white blouse I showed you."

Mama frowned. "With the high collar and the big sleeves? Very modern, these blouses, my dear Hinde," Mama said, shaking her head. Helen smiled and didn't answer. Mama constantly forgot and called her by her old name. Helen had stopped reminding her. She was going to always be Hinde to Mama.

Mama went on, "I'm going to wear the nice navy-blue dress you gave me. Aunt Rose is going to put my hair up at four in the afternoon. If you can get here by four thirty, she can do yours, too." Helen nodded.

As she dressed for work, she watched all the little ones wake up. They were relaxed because it was Saturday, and today they could play. She kissed each one and said, "Remember to wash your faces and hands before dinner." Each one promised earnestly.

Her hours at work went fast. Joe had her doing button holes for several hours, and she was tired by the time she was done. She was happy that she could head home, and excitement over the evening lifted her spirits.

Helen got to their building and felt a jolt of energy. She raced up the stairs. The whole building smelled of roasting chicken. Mama looked beautiful in her new dress. Aunt Rose was just finishing piling Mama's hair on top of her head in a becoming fashion.

"Come over here and let me fix you up, too," said Aunt Rose. "I have to work quickly so I can leave before the honored guest arrives," she said, winking at Helen.

Soon Helen's hair was also piled on top of her head. This was the Pompadour style recently made popular by the fashionable Gibson Girls illustrations. Aunt Rose was a skilled hair dresser, and left a few tendrils drifting down around Helen's face. They looked quite accidental and alluring.

Papa arrived home about five, washed up, and put on a clean, button-down shirt he had saved for the evening. It had rounded points on the collar, and he wore a navy-blue tie to match Mama's dress.

The children all came rushing in from outside at once.

The boys noisily took their places on the far side of the table on the bench close to the wall. Max, Bernard, Milton, and Julius. Mama and Papa always sat at the head and foot of the table. Selma and Helen would sit on the outside bench. Robert's place tonight would be between Helen and Papa. Helen had revisited the china pushcart and had managed to find one more willow plate to add to their collection.

The new tablecloth and the matching china looked beautiful. Mama had lit a pair of candles and had set them in small pattern glass plates that she had found at a moving sale. The little plates sparkled in the glowing candlelight. Helen looked at everything and felt that it was perfect.

Robert arrived and gave Helen a big smile. She reached out to squeeze his upper arm affectionately while they were still at the door where no one could see them. He put his hand over hers for a moment. Helen led him into the kitchen.

"Everybody, Robert is here."

"Hello Robert," said Papa. "So glad you could join us for dinner once again."

"Welcome," said Mama. "We are very happy you could join us."

"We're having roast chickens that I brought from my job," Max said proudly.

"I heard you have your own company," Bernard said to Robert. "I'd like to do that someday. How did you get started?"

"Slow down everyone," Helen said in a louder voice than anyone else. "Let Robert sit down and get comfortable before you make him answer so many questions."

"It's no trouble," Robert said, smiling at Bernard. "I'll

tell you all about starting your own business. First of all, you have to have a skill."

Helen knew Robert could go on about his business, his favorite subject. She hoped this wouldn't take too long, especially because he was still standing in his coat.

Robert continued. "I worked for somebody else for several years, learning the way things were done. It was hard work, but no one can understand how a complicated business works right away."

"Give me your hat and coat, Robert," interrupted Mama. "Sit down and be comfortable."

Papa started right away. "So, how is your wool shrinking business going these days? It's good that we all work in the *schmatta* trade," Papa added. "Things seem to be booming for everyone," he went on. "It's the right time to be in business for yourself. I was thinking I might start a chicken store, but maybe we should stay in the clothing business. What do you think, Robert?"

Helen thought Papa was testing Robert a bit, seeing if he could think on his feet. Robert agreed politely with Papa. "Yes, it's a wonderful time to be making clothes in New York. I read in the *New York Times* that here in the city, we make almost three-quarters of all the clothing in America."

It was obvious that Robert was knowledgeable about the garment business. "You are well informed," Papa said.

"I try to stay up on things," Robert replied. Robert and Papa looked at each other, man to man.

"Enough business talk," Mama interjected.

"Let's eat," said little Julius.

"Yes, let's eat," echoed all the boys noisily.

Mama brought out the golden roasted chickens on a

large wooden board that the family used for a platter. The birds glistened, surrounded by roasted onions, potatoes, and carrots. Helen breathed in the aroma with its delicious promise of tastes to come. Mama put everything in front of Papa, who expertly carved. Soon it was quiet with the simple pleasure of eating.

"So, tell us about your company," Bernard tried again.

"Merit National Shrinking Works is going to be one of the biggest companies in New York. We already are shrinking fabrics for major textile companies. We recently signed a contract with Milliken in South Carolina."

Robert turned to Helen for a moment. "Did I tell you we got it? I'm so excited."

"That's wonderful," Helen replied with an encouraging smile.

Robert turned back to Papa and continued. "It's cheaper for them to ship their woolens to us than to find someone down there who doesn't know what they are doing the way we do. In fact, a few weeks ago I had to take the train to South Carolina to meet with them and secure the contract. It's a big country, I had no idea how big."

Helen was happy that Robert was so comfortable with her family, truly having a good time.

"When are you going to marry Helen?" Julius asked Robert. "I want to be the ring bearer."

Helen felt her face grow hot. She imagined herself disappearing from her bench. Slipping down under the table would be the best thing right now. She looked over at Robert and was relieved to see him smiling broadly at Julius.

"How do you even know about ring bearers?" asked Mama.

"My friend from school was a ring bearer," replied Julius. "He said in the old days, the ring bearer carried the ring on the tip of a sword, but in modern weddings all the ring bearer gets is a stupid, pink pillow. Can we use a sword, Helen?"

"We might need a ring bearer," said Robert. "Probably no sword though. We'll let you know." Robert gave Julius a big smile. "Soon," Robert added, glancing at Helen. "There are a few people who need to be consulted, but once I talk with them, you will be first to know." Robert looked over at Papa. Papa nodded, a big grin on his face.

Then Robert turned to Helen. She noticed that she was miraculously still sitting on the bench. "Don't you agree, Helen?" he asked.

Helen looked around the table. Everyone was smiling at her and Robert. She realized that she was smiling now, too, and feeling quite happy. "Oh yes, I agree."

23

MEETING MRS. FEIN

As the weeks went by, Robert was often invited to stop by for dinner mid-week. Helen's whole family enjoyed his company. This week, he asked Helen if she would like to come to dinner at his mother's house. Their relationship moved along the well-trodden path of courtship, and Helen was thrilled at every step of the way. Helen's parents gave their consent for her to visit Robert's mother the following Saturday evening.

Helen and Robert made their way to the apartment on Clinton Street where Robert's mother lived. It was on the first floor, in the back away from the street noises. Robert led Helen down the hall and opened the door for her. Nervousness roiled in her stomach.

Robert held the door open, and Helen entered ahead of him into his mother's small bedroom, just like in Helen's family's apartment. Everything was neat as a pin. The bed was covered with a big, fluffy eiderdown quilt. Helen had seen these on the pushcarts, but no one she knew could afford one. Robert's mother had covered the quilt with a pale coral spread. The room looked fit for a queen.

Robert's father had died many years ago, before they came to America. Helen wasn't sure where his brother Abe lived, but assumed she would meet him later. This first dinner would be just the three of them.

Helen and Robert went through the kitchen into the parlor at the rear. Mrs. Fein stood up and extended her hand. She greeted Helen with a smile that seemed a little forced.

Helen saw a frail older woman, older than she expected, quite a bit older than her own Mama. Mrs. Fein's hair was blond like her son's, but streaked with silvery gray. She wore gold spectacles that sat down on her nose as she peered at Helen over the top of them. Her mouth was pursed, and Helen worried that she had somehow inspired disapproval. Mrs. Fein had a stern face.

"Mama, this is Helen. Helen, please meet my mother, Mrs. Ernestine Fein."

Helen held out her hand to the older woman, who grasped it. "Welcome, my dear girl," said Ernestine a little crisply. "I'm happy to meet you at last. Please sit down, you two."

Robert led Helen to a pretty burgundy velvet couch with wooden arms and legs. Helen thought that everything was much richer than what her own family had. There were lace antimacassars on the sofa and chair arms and backs. Everything matched, unlike the patchwork collection in her own home. Mrs. Fein was perched in a beautiful maroon silk wing chair with a pattern of diamonds where every other diamond was shiny, and the ones in between were dull and soft looking. It matched the couch perfectly.

Helen reminded herself that Ernestine and Robert had been in America much longer than she had, and they didn't have a big family with small children. If the apartment and its furnishings were any indication, it seemed that Robert was even more successful in his business than Helen had imagined.

"It's a beautiful day for November, isn't it? I hope you enjoyed your walk over here. We live close to one another, don't we? Robert tells me you live with your family on Delancey, practically around the corner. Can I offer you each a glass of cold tea? It's the thing to serve this year, I hear. I thought we should try it out since this is such a special occasion."

Helen was glad that Mrs. Fein could carry on a conversation without much help from anyone else.

Mrs. Fein reached for a metal pitcher that had beads of condensation over the outside. It sat on a side table with three tall glasses. Helen nodded and smiled, and Mrs. Fein poured out iced tea for everyone. "Robert recently brought home an ice box that we keep out on the fire escape, so this strong black tea is quite cold. Helen, I understand that you work in Joe's shop on Orchard Street? Do you enjoy your work? Have you made friends there?" Robert's mother had lots of questions about Helen's work and life in general.

Helen answered the questions, telling a bit about her life, careful not to complain about anything, and emphasizing how wonderful it was that her entire family was now united in America.

"Are you a good cook?" Mrs. Fein asked. "Do you go to Temple? What did your family do in the old country? And what do they do now?" She wanted to be sure that her son would marry into a good family. Helen did not enjoy being grilled in this fashion, but she did her best to answer and set the older woman's nerves at ease. Gradually, as Helen patiently explained things, Mrs. Fein seemed to settle down. By the time Helen had finished her glass of tea, Mrs. Fein smiled at her and seemed much more relaxed. Apparently, Helen had passed the exam.

Mrs. Fein nodded her head. "It's only the three of us now, Robert, his brother Abe, and me. I lost my husband when the boys were young. We lived in Germany originally, but everyone hated the Jews there, and with no husband, I felt afraid. We had all heard the stories of people coming into the Jewish quarter and breaking windows and beating up or even killing people."

Helen felt a tension near her heart just thinking about it. She recalled her own family's danger back in Lithuania.

"We moved to Rotterdam when Robert was only six years old. Jews have a much better life there. The Dutch themselves are Protestant, so it was alright not to be Catholic. If you weren't a Catholic, you could come to Holland to escape intolerance. Especially Jews. Jews came to Holland from all over Europe. It was wonderful to leave behind the terrible hatred that was so common in Germany."

Helen understood how good it must have felt to come to a country without so much anti-Semitism. She had the same experience here in New York. She knew how this changed everything, days lived in peace, without fear and hiding.

"Rotterdam is a seafaring town, you know, with visitors coming and going. To survive, I took all our savings and bought a small hotel near the docks where people could stay for not too much money. I served meals each day and cleaned the rooms and worked hard, and we made a good living. Robert was always a good son, and he helped me greatly, even though he was just a small boy."

Helen was impressed with Mrs. Fein. She had been a woman with small children alone in a new country, but she had found a way to support her family and give them a good life.

"Maybe we shouldn't have lived so close to the docks, because by the time he was eight, Robert had become obsessed with going to sea and traveling the world. He would sit up all night listening to sea stories from the old sailors who sometimes stayed with us, or the travelers from afar who came to Rotterdam from Spain, from India, from China."

Helen looked over at Robert, who blushed a bit at his mother's story, but managed to smile at Helen and laugh at himself.

"I knew Robert would be gone soon. I could never hold either of my boys back from their dreams. By the time he was eight, he lied about his age, saying he was twelve, old enough to be a cabin boy, and he enlisted in the Merchant Marine. I was fine because our little inn had done well. I could now hire someone to help me take care of the guests and the cooking and cleaning."

"Yes, I got to go to sea at eight years old," Robert said. "Most of the crew had a soft spot for the cabin boys, and they treated me well. I loved visiting a city like Hong Kong where everything was so different that it was completely incomprehensible. My shipmates and I would wander around town, not understanding the simplest things. We couldn't read any of the signs, so we didn't know where we were. We couldn't tell a restaurant from someone's home from a store. When I came home, I would turn over my pay to help support the family. Between Mama's hotel and my earnings as a merchant marine, we got by."

Mrs. Fein went on. "Of course, I always worried terribly about Robert when he was at sea, and I was happy when he came home one day and said his sailing days were over. He had been at sea for two years. He travelled all over the world. He told me that he had been to New York, and what he had seen there amazed him. This was going to be the land of the future. He wanted us to move to New York as soon as possible. Even though he was young, I trusted his judgment. We sold the inn for a good profit and set off for America. That was many long years ago, and I have never regretted it. My son Abe loves being here, too. He works for a company that makes games for amusement parks and carnivals, like that game where you toss a penny and try to get it into the cup. One time, Abe took me to a carnival, so I could see what he does. It was lots of fun."

Helen remembered how much fun she had at the amusement park at Coney Island. Abe worked in a business that was fun for the patrons.

"As you know, I work at the office with Robert every day. I keep all the accounts and take care of the details for him. I enjoy that part of the business."

Mrs. Fein refilled Helen's glass. Helen sipped at the cold tea, enjoying something she had never had before. It was black tea, lightly sweetened and cold, and she found it delicious. "No wonder iced tea is sweeping the country," she commented. "It is refreshing, thank you so much."

"I'm happy you like it, my dear," said Mrs. Fein, leaning over to pat Helen's hand. "I know we are going to share wonderful things in the future." The two women smiled at one another, and in that moment, Helen knew there wasn't going to be a problem. She relaxed in the peace of Robert's home. Robert's mother was smart, and she was ready to share her son. Helen knew how important a mother-in-law could be in Jewish families. He was devoted to his mother, and Helen was happy to find she could enjoy Mrs. Fein's company as well.

Dinner was a pleasure. Mrs. Fein had made a brisket and cooked it all day to perfection. In the same pan were potatoes and onions and carrots, everything cooked in the savory drippings that had so much rich flavor. There was even butter to go on the potatoes, an expensive luxury rarely seen in the Breakstone household. Mrs. Fein tried to assume an offhand manner as she asked, "By the way, did you see the pictures of Eleanor Roosevelt's wedding?"

Helen had followed this wedding closely, as it was the biggest news a few months earlier. The wedding had been held in New York on St. Patrick's Day, but the scene had been stolen by the appearance of Eleanor's uncle Theodore Roosevelt, President of the United States, who gave away the bride. The groom was a young law student at Columbia named Franklin, whom no one had ever heard of. "Eleanor did have a beautiful dress, didn't she?"

Everyone had seen the photos of Eleanor in her long white dress with a full train and the beautiful lace top. Helen knew that it probably cost more than they all made together in a year, but it was fun to dream.

24

KATZ'S DELI REPRISE

It was another Saturday night, a few weeks later. Robert had previously asked if he might take Helen out to dinner that night. Helen said she would love to go, and of course their chaperone would come too. Aunt Rose was free and said she was happy to go out with them again. There had been many dates by now. Helen knew if she wanted to go out with Robert, a chaperone was required. She was still amazed that they had gotten away with their unchaperoned trip to Coney Island. Helen felt a little guilty; she had not lied directly, but she knew she had left her parents thinking things that were not true, such as that she had spent the night at Kathleen's. She had never lied to her parents before, and it weighed on her mind. But not so much that she felt the need to confess.

As she combed her hair in the parlor before his arrival, Helen wondered what direction things would now take. They had been out many times, and she had enjoyed his company greatly. She thought it was mutual. He had introduced her to his mother, and that had worked out well. And Robert was becoming like family at Helen's house.

Then there had been the embarrassing discussions of marriage at the table before the whole family, thanks to the innocent questions of an enthusiastic child. The whole process of courtship was wonderful and terrible all at the same time.

Mama and Papa celebrated *Shabbat*, and Robert and Aunt Rose both arrived separately at sundown. Aunt Rose brought her children Morty and Josie, who had become great friends with their cousins. Everyone had been invited to come around sunset to participate in the ritual closing of the Sabbath day. There were four rituals to be performed: a blessing over the wine, a blessing over fragrant spices such as cloves and cinnamon, a blessing over the candle, and the final blessing over the separation of things, such as the sacred and the secular. Robert knew the Hebrew prayers because his mother had done these blessings all his life. Papa invited him to lead the last prayer and blow out the candle to end the day.

Once the Sabbath had ended, Mama lit the fire in the stove and made tea for them all. Everyone gathered at the table and enjoyed conversation with one another until the couple and their chaperone got up to go. They would skip Mama's dinner tonight, but Aunt Rose's children would stay for the meal. The couple and chaperone were headed to Katz's Deli. Helen felt they had lots to talk about.

Katz's was an excellent choice because it was where they had their first conversations together. Helen would never forget looking up into the blue eyes of the handsome man sitting next to her in the steamy restaurant, spilling her water all over him, and laughing together like it was the funniest thing that had ever happened. Her intuition told her they were returning to discuss their future.

As they walked out of Helen's building, Robert moved between the two women and folded Helen's arm into his own right, and Aunt Rose's into his left. Several times, he smiled down at her as they made their way to Katz's.

At Katz's all three of them wanted to have pastrami, the new brined beef that was like bacon but kosher for Jews. Everyone was crazy about pastrami right now. Robert and Helen both loved it, and Aunt Rose was always game to try something new.

They waited at the counter for their food, and Robert paid for everything at the big golden cash register. The three made their way to a corner table where it was quiet enough to hear one another.

Helen sat across from Robert at the small marble-topped table. She took a big bite of her pastrami sandwich on Katz's delicious marble rye bread. The pastrami was fatty and peppery and seemed to melt in her mouth. She swooned a little from the pleasure.

"I love this," she said to Robert. "It's supposed to taste like bacon, which Kathleen and Kevin rave about. I tried ham and liked it, but I don't think I'm ready for bacon."

"You are correct," said Aunt Rose. "It is delicious!"

Robert said. "It's got a smoky flavor like a hot dog. If someone handed me a piece of bacon, I'd try it out, but I'm not going to go looking for it. But this is good, salty and spicy. Beef, but not like beef," he pronounced. "And kosher to boot."

After demolishing half of his sandwich, Robert sat back in his chair and relaxed. He seemed to enjoy simply being in one of his favorite places. Nothing was quite like

Katz's. Then he straightened himself in his chair and smiled at Helen. "We had an interesting discussion last week at your family dinner, didn't we?" he began. Helen noticed the small grin on his face.

"We certainly did, thanks to my bratty little brother," Helen replied, offering an out if Robert wanted to take it.

He did not. "I was happy it happened," he said. "I hope you were, too."

"Yes," Helen said simply, and nervously returned Robert's smile. "I was happy it happened, too."

Aunt Rose was holding her sandwich, frozen in midair while Robert and Helen focused only on one another.

"Your little brother was cute. Someday I want to have a big family," Robert went on. "Especially since I was just one of two brothers. Having lots of siblings looks like fun to me."

Helen replied, "I've always wanted to have a big family. I couldn't imagine anything else."

Robert continued along his track. "I want you to know that I had lunch with your father this week, while you were at work. We had a long talk together about the future."

"Oh," said Helen, surprised. "I had no idea you and he spoke. What did you discuss?" she asked, already having a good idea. But she did not expect what happened next.

Robert stood up and bowed formally to Helen. Then he came around to her side of the table, reached into his pocket and, with a small flourish, took out a small box. Opening the box, he got down on one knee before Helen and held out a small but sparkling diamond. He looked into her eyes.

"Will you marry me, Helen?" he asked simply.

Helen felt her heart racing. Her eyes were locked with his. She was unaware of the smiles on the faces of the other patrons of Katz's, all of whom were suddenly frozen with their forks poised at various stages between plates and mouths, leaning forward to watch the drama unfold. Aunt Rose was still as a statue so as to not disturb the moment.

Helen's head was spinning and her stomach did a flip-flop. She had known they would talk and share with one another this evening, but she hadn't expected a formal proposal of marriage. Then a new feeling began, a sweet feeling of just how right this felt. It was strong and calm, and it was right. Her heartbeat slowed down to a steady rhythm as the sweetness spread through her.

"Yes," she said. "Yes, I will."

He slipped the ring onto her finger. Their eyes had stayed locked for a moment, then Helen looked down at her finger and smiled at how perfectly the ring fit. Aunt Rose finally put down her sandwich, which had been in midair for several minutes it seemed, then stood up, clapping her hands and smiling widely. Suddenly the whole restaurant burst into applause and cheers. Cries of *Mazel Tov* rang from the rafters, and glasses were lifted high.

Robert stood up and so did Helen. Their arms went around one another, and they kissed, right there in public, to the joy of all the watchers.

"My wife to be," Robert announced to the crowd, smiling down at Helen and raising his own glass with a flourish.

25

NEXT STEPS

Robert and Helen sat back down. Helen was too excited to eat any more pastrami and kept looking down at her new ring. A future with Robert was exactly what she wanted. He was kind and gentle and smart. He was handsome and Jewish, but not too religious. He loved her and had eyes for no one else. He was already a success in business, and she felt they would want for nothing through their lives. Never again would she face the insecurity and poverty that she had grown up with in Lithuania. They would live safely, welcomed into the community. Their children would be safe in this country and their futures secure.

While Helen's appetite had vanished, getting engaged seemed to have stoked Robert's. He wolfed down more of his pastrami sandwich. He smiled at her and talked with his hands all at once. "We have so much to discuss. I have ideas. I heard about land for sale out in the country, in the northern-most borough of New York City, the Bronx. It's cheap now, a good buy, but it's going to go up and up in price. It's way out in the north Bronx in an area no one ever heard of called Riverdale."

"So far away?" Helen asked.

"You can get there in thirty minutes on a train from Grand Central, and there are rumors that the subway is going to be extended to go there in the next year or two. We could buy land there and sell it gradually at great profit. The Bronx is going to be the big thing soon. People are tired of tenements and city streets. They want leafy neighborhoods and bigger houses where they can raise families. Of course, if you don't like the idea, we won't do it. I would love to make money, but I want to make you happy more than anything else."

Helen smiled and reached out to squeeze his hand.

"We could build a big house there and fill it with children." Robert was excited. He was going so fast Helen had no time to reply to anything. She laughed out loud at his enthusiasm.

Helen felt her appetite return and finally got interested in her own pastrami sandwich. It tasted even better than before.

That evening when the couple returned to Helen's, the little ones were asleep, but Mama and Papa were awake and sitting at the kitchen table reading and drinking tea. The couple walked in, and Helen stretched out her left hand so her parents could see. She waved her finger around as the ring sparkled in the light from the bare kitchen bulb.

"Helen!" exclaimed Mama. She jumped up and hugged her daughter, then turned to hug Robert too. "My new son to be. I am so happy you will be a part of our family, Robert."

"Ah, my beautiful daughter will go out into the world on her own with her man," said Papa. "As it should be." He stood up to shake Robert's hand and to hug Helen. "I'm happy for this."

26

PREPARATIONS

Mama told Helen to invite Mrs. Fein to dinner with Robert. Helen knew that Mama wanted to meet this woman who would soon be family. What if she was difficult and always complaining? What if she was not wonderful to Helen? Helen had met Mrs. Fein and didn't share Mama's concerns anymore. She felt confident that she could have a good relationship with her soon-to-be mother-in-law. Helen knew Mama wouldn't dwell on these thoughts and after a few worries, would assume the best until proven otherwise. No need to suffer over made-up stories.

Once the date for dinner was set, Mama decided it was time to buy a ninth chair for the table. They could squeeze Robert in on the bench with the children, but Mama wanted Ernestine to enjoy her visit without being crowded. Future guests would feel more comfortable too. Papa went out to the pushcarts and found a chair that wasn't too wide and would fit at the end of the outside bench next to Papa.

The evening came, and Mrs. Fein and Robert arrived

at the Breakstone family apartment. Helen showed Mrs. Fein to the new chair next to Papa. Robert sat down on the bench next to his mother, as if to offer moral support, but Mrs. Fein didn't seem to need support of any kind. She and Papa started talking right away. There was nothing shy about Ernestine Fein.

"Thank you so much for inviting me. I'm so happy to meet you now that we are going to be family." She turned and nodded to Robert and Helen as she said this.

Papa replied, "Yes, we're happy for this as well. Our eldest child is going to be married to a real *mensch*," Papa said. Mrs. Fein beamed at the expression. So did Helen, while Robert blushed a bit. "May this be the first of many visits we will share."

Mrs. Fein said, "And I would like to invite all of you to have dinner with us, soon. All the small children must come."

"You may regret that; small children are great creators of chaos," Papa offered.

"Papa, we want to go to Mrs. Fein's," Julius whined a bit. "Please can we go?"

"A little chaos is good for me as I get older and more set in my ways," Mrs. Fein replied, with a smile for Julius.

Bernard piped up, "I would be happy to come to your apartment and have dinner and make a special chaos for you." Bernard tried to describe the shape of chaos with his hands up in the air, but wasn't sure what it would look like. "What is 'chaos' anyway, is it something we can eat? I'm not a good cook yet, but I will try to improve before we come to visit so that I can make the best chaos you have ever had." Bernard looked right at Mrs. Fein as he pledged to do his best.

Everyone laughed. Helen was relieved that the ice was broken. She thought that this was often the case when young children were present. Nothing stays too formal or stiff when there are adorable children in the mix.

"Chaos isn't a food, little one," replied Mrs. Fein to Bernard in a friendly tone. "It is a time when all kinds of *mashugana* things go on, and more of them can happen at any moment."

"Oh," Bernard said. "Much easier than cooking."

Everyone laughed at Bernard's accurate reply.

Mrs. Fein was a great hit with the Breakstones. Her sense of humor was more than welcome, and Helen could tell that she enjoyed being with a large group of people. It was obvious why Mrs. Fein had been so successful as proprietress of her hotel in Rotterdam. She paid sincere attention to everyone. She learned all the children's names quickly and had questions for each of them that they enjoyed answering. Not only was she not bothered by the noisy discussions and everyone talking at once, she enjoyed it.

Papa took to her immediately. Because of her work at Robert's business, she knew the garment business as well as Papa and could discuss it intelligently.

Mama and Mrs. Fein were trading recipes before dinner was over. Helen chimed in, "Mrs. Fein made the best brisket when I came to visit. If that recipe isn't a secret, I know Mama would like to have it, and so would I." Mrs. Fein was quite a bit older than Mama, but they had lots in common and besides trading recipes, they shared tips on where to buy the best meats and vegetables. Mrs. Fein invited Mama to go shopping with her next week, so that she could show her the secret special places she knew about for food shopping on the Lower East Side. Helen could see that Mama was no longer so concerned over this new family member to be, that she saw Mrs. Fein as someone who would fit in with the family just fine. Just *Fein*, Helen thought to herself with a smile that no one noticed.

Mama served her chopped liver as a first course. She made the chopped liver with hard boiled eggs and *schmaltz*, rendered chicken fat. The chicken fat made it like a rich pâté. Mrs. Fein ate every bit of her serving, then complimented Mama. "This is delicious."

Mama answered, "I will be happy to share the recipe with you. You have to caramelize the onions for a long time to make it so sweet."

Next came Mama's pot roast, a family favorite. She had cooked onions and carrots and potatoes in the same pot all day long. The meat was so tender it fell off the bone, and all the vegetables were perfect. Mrs. Fein cleaned her plate, as did everyone else, and seconds were served all around. Eating the scrumptious food, Helen vividly recalled the thin soup and soured milk that had been the family's diet in Lithuania. What a long way they had come!

After the main course, Mama brought out a big plate of Rugalach, bite-sized cookies filled with nuts and chocolate. These were made with no dairy to keep kosher when served with the meat. "Start with just one," Papa admonished the little children, as a forest of small hands reached for the cookies. "Leave some for the adults."

The family always kept kosher, even if they hadn't ever been able to afford two sets of dishes. They ate meat and dairy on the same plates and didn't worry about it. But they wouldn't serve meat and dairy in the same meal; that would have been too big a break with tradition.

Papa stood up and raised his coffee cup as if he were going to make a toast. "I have an announcement to make to you all," he began. "I am planning to start a new chicken store here in the neighborhood." Everyone knew this except Mrs. Fein, so Papa wanted to make it clear. "As you know, all the young children are now in school, and Mama wants to work outside the home. I'm pleased to introduce you all to our new bookkeeper, Mrs. Chaim Breakstone."

Mama beamed. "I'm so excited to have a real job. I worked in the dairy with the cows in the old country, but this will be nice work in a clean office, and I'll be able to help the family business succeed. I can't wait to get out of the house each day, to talk to other adults and do a great job of keeping track of all the money we will make."

The little children applauded, and Helen, Robert, and even Papa and Mrs. Fein joined in.

"I very much enjoy my bookkeeping work for Robert's company," volunteered Mrs. Fein. "I would be happy to show you some things I have learned over the years."

"That would be wonderful," replied Mama. "I know I have a lot to learn, but I'm excited to become a working person again."

Helen knew how happy Mama was about this coming change. Mama had confided that there was only so much time one could spend with children and only children, without the brain becoming addled, only so much cooking, cleaning, and laundry a person could do without needing adult stimulation. When Mrs. Fein offered to help Mama set up her books, Mama was excited and grateful. She looked forward to her first job in America.

"Call me Devorah," she told Mrs. Fein.

"And you call me Ernestine, of course."

Helen watched the two women getting along. She was happy to see that Mama wasn't going to be simply Mama forever, that she planned to move out into the world in a new way, to pursue her own work once again. Not that Mama had ever not been her own person, but she had always put her children first.

As the evening neared its end, Helen felt the dinner had been a great success, and that the future boded well for herself and Robert. Helen felt that she had been silly to worry that Mrs. Fein might find their home too shabby. Even though Robert's mother had finer things, she wasn't a snob about it.

Weeks went by. Robert came around to Helen's even more often now, enjoying a standing invitation to dinner and showing up every few nights. Often, his mother came as well. The Breakstones all understood that Robert was reluctant to leave his mother alone so many nights in a row, and anyway, having Ernestine present was always a pleasure. It seemed that everyone wanted the two families to merge into one. No one cared that the little kitchen was crowded. Some days Mrs. Fein came early, and she and Mama would prepare the meal together.

At these times, Ernestine might bring a big pot, which Robert would carry over from their apartment, with enough food for everyone. Sometimes it was a cut of meat Ernestine had cooked for the family, sometimes more expensive than what Helen's family was used to.

Papa had enjoyed Robert's company since they met. The two men discussed business and the New York financial climate. Both thought they were sitting on the brink of a boom. Both looked forward to doing well for themselves and their family. New York was becoming the most important city in the country, and they could see the town taking its place as a world center like London or Paris. The subway had recently opened. Literally millions of people were living in New York, most of them Catholics and Jews who immigrated from Europe. More came every day as the dream spread all over the world.

Papa had big plans, and Robert was always interested in business plans. Papa was almost ready to open the kosher chicken store. He had dreamed about it for a long time. Mr. Bloomberg, Max's boss, advised him on how to proceed. Papa had found a suitable location, a ground floor storefront over on Hester Street near Aunt Rose. This was far enough away so that Papa wouldn't draw away business from Mr. Bloomberg. Max's boss had been kind, helping Papa with useful ideas, so the last thing Papa wanted was to take any business away from him. Max would help Papa for a few months until the next school year started. Then Papa would be on his own with the business as Max went back to school. Max's returning to school was the fulfillment of Papa's plan and his promise to Max.

The location on Hester Street was ideal because the living quarters in the rear were occupied by a widow. She wanted to rent only the storefront to Papa and Max and keep the living quarters for herself. That meant it was much cheaper than other storefronts on the Lower East Side, most of which included living quarters.

Papa's back had been hurting for a long time. His work as a jobber in the garment trade required him to stand all day, and this had taken too much toll. On top of that, he had to wield the big cutting knife through huge piles of fabric to make the pattern pieces that would be sewn into clothing, and his hands would only hold up so long. Papa was getting older, and he wanted to do something else, something that would be easier on his back and hands. He was almost forty-five, and his age was starting to slow him down.

By this time, Max was fifteen. He knew the chicken business on the Lower East Side inside and out. He had been involved in every aspect of running Mr. Bloomberg's shop. The plan was that Bernard would take over Max's job, and he too would have a chance to learn the business. In fact, Mr. Bloomberg was making enough money to retire and not have to work anymore. Eventually Papa and the boys figured they would buy him out and run two stores. They suspected Mr. Bloomberg might be thinking along the same lines. These would be their first two stores. Papa and the two oldest Breakstone boys had big plans.

Bernard coming into the business meant that until school started, Max could temporarily move over and be Papa's knowledgeable assistant in the new store. Once again, the family saved everyone's salary, as they had during the years of saving to bring over the rest of the family. This time they needed two hundred dollars to rent the store, to have signs made, and to buy the first round of chickens. Papa wanted the signs to say, "Breakstone and Sons - Kosher Chicken."

Helen loved how they all pulled together, how they all saw the goal clearly and were willing to sacrifice for the future. The chicken store was nearing reality. Exciting things were happening. America was like that, Helen thought. New York was like that.

But to Helen, nothing was more exciting than her up-coming wedding. In her heart of hearts, she knew that she wanted a family more than anything. Family had always been her source of true happiness. Papa and Mama had provided a warm and loving home where everyone sup-ported everyone else. Helen wanted to make that happen again for her own children. She and Robert had discussed this and were in perfect agreement.

Helen certainly looked forward to walking down the aisle in a white dress, one that might not be as rich and elegant as Eleanor Roosevelt's, but was nonetheless going to be the most amazing dress anyone on Delancey Street had ever seen. She could imagine her handsome and lov-ing husband-to-shortly-be, standing there awaiting his bride at the altar.

Helen planned, and Kathleen helped. On Joe's stoop after work, the two girls would talk and talk about what would be best. Long or short? What color of white, pure white or a beautiful creamy color? A veil? A train, of all things?

Kathleen and Kevin were now engaged, too. The girls planned to focus on Helen's wedding first, putting all their energy and ideas into that event. Then they would plan Kathleen's wedding, going over the dress, the cake, and which of the many Catholic churches would be best. Nei-ther Helen nor Robert had ever been in a Catholic church, and they looked forward to Kathleen's wedding as a chance to see the inside of a real church. Helen and Kath-leen had different churches, different services. But their weddings would have the same wonderful feelings, the same wonderful dresses and dreams.

Sometimes Helen and Kathleen would skip eating and

spend their lunch half-hour walking around the nearby fabric pushcarts, looking at lace and satin and even white velvet. They always reached out and felt the goods; they knew that was the only way to know if fabric was of superior quality. Helen thought of the miles of fabric that had passed through each of their hands over the years they had worked together at Joe's. How lovely it would be now to sew glamorous silk and satin dresses instead of knickerbockers.

Helen and Robert chose a synagogue for the ceremony. Both would have been happy to get married at City Hall, an elegant building almost one hundred years old, but they understood how disappointed their parents would be if they didn't marry in a synagogue. Their parents were liberal and open minded, but they were still attached to the old ways. A wedding that took place at City Hall wouldn't be a real wedding, neither to Helen's parents nor to Robert's mother. They wanted to join their families on the right foot, and to do so required respecting their parents' views.

Helen and Robert chose to have the ceremony at the Ansche Chesed Synagogue. They both liked that the name translated into English as "People of Kindness." This was the same temple where Aunt Rose had taken Helen when she first came to America, the one that was designed to be like the Sistine Chapel. This was the synagogue where Helen had come many times to rest and enjoy the familiar ways of the service. The congregation wasn't exactly Reform Jewish, but it was a liberal Conservative Jewish, so both Helen and Robert were happy. It was also the synagogue that Mrs. Fein attended every Saturday.

The Rabbi at Ansche Chesed Synagogue was Rabbi Jeff Marx. He would perform the wedding ceremony. Rabbi Marx had an excellent reputation in the community. He was deeply religious, of course, but also a man of science, smart and forward-thinking. Many people in the neighborhood relied on Rabbi Marx for good advice on how to live their lives, and also for someone to talk to in tough times.

Helen and Robert made an appointment to meet with Rabbi Marx. It was part of their obligation if they wanted to marry in the synagogue. Remembering the teacher Rabbi David back in the old country, and how he insisted that every word of the Bible was true, made Helen feel concerned. She knew this Rabbi was well-regarded, but she was worried because of her previous experience and her lack of religious fervor. She was also worried that the Rabbi would disapprove of her because she wasn't a very observant Jew, and Robert was even less so.

The day of their appointment arrived. Helen had to remind herself not to bite her fingernails, a new nervous habit that sometimes appeared when wedding plans were discussed.

Rabbi Marx welcomed them into his office at the back of the synagogue. He was young, only in his thirties, which surprised Helen. "So, you want to marry in our synagogue," he said, getting right to the point.

"Yes," replied Robert. "My mother, Ernestine Fein, is a member and comes every Friday night and Saturday."

"Yes, I know your mother, Robert. She is a lovely lady and active in the Hadassah and in other ways. What is it that inspires you to want to have your wedding here?"

Robert began, "We have heard that this synagogue has

a congregation of people with liberal attitudes. Neither Helen nor I embrace Orthodox views. We want to get married in a synagogue that shares our values. I know the Germans Jews who came to New York fifty years ago were quite liberal, and that they founded this congregation. The Feins are German."

Helen thought she might as well move the conversation toward her areas of concern and get it over with. "I'm from Lithuania, and many of the Eastern European Jews are strict. I don't agree with them. I like the Jewish principals, where science and religion can both be right." Helen hoped the Rabbi would understand and not try to convince them of anything.

"Why don't you two tell me more of your thoughts about Judaism," the Rabbi continued. "You can speak freely," he added.

Helen took a deep breath and decided to speak up and say what she thought. "Our Rabbi in the old country insisted that every word of the Bible was literally true, and I couldn't go along with that. I love our Jewish traditions, and I will always be a Jew. I will raise my children as Jewish, and I will come to schul sometimes, but not every week. And I simply cannot believe in every word of the Bible."

Robert continued her thought. "I feel the same way, Rabbi. I have the utmost respect for our traditions and history, and for you as a learned Rabbi who can guide the community, but I don't get much inspiration from services or from rites and rituals. I, too, will always be a Jew. I, too, want my children to know their heritage and traditions."

Helen was happy to hear Robert saying just what she thought. The Rabbi was not smiling at them particularly, and she was worried about what would happen next. He could easily turn them away as not religious enough Jews to merit a wedding in this synagogue. Perhaps he thought badly of the two of them, for not ever participating in synagogue gatherings and for rarely even coming to *schul*. His next words might be to condemn them both for being insufficiently God-fearing, and for not keeping the important rituals of Jewish tradition.

The Rabbi nodded at them both. He stood up, clasped his hands behind his back, and walked around the room a little. Helen was sure he was about to condemn the two of them.

Rabbi Jeff Marx spoke carefully. "I want to thank you both for your honesty. I know it takes courage to tell a Rabbi about your religious reservations. Today, many young people feel the way you do. I sometimes wish young people would be more observant, but I understand there are so many concerns here in the New World, and the old rites and rituals seem to have less meaning. But it is not the rites and rituals that make Judaism a wonderful religion. It is our ancient teachings, and our caring for one another, and our beautiful culture that bring us together. These things, I am happy to see you both appreciate."

The Rabbi continued, "As a liberal Conservative Jew, I do not believe every word of the Bible is literally true. Maybe the Red Sea parted and maybe it didn't. Maybe that was just an image to show how the forces of goodness came together to help the Jews in their exodus from Egypt. I think your attitudes toward Judaism are very much in line with our congregation's and with my own thinking."

Helen breathed a huge sigh of relief.

He continued, "It makes me very happy to welcome you to have your wedding here at Ansche Chesed Synagogue."

Helen smiled at the Rabbi and said, "Thank you, Rabbi. I'm so happy that we will be married here, and I look forward to this synagogue being part of my family's future."

"Yes, Rabbi, thank you very much," said Robert. "We are both happy that we may hold our ceremony here. Will you conduct it for us?"

"Of course," said Rabbi Marx. "That comes with the package. We will always welcome you both here. Please do come and join us from time to time. Later when you have a family, show your children where the *schul* is, what the service is like. Maybe even light the candles on Friday night, even if you don't keep *Shabbat*, it doesn't matter. Do whatever you can. Relax on the Sabbath, take it as a day to be together with family and to relax from the work week. Be who you are. Be true to how you see the world. Don't let science and the world's expanding knowledge be separate from Judaism. It can all work together."

Rabbi Marx continued, and he gave them ideas about how to present their plans to Helen's parents so that they would understand and not feel alienated by the new ways.

"Rabbi Marx," Helen said, "You make me happy that Robert and I can belong here without having to pretend anything. We can just be who we are." Rabbi Marx was a truly spiritual man, and if she ever needed wise advice in the future, Helen knew that he was the person she would turn to.

"Well let's set a date for the wedding," Rabbi Marx said.

Helen and Robert looked at one another. When she

saw the relief on his face, she realized that he, too, had been anxious about this meeting with the Rabbi. In their silent exchange, Helen realized that she and Robert spoke the same language, even when they said nothing at all.

"Yes, Rabbi," Robert said, his voice bolder now. "Let's set the date."

27

THE BIG DAY

Everyone in the Breakstone household was full of energy and plans. Bernard and Julius were now the proud owners of suits with knickerbocker pants and long woolen socks that tucked neatly under the bottom of the pants. Max had been fitted with a real grown-up suit with long pants. All the boys had white shirts and ties. The entire family was going to look prosperous and happy at Helen's wedding today.

Helen had gone all out. She and Mama had found satin, lace, taffeta, and organza. They made a beautiful wedding dress inspired by the one worn by Eleanor Roosevelt that had appeared on the front page of the *New York Times*. This dress had set styles in New York for months after the big society wedding the previous March.

The full skirt was a bright white satin meant to be worn over a horsehair crinoline. The crinoline was scratchy, but Helen was willing to put up with it because it made the dress look perfect. The neckline of the dress was round with a satin rose on one side. Big ruffles at the shoulders gave way to long thin lacy sleeves, old point lace bordering the bodice, and a point lace veil. Helen loved the point lace.

Aunt Rose had made the intricate pattern with just a needle and thread. Point lace was the most delicate lace of all.

Selma would be Helen's maid of honor, and Helen had designed a dress for her to wear, a pale rose satin. It was like Helen's dress in several ways—the ruffled shoulders and a round neck, with a pretty rose at the neckline in pink satin.

Mama had taken over and completed most of both Helen's and Selma's dresses from pictures that the girls had drawn, and no one could sew like Mama. Helen would carry white roses, and these were the first flowers she had ever purchased from the flower peddler's pushcart. She had tied the flowers together into a bouquet with a matching bright white satin ribbon trailing down. She had bent over the bouquet to deeply inhale the scent of the roses that so perfectly matched the many sensual luxuries of the day: silks and satins, wonderful food, and above all, family and friends gathering in celebration of love.

Helen hoped she would be an attractive bride. She never thought of herself as pretty, much less beautiful. But she knew she would look charming in this dress, her hair dark and shiny and her face glowing with happiness on the day she married Robert. And why not? Tall, blond, smart, successful, and kind—he was the prince of her dreams. Most of all, he loved her as much as she loved him. Maybe she would qualify as a beauty on this one special day. At the least, everyone loved a bride and would feel inspired seeing her.

Robert's mother wanted to wear a pale mint green dress. She was tall and thin, and Helen thought she would look quite elegant in that color.

Mama would wear a shining golden dress with fringe. Fringe had become popular lately, ever since New Yorkers had seen pictures of Native Americans with fringed clothing. You never knew what was going to start a fashion. People who worked in the garment industry, like Helen and Robert, paid special attention to fashion and enjoyed watching the trends come and go, understanding what set off the newest thing.

Mama had a strong sturdy build and was not tall. The gold color suited her dark coloring and her shiny and still mostly dark hair. "Mama, you look like you have just come down from Astor Place dressed in the height of fashion. Have you wandered away from a big party at your mansion? I would be happy to help you find your way back uptown." Mama laughed off the compliment, but Helen could tell she enjoyed looking the part of a sophisticated New Yorker. No more greenhorns in the Breakstone family.

Papa had a new suit of a beautiful, silky navy-blue wool with a pinstripe, the finest goods the garment district had to offer. Normally all these expensive fabrics would have been too expensive, but because Papa and Helen worked in the garment business, they knew how to get the best for the least. Helen's boss Joe had helped them find wonderful fabrics for a fraction of the price. Papa's suit had a fashionable cut that showed off his tall, solid frame to best advantage. He looked like the successful businessman that he was. Helen had no idea what Robert would wear, but she had never seen him in anything less than perfect for whatever the occasion, so she didn't worry. The wedding party would be a picture of New World happiness.

Robert's brother Abe would be best man. Helen had met him a few weeks earlier. He loved his work at amusement parks and carnivals, setting up games and booths. Helen enjoyed listening to him talk about the carnival life, the performers and carnival workers. He seemed like an interesting fellow, and Helen looked forward to getting to know him better in the future.

Everyone would come back to the Breakstone's De-lancey Street apartment for the reception. Mama, Selma, Mrs. Fein, and Aunt Rose had all been cooking for days. Max had invited Mr. Bloomberg from the chicken store and his whole family. Joe, Helen's boss, and his wife and two little boys would come. Papa had invited all the men he used to live with, as well as those with whom he worked. Robert had invited everyone who worked at Merit National Shrinking Works. All the Breakstone neighbors would come. It would be a good crowd, completely filling the small apartment, and probably spilling out into the hallways and down the stairs into the street itself.

Helen had invited everyone from work, including Joe and his whole family, Kathleen and Kevin, and the Katz's Deli group. Everyone had accepted her invitation except for one person. Of course, it was Esther, the third sewing girl who was always so unhappy and who had treated Helen and Kathleen so badly. One day, when work was over, Helen waited to leave until everyone was gone except Esther, who was just about to leave. She followed Esther out the door and down the stairs. She waited to speak until they reached the stoop at the front of Joe's building.

"Esther, I especially wanted to invite you to come to my wedding. We have been sewing side-by-side for four years now. It won't be the same unless you join us."

Esther stopped cold on the white marble stoop. Her shoulders had automatically hunched up as Helen spoke. "I am so sorry, Helen, but I cannot come. I have other plans." Esther did not turn around.

Helen decided to take a chance. The situation with Esther could not get worse, so there was nothing to lose. She spoke to Esther's back, "I heard what happened to your fiancé. I am so sorry you had to live through that. I cannot imagine how hard that must have been. You may have heard that my brother was also beaten up for being Jewish. I thought of you so much during that time. If my brother had died, I think I might have died, too. But you didn't die. You have been brave enough to go on. You are still here, and you have a whole life in front of you. You are probably my age, not even twenty yet. So many good things could still happen for you."

Esther did not reply, so Helen went on, "Everyone at work would love to get to know you better and be friends with you. No one wants to say anything about what happened. But I am talking about it. It's better to acknowledge it and move on. It's not disloyal for you to have a life. Maybe it is time for you to have a friend."

Esther turned around slowly. She had dark eyes like Helen's own, and they were filled with tears. Esther looked at Helen with the saddest face Helen had ever seen. Helen reached out and took Esther's hand. Esther grasped Helen's hand as the tears began to fall down her face. Together, the two girls sat down on the marble steps.

"I have no friends," said Esther, choking with sobs. "I have barely spoken to another person for a long time."

Helen held Esther's hand and waited for her crying to ease. "I want to be your first new friend," Helen said solemnly. "I want you to come to my wedding. It would be a first step for you to a new life."

Esther took a handkerchief out of her pocket and dabbed at her wet eyes and red nose. "Thank you, Helen.

I've been so mean to everyone, no one has dared to speak to me until you, today. People will not forgive me. It's too late."

"No, Esther. Everyone understands how bad you felt. Everyone will forgive you."

"Okay," Esther said. "I will come."

"This makes me so happy." Helen leaned over and again put her arm around her newest friend. "Your coming to the wedding will make us doubly blessed."

Helen and Robert had spent weeks after work and on weekends looking for an apartment to move into immediately after the wedding. Mrs. Fein had offered, and they had considered moving in with her, but there was little privacy in Lower East Side apartments. Helen and Robert both wanted to start out on their own. They had finally found the perfect place a week ago. It was near Robert's mother on Clinton Street, and it was in the back of the building on the second floor, which was desirable as it would be away from street noises.

They saved to furnish the apartment, and they had found good bargains. They had a well-made wooden bed with soft bedding and a curved headboard in deep mahogany. They got a deal on a heavy kitchen table and four chairs, all of which had gracefully turned legs. A pink velvet sofa and small table fit perfectly into the parlor. Other things would come with time. Helen felt they didn't need much to get started.

Helen couldn't imagine what it would be like to have this much space to herself. Most of her life, she had shared one room with seven other people. Now she and Robert would have three rooms all to themselves. She had taken to stopping off at their apartment after work, if only for a few minutes, to breathe in the air and space and to take in being on the brink of a new life.

Finally, the day had arrived. It was a Sunday. They had chosen Sunday on purpose because none of the guests would have to be at work. Helen awakened in the parlor. She had put her hair up in rags to add more curl. Kathleen had shown her how to cut an old cloth into strips about an inch and a half wide and then wrap the rag strips around plaits of hair. She had moistened her hair, so the curls would last all day long.

Helen's brothers and sister were all still sleeping, and she was happy to have the first moment of this day all to herself. She sat up and looked out the window. It promised to be cold but sunny. This would be the last time in her life to awaken as a daughter in the home of her mother and father. Tomorrow she would awaken as a wife in her own home with her husband Robert beside her.

Quietly Helen arose and went into the kitchen. There was Mama, with coffee ready for the two of them. They hugged and smiled and needed no words. Papa came in after a bit, and Helen poured him a cup of coffee, too. The three of them sat together without needing to speak. Their communication was perfect, their happiness palpable. This would be their last early morning as parents and child at home together.

In time, the other children awakened, and the house began its usual hum. Selma was the first to come running into the kitchen. "It's your big day," she said, bending down to throw her arms around Helen's neck. Helen reached up to hug Selma. Soon all the boys came romping in, and the kitchen transformed itself into the usual busy and boisterous heart of the home.

Helen planned to get dressed at Aunt Rose's. Her wedding clothes awaited her there. After a bit, she put on a simple dress and her warm coat. She left her parents' home for the last time as someone who lived there. From now on, she would be a visitor. This felt a little sad, but she thought about her new home, and she was comforted.

Aunt Rose answered the door. She was practically jumping around, fetching this and looking for that as she helped Helen get dressed and ready. Aunt Rose and the children would walk with Helen in all their finery for the seven blocks to the synagogue. Morty and Josie had new clothes, too. Morty was already sixteen years old and gained early acceptance to City College where he had always wanted to study engineering. Josie was thirteen and in high school. Helen thought how much time had gone by since that first day in New York, when she had met these two children, who were children no more.

Josie showed Helen her new flat Mary Jane shoes, named after a character in the Buster Brown comic strip. Helen also had Mary Janes, in white to match her wedding dress. Helen's shoes had small heels and were easy to walk in. She didn't want to take a chance of tripping as she walked down the aisle. The white shoes could be dyed to a dark, more practical color after the wedding.

Aunt Rose combed out her rag curls into a sophisticated arrangement atop her head. "Your hair looks beautiful," she told Helen. "It's glossy and curling as if you were born that way." Aunt Rose left a few charming tendrils.

Helen found herself alone in the parlor for a few minutes and took advantage of the moment to look closely and enjoy her wedding dress. Its whiteness symbolized to her a new beginning, nothing yet written, a future that would gradually unfold. She looked at the tiny stitches sewn by Mama and Aunt Rose and herself. They ran in different directions, up this seam, around that gathering or gusset. She remembered the hours one evening when she was sewing the hem, and another time when she watched as Aunt Rose created the point lace. It was delicate, carefully wrought, and new to the world, just like her marriage to Robert. Each stitch was another step in a certain direction. Stitches of the dress, stitches of her life. She thought of her first days at her sewing job, where the whir of the sewing machines was so frightening at first, and her father cutting fabric, and Robert shrinking it. Stitches sewed the garments together, stitches brought her family to America. Now, she and Robert would be sewn together in marriage.

Helen put on her dress, raising her arms and letting it float down over her. She slipped on her shoes. She was ready. Aunt Rose called from the kitchen that it was time to go. At the sound of her voice, Helen remembered how kind Aunt Rose and her children had been when she arrived.

Her mind went all the way back to Panemunė, to the turning point, that terrible day when the Russian soldiers had come to the family home, the day when she had hidden Max under the floor to save him. Never again would their family face that kind of terror. In America, Max and her other brothers could look forward to a life where they weren't hunted. Of course, there were always people who had to hate someone, and the Jews were often their target. But in America, this was the exception, not the rule as it had been under the Russian tsars.

Her siblings could get a good education, find the work of their choice, and look forward to passing their days in a peaceful country. They were building lives that were safe and full of opportunities. The New World had truly turned out to be everything the family hoped it would be.

Helen looked up at the sound of Aunt Rose's voice. "What are you daydreaming about? Today is your wedding day. You don't want to keep Robert waiting." She had been years away and thousands of miles, remembering the difficulties and good fortune that had brought her to this moment.

Helen walked into the kitchen and smiled at her cousins. "I'm ready to go," she said.

The four of them walked over to the Ansche Chesed Temple. Everyone on the street stopped and looked at them. They smiled at the fortunate occasion, and a few even whistled and applauded their procession.

At the synagogue, rows of chairs had been set up in the small courtyard out back. The chairs all faced a huppah, the traditional canopy that the couple would stand beneath as they said their marriage vows. The huppah symbolized the sacredness of the occasion. It was covered with the beautiful tablecloth that Mama had stitched, the one with Lithuanian patterns, the very tablecloth that they had used the first time Robert had come to dinner. Selma and the boys had bought white daisies and green leaves to further decorate the huppah, and Helen was charmed at how beautiful it all looked.

Helen's whole family sat in the front row. Kathleen and Kevin were there behind them. And on the other side of Kevin was Esther. Helen noticed her new friend's beauty for the first time. Until today, her looks had been hidden behind a veil of sadness.

Helen noticed Mama brushing away a few tears at the sight of her firstborn daughter in the white wedding dress. Mama got up, and she and Aunt Rose led Helen inside the synagogue and into the Rabbi's study. Kathleen came along.

"You are ready?" Rabbi Jeff Marx asked. "I always check one last time to be sure you haven't changed your mind. Now is the time if you are not completely sure."

Helen smiled at Rabbi Marx.

"Are you ready?" He asked again.

"I'm ready," she said. "Ready for our new life."

EPILOGUE

Helen and Robert Fein were my grandparents. Almost everything I know about them is included in this story. I invented the conversations and some details. I know she was in love with him. I can see from the photos that he was handsome with his blond hair and blue eyes. They met and married and lived on the Lower East Side and had the first six of their eight children in a tenement apartment.

Many Lithuanian Jews bought land in the Bronx. Robert's dream of buying land there came true. In 1913, he saw a business opportunity and bought land in the country. Today that land is in Riverdale, a leafy residential area along the Hudson in the North Bronx. Over the years, Riverdale became a good neighborhood. Residents enjoyed the peacefulness of more distant suburbs with a short commute into Manhattan. Helen and Robert were able to sell off all the lots they owned, but kept two adjoining lots at 6027 Tyndall Avenue. Robert always had a head for business.

The couple hired architect Dwight Baum to design a three-story Dutch Colonial brick house with four bedrooms and two baths. Baum later received a medal from President Herbert Hoover and the AIA for his beautiful homes in Riverdale. The Fein residence at 6027 Tyndall Avenue was the bustling hub of the Fein family for more than sixty years.

~

Helen's family prospered in the New World. Each of her brothers had a good career. The chicken business did well for Helen's father, and was carried on by the next two generations. Great Uncle Milton became a lawyer and a truant officer for the New York Public School system. The family story is that he apprehended a young truant named Bernard Schwartz, who later took the stage name of Tony Curtis. Back then it was a fact of show business life that no one could work in Hollywood with a Jewish name.

I remember Nana Helen's extended family came to visit when I was six years old, about 1950. Nana called me over and asked one of her relatives to roll up his sleeve, so I could see the numbers tattooed on his arm. I didn't understand, but Nana told me that it was important and not to forget it.

I remember Great Uncle Julius as fun and friendly when he came to Helen's house when I was no more than five. Great Aunt Selma had wanted to be a doctor, but it was too difficult for a woman at that time. She married Mr. Leonard, who went out one night to buy cigarettes and was never seen again. After that, Selma lived with Helen and never remarried. Most of Helen's family lived in Brooklyn, and she took me on the long subway ride from the North Bronx to Flatbush for holiday celebrations. I remember lots of cousins and lots of laughter. I loved being part of a big, noisy Jewish family.

In her life after the time covered in this book, Nana devoted herself to her children. Grace was Robert and Helen's first child, the apple of her father's eye. She was born on the Lower East Side in 1907, two years after the wedding. No doubt the couple lavished enormous attention and tenderness on their baby daughter. She grew into a confident and beautiful woman. Grace was a dynamo and a social genius. She married Julian, a young salesman who later became a prosperous Vice President at Hudson Pulp and Paper Corporation.

They did well, and Grace led a long and happy life in New York, where she lived on Sutton Place. She spent summers in East Hampton and later retired to Palm Beach, Florida. Grace's brilliant and talented son, Julian Barry, was Nana's first grandchild. He was only four years younger than his uncle Ernie, old enough to hang out with Ernie and Marvin. Julian Barry started out as an actor on Broadway, but he became a writer and wrote the hit play *Lenny*, about Lenny Bruce. The play was later made into the award-winning film *Lenny*, and Julian was nominated for an Oscar for writing the screenplay.

Joe was the next child after Grace. Joe was the first child to attend college, graduating from the University of Illinois. Joe married the lovely Helen Bloom, an elegant lady who looked like Marlene Dietrich and was a gifted painter. Joe joined his father at Merit National Shrinking .Works, the only child to work in Robert's business. Although he wanted to be a journalist, the Depression was in full swing by the time he entered the workforce, and nobody in their right mind could turn down a job.

Next came Murray, the family athlete. Murray was built like his father, big and strong. He played on local teams, especially as a stringer for the St. Margaret's Catholic School team. They always won when the Jewish boy from Tyndall Avenue was allowed to play. At one game, Murray said a swear word. The priest told him to sit on the bench and say, "I will not take the Lord's name in vain," one thousand times. But then the team started to lose, and the priest cut it to 250 times and put him back into the game in time for a win. Murray also married a beautiful and elegant woman, Pat. The Fein boys all had an eye for fabulous women. Murray went into his grandfather Chaim's chicken business.

During World War II, Murry was an MP, and he supervised German prisoners of war, bringing them to the United States to be interned. His strength and size made him a natural as an MP.

Helen and Robert Fein had two boys with intellectual disabilities, Herman and Alvin. They kept the boys at home and cared for them as part of the family. There was, in the 1900s, a great deal of shame in families with "defective" children. Helen and Robert were not ashamed. They supported their two boys throughout their lives. The two were like children, sweet and loving. I remember they were my playmates when I was six years old. They were just like me, only bigger.

The last child to be born on the Lower East side was Shirley. Aunt Shirley told me, "We lived in a very nice tenement building." Shirley also graduated from college, attending Hunter College and majoring in Physical Education. She was an independent woman and an adventurer. She worked in France and Germany during WWII for the American Red Cross. After the war, she helped to rehabilitate American soldiers who had been released as prisoners of war. She attended the proceedings at Nuremberg. Many years later she received the American Red Cross Legacy

Award for her service. Her time in France added a special sophistication and an appreciation for elegance and style. Shirley married late in life to Joseph Sheriff, a widower. Shirley was open-minded and embraced the social changes of the late twentieth century. She was an excellent yoga instructor, making good use of her degree, and she believed in a balance of body, mind, and spirit. By the time Shirley was born, Helen could quit working because Merit National Shrinking Works became more and more profitable. Helen stayed home with the children.

In the new home in Riverdale, Marvin and Ernest, the last of the eight Fein children, were born at home. Marvin was the first Jewish boy ever to attend Georgia Tech, and he became a successful electrical engineer. His father always said science and engineers would save the world, and this influenced his son's choice of career. During WWII, Marvin worked as a civilian on the radio equipment in submarines in Charlestown, South Carolina. He spent a year near Bogota, Colombia, where he installed the world's largest transmitter. Marvin lived a long and happy life, ending his days in sunny California, which he adored. He was a loving father to me. I miss him very much.

When the vegetable man came down Tyndall Avenue with his horse-drawn cart, Nana could buy vegetables on credit. My father told me that the vegetable man kept her credit record on a sheet of paper with the heading "Jew lady, lotta kids." It meant nothing harmful, it was just a way of keeping track of all the different people on his route.

My father and mother's marriage only lasted four years. They had insurmountable difficulties due to cultural differences and my mother's young age. Nana Helen stepped in and offered me a warm place in her home and her heart. I adored my Nana, and I truly believe today it was her kindness and generosity to me that saved me from a life of unhappiness.

Nana loved me unconditionally. She saw something special in me when no one else had the time or attention, the other adults in my young life being wrapped up in their own dramas. Without Nana, I would not have survived. I wrote this book to honor her memory and to share my gratitude.

I spent every summer with Nana and my dad. I loved the summers and could not wait each year for school to be over so I could fly back to New York. My memories of that time are vivid and happy. Nana swept the sidewalk along the tree-lined street every morning, and I had a little red broom and would sweep along with her. There were lots of kids my age on Tyndall Avenue, and we would roller skate up and down the street for the entire day. I always slept in the big second bed in Nana's own bedroom, with an oversized yellow wing chair pushed up close to the bed to keep me from falling out. The wing chair had a pattern of diamonds where every other diamond was shiny, and the ones in between were dull and soft looking. When I think of that pattern, I feel the safety of being with my grandmother. I put Robert's mother Ernestine in a maroon version of this chair. I don't know anything about Ernestine, but the character I made up would have liked that chair.

Helen's youngest child was Ernest. He was named for Ernestine. Ernie inherited the ocean-going gene from his father Robert. Ernie was a merchant marine. He was the black sheep of the family, not that we knew of anything specific that he did that was bad, as no one knew exactly what he did. There were some hashish stories from the older cousins. My Uncle Ernie had a twinkle in his eye. He was always fun when he was in port. One day, he brought home a wife from the Dominican Republic, Louisa. Louisa was a gentle woman without much English. She became Helen's companion and caretaker at the end of her life.

On November 2, 1944, Robert died of a heart attack. He was sixty-four. Helen outlived him by thirty-one years. She died in her own apartment in Riverdale, on November 11, 1975. She was ninety-one.

She lived in New York from the age of sixteen. She saw World War I, the sinking of the Titanic, the Great Depression, and World War II. She lived through the amazing prosperity and growth of the 1950s. Helen was enthusiastic, yet even-tempered and always kind. She had a dry humor and a way of accepting what happened in her life with generosity and peace.

Thank you, Nana. You saved my life. I send you great love and appreciation. I hope I will see you in heaven, if it turns out that heaven is a place.

ACKNOWLEDGMENTS

I would not have undertaken this book about my grandmother were it not for the encouragement of my first cousins Julian Barry and Deborah Schiavo. The three of us share fond memories. My editor, writing teacher, and friend, Patricia Dove Miller, helped me over many years to find my voice, and more recently to tell this story. My editor and coach Betsy Graziani Fasbinder became a true friend as she read the book at least three times, each time offering valuable feedback and encouragement. My friend Jozeffa Greer is a therapist, and she read this book for the characters' emotions and the accompanying bodily sensations. I like to think that Jozeffa gave the book therapy, helping the reader to experience what the characters feel. Many thanks to Rabbi Jeff Marx for his wonderful website on the Breakstone family, for finding the ship's manifest with Helen's name on line 11, and for his advice and counseling about Reform Judaism. Thanks to my wonderful writing groups over the years for amazing feedback and support. I am blessed with a wide and wondrous circle of friends, and I always know they are in my corner. Thanks to She Writes Press and SparkPoint Studios for their help. Any inaccuracies are solely my own.

ABOUT THE AUTHOR

Credit: Mike Martin Photography

Mary Helen Fein was born in New York City, in 1943. She attended schools in New York and began writing at the age of twelve when her mother died. Writing has ever since been an important part of her life, a way to understand and process life's events. Mary Helen holds a BA in English literature from Temple University and an MS in computer science engineering from the University of Pennsylvania; she also studied painting at the Pennsylvania Academy of Fine Arts, America's oldest art school, for two years. Today she lives in Northern California, where she owns her own website design company, writes, paints, and teaches Insight meditation. In 2014, she published her first novel, *Loss of Deliverance*—the story of a young woman's adventures in the drug trade during the 1960s.

Please visit the author's website at:
www.maryhelenfein.com

Printed in the United States
by Baker & Taylor Publisher Services